SILVER HARVEST

Recent Titles by Kay Stephens from Severn House Large Print

LATE HARVEST

SILVER HARVEST

Kay Stephens

Severn House Large Print
London & New York

This first large print edition published in Great Britain 2003 by
SEVERN HOUSE LARGE PRINT BOOKS LTD of
9-15, High Street, Sutton, Surrey, SM1 1DF.
First world regular print edition published 2002 by
Severn House Publishers, London and New York.
This first large print edition published in the USA 2003 by
SEVERN HOUSE PUBLISHERS INC., of
595 Madison Avenue, New York, NY 10022

British Library Cataloguing in Publication Data

Stephens, Kay
Silver harvest - Large print ed.
1. Fruit growers - England - Kent - Fiction
2. Antiques - England - Kent - Fiction
3. Domestic fiction
4. Large type books
I. Title
823.9'14 [F]

ISBN 0-7278-7213-3

Printed and bound in Great Britain by
MPG Books Ltd, Bodmin, Cornwall.

One

'Don't be surprised if I don't come back!'

Amanda knew no one had witnessed her outburst, but she felt better already. She slammed the door behind her, ran to the car, and sped off, never more thankful to be driving towards her mother's home.

The weekend had been dire; she had fixed her mind on Monday at The Sylvan Barn and her work with Caroline's PR company. After all the years following her parents' divorce, living with her father seemed like a huge mistake. She needed to extend herself – earning the freedom to exercise her flair might compensate for the situation at home. She loved handling a responsible job which created the ambition to tackle further challenges. And today Amanda sensed that Caroline needed her far more than her father ever had.

Of course, she understood that Julian should have different priorities since he'd remarried, just as she realised he and Emma needed to take time over planning their visit to Spain and Portugal. Amanda *wanted* them to go. If Emma hadn't accused her of being jealous of their plans, and in such a patronising voice, she would have left them to their discussions. She needed to find something that really interested *her*, and she'd not discover that in their home.

She would have explained but Emma's gaze, which Amanda rarely could quite read, had stopped her. 'Your father did ask if you wished to join us on this trip, remember. You'd not be envying us if you didn't prefer to work.'

Overnight, Amanda had begun to understand that Julian might have been hurt by her insistence that Caroline relied upon her more than ever now.

In the car driving towards Kent, Amanda went hot, recalling how she had flared back. 'I'm not envious at all. I only thought there might have been some space, at some time during the weekend, for something other than your holiday.'

She could still picture her father's look that said he thought her unreasonable. 'There's a lot of mileage involved; the logistics warrant careful attention.'

Amanda didn't need his explanation. She was twenty-six, not the child that her stepmother seemed to consider her. But Emma and Julian were both there together throughout each week – didn't that provide time enough? They had bored Christopher into leaving within minutes of calling in on Saturday evening. He was soon driven to escape to the pub. Amanda would gladly have gone off with him.

When he didn't suggest that, the atmosphere in the bungalow had grown even more intolerable. She had realised during the past few years what a fool she'd been, had seen that becoming so involved with her father's life had prevented her from making many friends. No one knew how much she'd looked forward to having Chris spend a few hours with them. No one knew how greatly Christopher Parker mattered to her.

'Can't wait to see you busy around The Sylvan Barn again!'

Remembering Caroline's words was making Christopher smile, increasing his elation that autumn morning as he drove over the Kentish downs towards his old home. He certainly was pleased to be working with his father again, however temporarily. When Malcolm first asked him to advise about creating a vineyard there, Chris was delighted. Their ensuing discussions were proving agreeable and stimulating. He was excited today about finally preparing the ground.

He steered his classic MG into the familiar drive, and saw the ambulance parked by the front door.

'God, not Dad's heart again!' Severely

shocked, he braked, switched off the ignition, and sprinted towards the house.

Malcolm was standing there, unlocking his own car. Then who...? And whatever was wrong?

Seeing his son, Malcolm sighed, gave a helpless shrug. Before Chris could ask what was happening his father was telling him.

'It's Caroline – passed clean out just as we finished breakfast. She came round, but paramedics can't tell why she flaked out like that. Going to get her checked over.'

'Right. I'll come with you.'

Malcolm shook his head. 'No, better have someone here. Can't expect Mrs Dacre to cope alone – she's getting older – no matter how good a housekeeper she is.'

The ambulance doors had closed; it was reversing, about to depart. Malcolm flung himself behind the wheel of his Jaguar.

'Ring you from the hospital, Chris.'

'But how bad is Caroline? Which hospital...?'

His questions went unanswered while Malcolm roared off down the drive.

Perhaps his stepmother's condition wasn't too serious, Christopher hoped; the ambulance wasn't sounding that appalling siren.

Mrs Dacre was at the door of the elegant hall, her grey-green eyes moist. She had been with the family too long to be unaffected by sudden illness.

'Thank goodness you're here,' she exclaimed. 'It all happened in such a rush, just as I was arriving.'

'But what was it exactly? Some sort of a blackout, Dad said.'

'So I gather. They were already helping Caroline out to the ambulance.'

'We'll just have to hope she's no worse for passing out. Where're they taking her?'

'Can't say – sorry. Didn't know themselves; they were on about having to radio ahead en route.'

'Must depend which hospital's admitting emergencies today. So, what can I do here?'

'Not much, is there? Your father said not to let your brother know until there's more definite news. Likewise, your aunt and uncle. There's Amanda, though – she'll be here any minute. Caroline was insisting that she didn't want Amanda to be alarmed. "Do tell her not to worry. Just to get on with the job she started on Friday." '

'Give me a second. Then I'll talk to Amanda.'

He wasn't granted even that short time to compose himself for reassuring her. Caroline's daughter was there already, parking her car as she gave the MG a look.

'What's up, Chris?' she called with a grin, after hastily checking her reflection in the rear-view mirror. 'Run out of petrol before you could reach the house?'

As she walked towards them Amanda saw their grave expressions. 'What's going on? Family crisis?'

'We hope not,' he began, taking her arm and leading her through to a sofa in the large entrance hall. 'You're not to panic – we believe there's no need. It's just ... your mum's had to go to hospital.'

Her brown eyes darkened in concern. 'You mean the baby's on its way? But it's not due for—'

'Don't think that was it – Dad never mentioned the baby. Just said your mother had a ... a sort of blackout.'

'A blackout? What caused that?' Amanda felt sick.

'I don't know. Just ... some kind of faint, I suppose.'

'Bad enough for them to send for you, apparently.'

'No, no – nothing like that. I was due here, had you forgotten? To continue preparing Dad's vineyard.' He shrugged. 'Guess there's not much else I can do in here; might as well make my way down there.'

'Chris, how can you! Don't you care at all? You ought to come to the hospital – *with me*. Learn how Mother is.'

'We can't go anywhere as yet, Amanda. Don't know which hospital.'

'Then we've got to find out.' She stood up hastily.

'Dad'll let us know. Meanwhile...' Chris took Amanda by her shoulders, steadying her. 'Meanwhile, Caroline said you mustn't worry – she specifically asked that you should get on with the work you were doing on Friday.'

'What? You can't be serious.'

'*She* was – serious enough to leave you the message.'

'Nobody's PR job can matter more than my mother being ill.' Half an hour ago she would have relished the chance to prove how reliable she was. She also had sensed that Caroline needed her more than usual.

'Not when it's *her* company? You wouldn't want to upset her by neglecting work.' Amanda always looked vulnerable, but he'd learned she responded to a challenge.

'OK. But only until we hear something. You will let me know the instant—'

'I promise. I'm off down the fields now, but I have my mobile. Let me know if you hear anything at all. And I'll contact you if Dad should ring.'

Christopher was relieved to be out in the open, on the hillside where ground adjoining the Channel Tunnel rail link was being redeveloped. The dreaded construction, churning up a swathe of rough brown earth through the countryside, provided one benefit, after all: causing Malcolm to rethink on utilising this part of his land.

With his experience as Julian's vineyard manager, Chris had needed only a few discussions with his boss to confirm that grapes should thrive on this south-facing slope. Being granted leave to ensure the essential groundwork went satisfactorily was good. Labouring alongside his father while not being employed by him was proving ideal. Even when this wettest of autumns rendered every spadeful heavy.

Chris was also pleased to be becoming a bridge between his father and Julian – a relationship which had remained predictably uneasy. Being Caroline's present and former partners could hardly be expected to generate a bond. Now, though, he didn't doubt that by the time the vines here were productive Malcolm would be agreeing terms for supplying to Julian's wine-processing plant.

Beginning to dig was satisfying, a welcome physical antidote for the anxiety that had tightened his throat and every muscle in this body from the moment when he'd seen that wretched ambulance. He wondered if Amanda's guess could be right, that the baby might actually be the cause of Caroline's collapse. He rather thought not: as the girl had said, it wasn't nearly due yet. Maybe his stepmother quite simply had been doing too much – she never had known the meaning of letting up. It seemed likely to him that the trouble was down to exhaustion.

Neither he nor Amanda had any news by the time Chris stopped for lunch, but he phoned around until he learned which hospital Caroline was in.

'May I speak with my father, please?'

That got him no further. The nurse merely said that Malcolm was with his wife, and not to be interrupted. She hung up on Chris, frustratingly, to dash off without responding to questions about his stepmother's condition.

'Whatever does that mean? Is Mother so ill your father can't leave her?' Amanda demanded, running her fingers through her golden-brown hair.

'Shouldn't think so.' Chris tried to sound reassuring, but he was concerned, could never have cared more about Caroline if she'd been his natural mother. 'You know what hospitals are like. Nurses too busy to keep an eye on everybody. I bet they're just glad he can stay with Caro while they attend to other patients. Ones who are more critical.'

Amanda wasn't satisfied. She was about to call the hospital herself when Chris prevented her. If, heaven help them, the news were bad, he'd got to be the one to tell Amanda. He couldn't expose her to learning of trouble over the phone.

'I'll speak to them again,' he promised. 'Just give them time to sort out Caroline's problem.'

Despite his own words, Christopher was greatly perturbed, more uneasy than he would ever admit to Caro's daughter. No matter how keen he was to continue with the hard graft of turning the soil out there, his mind – and his heart – was with Caroline and Malcolm.

Life had been tough until this past couple of years for his father, and no less so for Caroline. For longer than Chris could remember clearly their fruit farm had been on the decline; the consequent worry had contributed to that dreadful time when Malcolm's heart had all but given out. His eventual recovery owed much to Caro, whose determination to provide a healthier diet had been just as important as the care received from Anne Newbold, their doctor.

His father's steadily improving health had coincided with the time when the stresses of running the farm eventually decreased, and before the end of 1999 he was employing Hugh Edmonds to assist him. The whole family now appeared ready to really appreciate the life they shared here.

Looking beyond the course of the new railway line, Christopher's smile was rueful. No matter how strongly their village and others had battled against the route of this link to the Channel Tunnel, it nevertheless was a reality now. Maybe, given a few more years, the scarring of this landscape would appear less obtrusive. The line might even do some good, although he himself rather doubted that it would ever justify the costs. In investment, or human disturbance.

These vines they planned, however, would provide some measure of screening while they matured, even before they produced the harvests he anticipated. Dad might be surprised and forsake any earlier scepticism, he reflected. This land should in time yield a good profit for the acreage. I shall ensure that it does precisely that for him, Christopher vowed.

He was established well enough with Julian now to suggest taking the occasional day off to assist his own father. In that way he would at last make up to Malcolm for quitting all those years ago. Chris knew that his father had been as much to blame as he himself for the trouble that had sent him looking for a position elsewhere. But that fact did not preclude the everlasting awareness that he had caused Malcolm Parker intense disappointment.

Today's anxiety concerning Caroline was increasing Christopher's determination to do all he could for the family. Not knowing how he might help ease everyone through this crisis was making him frustrated.

At last he saw his father trudging down the field towards him.

'Dad? How's Caroline?' Chris called, scarcely daring to breathe.

He was noting Malcolm's slow progress. The weight loss which once seemed to restore his father's vigour was bestowing instead the appearance of a man far older than forty-eight, shrunken. The tan, won through years of tending his orchards, was drained away, leaving cheeks grey-tinged from strain.

Reaching his son, Malcolm extended both hands towards him and somehow conveyed an impression that he needed support.

God, thought Chris, not that! Not *Caroline*...?

But Malcolm smiled. Christopher felt strong arms come round his shoulders.

'She'll be fine, Chris – they both will.'

'Both?'

Releasing his son, Malcolm smiled into his blue eyes, let his own eyes release tears to trickle unashamedly down his cheeks.

'A daughter, such a scrap of a thing, but whole – and none the worse, I'm assured, for being those few weeks early.'

'And Caro – was it really just, well, the labour starting and that? Making her pass out, I mean?'

'So the doctors say. I pestered them repeatedly, to be reassured.'

'Thank God. I've never been more scared since ... since the time you were rushed off in that ambulance.'

'Me too, son, given her age. Anyway, there we are. Caro's resting now, naturally, but the worst's over.'

'What's the baby like?'

Malcolm grinned. 'Wrinkled, a bit red, but very sweet. With her mother's gold-tinged hair. She tells me that might change. Hope it doesn't.' He paused, reflecting. 'Oh, Chris – I'm so glad you were here, that you're here still.'

'Don't suppose you'll be putting in much time on preparing this vineyard as things are, with the new arrival.'

'Maybe. Hugh's on holiday, too. But it's time you stopped for the day now. I'm going to find that champagne...'

'Wait another hour and I'll join you thankfully. It'll be time then for a meal, and I don't have to go back to the flat tonight.'

'It's a deal.'

'I'll walk back to the house with you, just for a few minutes. Got to tell Amanda.'

'No need. Went into the office soon as I got home. Well, I knew the poor girl would be in a state about her mother.'

Christopher smiled, pleased that his father had considered Amanda. Malcolm made no secret of the fact that, years ago, he'd had no time for this daughter of Caroline's from her marriage to Julian. And even well into her twenties, Amanda was still insecure enough to need the approval of this extended family of hers.

'Why don't I change, come back out here,' Malcolm said. 'May not be much use, but I can't see myself settling to anything the rest of today. I am so elated.'

Covertly, Chris watched Malcolm as he headed up the field towards the house. He could understand his father's reluctance to sit alone in The Sylvan Barn. Could be as well to have him out here, while he himself kept an eye on his condition.

Amanda had been surprised when Malcolm came straight towards the PR office as soon as he arrived home. During the years that she had worked alongside her mother, he couldn't have called in there more than a dozen times.

'Amanda,' he began, smiling a little awkwardly as he walked towards the desk. 'You'll have spent the day worrying, so you'll be the first to hear. You've a tiny sister, arrived an hour or so ago. And she and your mother are going to be fine.'

'A sister! Oh, that is good news. Great.' Her brown eyes gleamed with emotion as she looked up from an incoming e-mail. 'And Mother really is OK?'

Malcolm reached across the desk, rested his hand on hers. With those gold highlights in her brown hair, she looked touchingly like Caroline. 'She really is. A few hours' sleep and she'll be itching to show off the infant to you.'

'That's brilliant. I am so relieved. You must be as well. It must have been horrible to have her rushed off to hospital like that.'

'I was mighty scared. The paramedics couldn't be sure why Caro blacked out. Then when they whipped her off to the labour ward no one would reassure me until the baby was delivered.'

'By which time Mother would be thankful to have you there.'

'You understand why I couldn't take a break to phone through?'

Amanda nodded. 'Sure.'

Malcolm smiled. 'I didn't want to give out any news until I was positive they'd both be all right. Sorry you had to wait so long.'

'You're the one who should stop worrying, Malcolm. The months of wondering how it will go are over at last. We all found it a bit of a strain, haven't we?'

He grinned. 'So, you'll have a while when you're in sole charge of Caroline's company. Think you'll enjoy that? I reckon it won't do you any harm. Everyone needs the opportunity to show what they're made of.'

When he had left, Amanda remained at the desk, smiling. Malcolm was right about her relishing the opportunity to run the business. Much as she loved working with her mother, Caroline Parker always had a certain reluctance to delegate some of the more crucial responsibilities!

Life suddenly felt good; Malcolm had been particularly considerate towards her, seemed finally to have discovered how to manage relations between them. She'd always understood that her father's previous marriage to Caroline had created unease in Malcolm's attitude towards Amanda herself. Things might have been simpler had she lived at The Sylvan Barn, instead of merely working here. She was beginning to believe Malcolm could have filled the role of stepfather quite readily.

Out on the hillside, almost too exhausted to even stand around, Malcolm was doing no more than watching. Christopher's spade struck something hard, more unyielding than the rough ground he'd been working all day. He drew back, thrust in the spade again, wondered who the hell had left something this solid a couple of spits beneath the surface. The contractors, he supposed. He glanced towards his father.

'Something strange here, Dad. Great chunk of stone. I'm surprised the mechanical digger we brought in didn't unearth it.'

Although curious, Malcolm couldn't offer

any suggestions, wasn't sufficiently interested to care. He stood by while his son continued heaving out spadefuls of earth, turning it, discarding weeds and a multitude of stones. There was no easy way, despite the machinery they had hired to work the soil ahead of this hand-digging. Adjacent to the mass of brown earth disturbed during preceding stages of the rail link construction, this part of their land had been seriously compacted. Although this steep slope preserved them from the flooding wrought elsewhere in Kent by the recent incessant rain, the ground was severely waterlogged.

Not that it had ever been brilliant. He could recall his grandfather being obliged to give it over to sheep. The old man had been annoyed – thinking to enlarge their farm, the family had bought this further acreage from a neighbour. Now Malcolm trusted that Chris really did know his stuff, and the vines would thrive here.

'This has got me beaten,' Chris admitted at last. 'Had a shot at it some time ago – just came back to it now. Want to have a look?'

Malcolm anchored in a trench the spade which he'd been disinclined to use, then stomped across the corrugations Chris had dug to where he was crouching.

'Like a paving slab or something, Dad. Can't think who'd have buried that here, or for what reason. Don't believe they'd be using this stuff for the rail line.'

Malcolm shook his head, bent down to examine the corner of the stone protruding from the trench. Together, they grasped as much of the stone as they could, feeling the sharp soil grazing their fingers. The force of their combined efforts raised the slab by a centimetre at most.

Malcolm sighed. 'More hard graft, from what I see. We shall have to work towards it from all sides. Until we expose the full surface of the thing we'll achieve nothing. Unless ... I suppose we could leave it where it is.'

'And lose space for good vines? Not if I can help it – there's going to be few enough as it is.'

They attacked the job steadily, facing each other from a couple of metres apart, digging down, plodding forward, until their spades each struck edges of the stone slab.

The day, once cool, seemed cool no longer while curiosity added urgency to their task and sweat streamed from heads and shoulders.

The stone, exposed at last, was about a metre square and five centimetres thick. Heaving it up from the earth and moving it aside required their combined strength.

Chris was the first to notice something that had lain beneath the stone: dark cloth, mildewed from evident long contact with the soil – an invitation to complete further digging.

Neither Malcolm nor his son suspected that the investigation now becoming obligatory would prove rewarding. Compared with unearthing that stone slab, retrieving the musty-smelling bag then slitting the rope at its neck were simple. Seated on the ground, they both gasped, grinned at each other.

Darkened and tarnished though they were, there could be no mistaking that the candlesticks, ornamental flagons, coffee pots and drinking vessels were silver.

'Who on earth do these belong to?' Chris pushed back the brown hair that always flopped forward now that his ultra-short cut was growing out. 'Where can they have come from?'

'Not from family, that is for sure. Or not in my lifetime.'

'No, well, looks to me as though this stuff's much older than that. Even so, how long have the family been here?'

'Parkers have farmed fruit here for generations, as you know. Precise dates for the length of time we've had a home here will take some researching. That should be interesting. Provide a bit more background for the infant. For you and Nick as well, of course.'

Christopher concealed a smile, wondered

already if this new baby would be given preference in their father's affection. Not that he would mind too greatly – not while he had his own position away from here. His own home, too – he was fond of that flat he'd bought over the border in Sussex.

'I'll fetch a carton for this,' he said. 'One that'll take the bag as well, leave the lot together like that. Should yield a few clues when we start investigating.'

The moment she had parked her car that evening Amanda went rushing through the bungalow to find her father. She found instead her stepmother, and received a curious glance.

Amanda tried not to laugh. Emma was too accustomed to seeing her bored out of her skull to have anticipated this sudden excitement.

'I've got a tiny sister,' Amanda exclaimed. 'Early, but fine. They're both fine, Malcolm assures me.'

Emma felt her face close blankly, cleared her throat, managed the smile expected of her. 'Very nice. Have you seen the baby?'

'Not yet. Mummy was exhausted, naturally.' She felt her colour rising; this was the first time she remembered calling Caroline 'Mummy'. Something about Emma created the uncharacteristic urge to cling to her real mother.

'I shall go in tomorrow to see them,' she added.

'If Caroline is up to having you visit,' said Emma. 'The birth is bound to take more out of an older woman.'

'She's only in her forties.'

Emma clamped her lips together. From the day that she heard that Caroline was about to produce another child, she had felt uneasy. It wasn't that she feared Julian might be over-concerned about his former wife, but *everyone* did always speak so well of the woman. Emma often wondered why, if the sainted Caroline was so marvellous, she had not lasted here!

Dismally, she willed herself not to bitch about her predecessor, and certainly not to Amanda. Neither the girl nor Julian knew how she really felt, how inadequate she would always feel because of not having children. Even her dearly loved first husband had never quite understood. No matter how kindly John had been – and he had been everlastingly kind – he had failed to comprehend how her inability to bear a child continued to gnaw into her.

'Your father's out in the sample room, I believe,' she told Amanda now. 'He'll be glad to know that Caroline's safely delivered. Just don't be surprised if he doesn't enthuse too eagerly.'

Her words hadn't dimmed Amanda's

excitement. She watched as the girl sped out of the house in search of her father. Emma hoped she was right about Julian not enthusing – she would never be able to bear it if Julian went on and on about what a splendid mother Caroline was, and how no one would be better able to cope with a baby late in life. She couldn't forget the way he'd reacted when first told of Caroline's pregnancy.

'Trust her! I hope Malcolm appreciates how brilliant she is, realises that he is extremely fortunate.'

Fortunate? Emma could have reminded her husband that Malcolm Parker had simply taken on *his* cast-off!

She was thankful that she still refrained from implying any such thing. She and Julian had a good marriage, and Emma herself had no regrets about their life together. It was too late now, anyway, for having children. It was her misfortune that her personal time clock seemed unaware of those physical factors; the relief would be enormous if she could only *forget* this great gap in her life. She wished the premature greying of her hair were accompanied by adjusted yearnings.

Emma turned, walked away from the window. Arm in arm, chattering, Julian and his daughter were coming back to the house.

Is it just me? Am I really so cold? Emma

wondered. Never once had Amanda taken her arm like that, never responded when she'd attempted to hug her. And she *had* made an effort. Sensing that she might make this bungalow a real family home, perhaps subconsciously hoping that contact with the girl might alleviate her own deepest needs, she'd tried putting an arm around Amanda.

She hadn't actually shrivelled at Emma's side – that couldn't have been so – but that was the way it had seemed.

There must be a reason, Emma thought now. Maybe things will get better if I begin to understand. This past weekend had reminded her of the constant need to work at the relationship with her stepdaughter.

She asked Julian that night, when Amanda had gone to her room. Taking care to smile – she didn't wish to deflate him while the evening's news appeared to be pleasing – Emma began: 'Amanda seems delighted about her new half-sister. I'm glad, and it's made me aware that I could do more for her, now her mother's likely to be preoccupied with this baby.'

'You've always done everything expected of you where Amanda's concerned – you mustn't think otherwise, darling,' Julian assured her.

'Everything I've been allowed, perhaps. But it's as though there's always a barrier there...' Emma's voice trailed off helplessly. She couldn't say how affected she was by seeing him and Amanda close. Really close, arms entwined.

'Barrier?'

Julian wasn't helping; she would have to state the bald truth. Emma felt unwelcome tears rising to her eyes.

'She never lets me hug her, not even place an arm around her shoulders.'

Julian grinned. 'Not just you, Emma darling. Didn't you know? Amanda's like that with her own mother, always has been. Well, almost always.'

'No. That can't be right. Not with Caroline.'

'Not right, agreed. But it is the way it was. Caroline was upset, but there appeared to be nothing we could do.'

'You mean when you split up, when she saw her mother afterwards?'

'Ages before that happened.'

'But I don't understand.'

'Nor I. All we can do is accept that's the way she is. Nothing you need feel responsible for.'

Emma felt slightly better for learning the truth, felt nowhere near so inadequate. She meant to use the knowledge to further a greater understanding between herself and this stepdaughter of hers. There would be no future attempts at forcing any physical contact, but she must think this one through, try to discover why Amanda had withdrawn. What could make someone shrink from affection, from a hug?

Strangely, the possible explanation came to Emma later that night. In memories which she had sealed away beyond even subconscious thought, because they were too hurtful.

It had happened with her first husband, during his terminal illness. She had spoken to John's doctors then, distressed by the way that he had shrugged himself free of her attempts to hold him. Their rationalising of this had helped only a little, but she could see that he had needed to prepare himself for the time when he was parted from loving gestures.

Poor young Amanda, Emma realised. You sensed at an early stage, didn't you, that your mother's presence would be withdrawn from here.

Anne Newbold was hurrying to lock up after evening surgery when the telephone rang. Hearing Malcolm's voice on the line produced that old familiar tug at her senses. He went gabbling on, near-incoherent with elation.

'It's a girl, Anne – we're calling her Rebecca. They're both fine now, after all the panic this morning.'

'What panic?'

'You didn't hear then? Caroline was rushed there by ambulance. Passed out at home, you see...'

'Strange. But you say she's all right now? Was it a faint, or something?'

'Don't think anyone really said; I can't be sure any longer. Only that we have this gorgeous little daughter. Soon as we got to hospital they realised Caro was in early labour. That seemed to go on for ever, of course. Anyway, all's well now. Can you come round tonight? Having a bit of a celebration later, when I've been in to see her – *them* – again. Crack open a bottle or two, say, around nine?'

'Thanks, Malcolm, but I can't make it. Meeting of the Retirement Housing Trust. Glad everything's OK, though. Many congratulations! Early, wasn't it?'

Anne was relieved to have good reason for not joining the Parker family that night. She had been pleased for Malcolm and Caroline when confirming the pregnancy months ago. That did not mean that her subconscious had relinquished all recollections of the hopes she herself once had nurtured. And nor could she overlook what she had learned of the covert friendship which had, for a time, threatened Caroline's remaining in that marriage.

Setting out from Birch Tree House, Anne

gave her mind to the road towards the village, and the prospect of introducing the Reverend Keith Clifton to the committee this evening. She herself knew him hardly at all; she had attended the service when he was inducted as their new rector, and subsequently had spoken to him a couple of times after Evensong.

His call today asking how he might reach the meeting had been a surprise, until he started to explain that his ancient Ford Escort had let him down.

'Forget buses,' Anne had interrupted him with a smile. 'They don't run, anyway, after seven. I'll pick you up en route.'

Keith was waiting as promised at the lych-gate, his smiling brown eyes witnessing to his relief and lightening the austere effect of his dark hair plus the black cassock that emphasised how tall and lean he was.

'Don't mind admitting I'm thankful we shall arrive together. This succession of introductions is rather beginning to pall.'

'Oh?' Anne had expected that anyone joining the Church would be only too happy to meet more people. Surely he must have a good grounding in getting along with everyone?

'Finding it a bit tough, are you?' she enquired when he didn't enlarge on his admission.

Keith laughed ruefully. 'My own fault, I

fear. It's not that the parishioners are setting out to be difficult – you mustn't think that. It's more that they are set in their likes – or *dislikes*, perhaps – regarding services.'

'Ah,' said Anne. And felt him giving her a look.

'Should I say no more? Do I tread my usual heavy way on delicate ground?'

'Not at all; you must have noticed I'm not deeply involved at church. Do feel free – doctors also, remember, are accustomed to keeping confidences! And to reserving judgements.'

'It's just ... I can't seem to get the hang of pleasing all of them. Parish Council meeting last night.'

'And wow, do they ever love their exuberant services,' she suggested.

'We referred to them as "happy, clappy" when I was training at Mirfield. The Community of the Resurrection, you—'

'Know,' Anne finished, nodding. 'Yes, I know Mirfield, Keith. I'm from Yorkshire originally.'

'I respect their wishes regarding the services they like, but I'd be happier if they would be prepared to respect mine. All I suggested was an occasional trial of something different. A Sung Eucharist.'

'With incense, I hope, and bells.'

'Smells and bells, yes.' There was a smile in his attractive voice. 'Do I detect one supporter in this village?'

'Count me as an ally, at least. *Pro tem,* until I've got you weighed up!'

She had sympathised privately with Keith Clifton already. Several of her more forthright patients had filled her in on his attitude towards them.

'No thought of biding his time, feeling his way gently while he gets used to us,' someone had said. 'Straight in, suggesting changing services, if you please. "Sung Eucharist" indeed! Why doesn't he go the whole hog, turn Roman Catholic?'

One of the churchwardens had sounded no less intransigent. 'We've given our people what they enjoy – why consider fresh ideas?'

'Perhaps they'll come round to allowing that the occasional experiment with something different might be good?' Anne suggested, one eyebrow raised.

'I doubt it, but I'm prepared to shelve my ideas. If only for a month or so.'

Even if attitudes altered, he'd still be disappointed – this job wasn't about projecting his own will regarding liturgy. He had trained for ordination hoping to make a difference in people's lives – not only the time they spent within the walls of a church.

Despite his inclination towards straight-talking, Keith slotted in well among the committee who ran the local retirement homes. His predecessor as rector had been its chairman and he readily succeeded to the post.

'If just for a probationary period,' he confided with a disarming grin. 'At least until you have the measure of me!'

With only an occasional interruption to request an explanation of references in the minutes, Keith did more listening than speaking, until it was his task to move them on through the agenda. Much of that night's business was routine, evoking little contention. Anne noticed his courteous yet firm direction, which prevented some committee members from waffling on about their pet causes.

Only towards the close of the meeting did their new chairman reveal a tongue which could be sharp. The subject was fund-raising for refurbishing the communal hall where their elderly residents could meet, and to which outsiders were invited for social events.

'You must have some experience of bringing in contributions, Rector,' the treasurer suggested. 'We're hoping you're here with lots of fresh ideas.'

'Not my function, I'm afraid,' Keith responded firmly. 'I've already told my parishioners that I've been trained for something more vital. I think they've begun to accept that if they really want funds for some project they will find a means of raising money.'

A sudden silence threatened to become awkward. Anne glanced around at her fellow members, noting the eyes that were veiling, the lips clamped in irritation.

She made an effort to smile as she spoke quietly. 'Fair enough. If a parson's commitments are anything like a GP's, there never is a day that contains enough hours! Keith *isn't* in the village to boost our funds, that's true. And we do have several people – some here tonight – who've always succeeded spectacularly in raising the resources needed.'

To her relief, one or two of the stalwarts of the village began to smile.

'We'll show you how it's done then,' the local postmaster said. 'As Dr Newbold says, we've managed before. I'll organise a sub-committee, if you agree. The older residents do deserve somewhere better for getting together.'

Anne was a little surprised on the way home in the car when Keith asked if he had shaken her by being so adamant in rejecting their suggestion.

'About responsibility for fund-raising, you mean?' She shook her head. 'I certainly prefer someone who's straightforward to a person who says what people want to hear, only to protest later on that they cannot commit to helping.'

'It's only that, well...' Keith's voice trailed

off while he worried that he might be making his own role sound too self-important.

'You're here to do other things?' Anne suggested. 'Not just conducting services, but being there for people who're bereaved, those who're depressed, youngsters who seem to have found no guidelines...'

'Glad there's one person I don't have to explain it to. And *you* also have a home taking your time and energy. No doubt your husband is understanding.'

Anne laughed. 'What husband? No one's ever taken that risk!'

Slowing the car outside the rectory, she read the surprise in his eyes, and was pleased. It felt like it was years since any man had appeared astonished that she had remained single. And that person had been Paul Saunders, she reflected. It was strange she should think of him today. The man who once seemed to have all but become a wedge between Caroline and Malcolm Parker.

She was thankful that no one had come between husband and wife; and now just along this hillside Malcolm would be toasting the arrival of his daughter.

'I think we both deserve a drink,' Keith was saying. 'The end of another long day, and neither of us going home to someone who'd help with the unwinding process.'

'Why not?' said Anne, and thanked him.

She hoped that Keith's apparent intention of using her to offset difficulties with his congregation somehow justified her need to delay returning to that empty house.

Until tonight she had believed she truly understood herself. She had assumed that she'd relinquished every last grain of the affection she had felt for Malcolm. And never before had she been acutely conscious of possessing maternal feelings.

'I gather that you live on top of your job, as well,' Keith was saying as he led the way into his home. 'So often we feel there's no real escape, don't we, no place providing space for recharging. Maybe, well, you'd be welcome to find sanctuary here, any time that I am in.'

'Thanks. We'll have to see,' said Anne.

This wasn't the day for committing to any arrangement. Although this somewhat untidy rectory, so evidently the residence of a lone male, *did* feel to be offering a welcome degree of tranquillity.

Welcome? Did this really mean she was growing old? Where was that old compulsion to *live*, to go for challenge, *excitement?*

Two

Coming home with Rebecca on that wet October Monday was an experience no amount of rain could dampen for Caroline and Malcolm. The hospital had approved discharging their premature infant and at last the waiting had ended.

'Do you think they were right back there, and she is nearer full term than you supposed?' asked Malcolm. He needed some indication that they might be justified in feeling easier about assuming responsibility for their daughter. She still looked so tiny. And so fragile that he had to keep looking at her, just to be sure she was quite well.

Caroline – who had reasons to recall precisely when Rebecca was conceived – decided yet again to let Malcolm believe whatever made him more comfortable.

'I suppose they know about likely dates. The important thing is that they finally consider she's strong enough to be entrusted to us.'

The days of waiting until the doctors gave the all-clear had seemed so very long and wearisome. For someone forty-seven, she'd recovered swiftly from the birth, and had hated remaining hospitalised. Although torn between this new scrap of humanity and concern for Malcolm at home, Caroline had refused to contemplate the option of *not* staying there to keep an eye on Rebecca's progress.

'Do you think Chris will still be at the farm?' she asked. The rain lashing into the windscreen suggested that he would be finding the ground too saturated for working.

Malcolm shrugged. 'Could be he'll have headed for home. Doesn't matter – he's been in to the ward, hasn't he, to approve his sister.'

'I know, I just...' Caroline let her voice trail off. She had so wanted to include her stepson in all the excitement. She'd missed several precious days of having Chris around The Sylvan Barn again, longed now to ensure that he still felt really involved, as family.

'Amanda can't wait to welcome you both – said to be sure and tell you she wouldn't dream of leaving the office before you arrive.'

The warmth in Malcolm's voice made her smile, eased the concern she'd been experiencing over Christopher. This husband of hers had been working at the relationship with her elder daughter; she'd never be able to thank him enough for his skilful handling of a delicate situation.

Amanda herself did, indeed, confirm that as soon as Malcolm halted the Jaguar in the drive. Rushing out from the side office entrance, she surged across to fling open the passenger door.

'Mum! It is so great to have you here again. And looking so well.'

She drew Caroline to her in a hug even before looking at Rebecca, who was sleeping in the carrycot.

Her mother's eyes misted. Infinitely thankful though she was to have the baby in their lives, nothing detracted from the delight of being embraced so uninhibitedly by her elder daughter.

'Let me give you a hand,' said Amanda, easing away with a smile to turn and open a rear door.

'Should I, perhaps?' Malcolm suggested. 'The way that carrycot is fixed is really complex.'

'Got to learn, haven't I?' Amanda continued. 'I mean to make myself useful in all kinds of ways, you know.'

Between them, she and Caroline released the restraints, and Amanda insisted on carrying the tiny girl into the entrance hall.

'Welcome home, baby,' they heard her murmur. 'I'm your big sister – the one who's going to teach you everything.'

Through the kitchen doorway Christopher was watching. He laughed.

'Smart-arse!' he observed affectionately. 'Anybody'd think you were the only one around here with any *nous*.'

Privately, however, he was very glad to hear Amanda's assertion. She had been such a hesitant, gauche individual when he'd first met her.

Setting the carrycot down, Amanda gave Chris a look from beneath long lashes. Normally, she'd have torn across to give him a thump, might perhaps have had that develop into a friendly tussle. No one had ever been a closer friend, no one made her so relaxed that she could have fun.

Today, though, she felt somehow different: towards Chris as well as towards her mother and Malcolm, she'd developed a strange tenderness. Amanda had always known how much she owed Christopher for encouraging her to be herself – the person she was meant to be. Without his influence, she'd never have had the guts to study journalism, and later to work alongside her mother. Until having Chris around, she hadn't discovered that love could have so many facets.

After taking a look at Rebecca and checking with Caroline that all was well, Chris returned to the silver that was set out on a kitchen work surface.

His stepmother came to stand at his shoulder, and smiled.

'So this is the silver you were telling me about when you came in to see us. Got yourself quite a job there, haven't you?'

'You can say that again. Interesting, though, especially now we're beginning to decipher hallmarks through all the tarnish.' Searching a book that he'd found for the relevant date letters was exciting.

'How old do you reckon it is then?' Caroline asked, pleased to be actually seeing the discovery from which her hospital stay had excluded her.

'Hard to tell about some of the pieces. But this one, for instance, appears to be eighteenth century. Early, so far as I can see.'

'We're planning on contacting an expert,' Malcolm revealed. 'See that crest – the initials indicate that most are family pieces. GP – and there's always a Graham Parker in every generation. Seems we're justified in paying for proper evaluation.'

'If they can discover how you locate such an expert,' Amanda put in. 'Chris doesn't quite know where to start.'

'And *you* do?' he demanded, blue eyes gleaming wickedly. They'd had fun together polishing the silver, gradually revealing the initials on it, trying to identify hallmarks. His teasing now concealed respect for Amanda's knowledge of history.

'You know I'd have said.' She faced her mother. 'Actually, Chris is right, but this stuff's got to be cleaned up a bit before anyone can read any markings accurately. He might let me help again, now I'm not totally tied up in the office.'

'Has it seemed tough, coping on your own?' Caroline enquired. She had worried about how Amanda might have been managing, although being in that ward had lent distance and a certain unreality to her business life.

Her daughter grinned. 'Dare I say I've loved having my head? There have been odd days, of course, when there've been problems. So far as I know, nothing insoluble.' She was looking forward to showing Caroline all that she'd achieved.

'That's good. In the morning I'll carry Rebecca through and you shall bring me up to speed on everything.'

'Does it have to be morning? I've arranged things so I needn't be in until later. When you said Gran Lucy was coming I rang her. I'm going to pick her up. Unless you want to?'

'I couldn't want anything better. You're a darling to think of driving over to Folkestone for her.'

Lucy Forbes was such a special mother, and Caroline was aching for her to see the baby.

'You will take care tomorrow, won't you?' Caroline said when Amanda was leaving for home. 'I don't know if all the flooding has subsided yet.'

Her daughter groaned. 'I've heard all that already, from Father. Even just about the drive here from Sussex. Something I've tackled every day for ever. I am quite grown up, you know.'

Behaving responsibly was, in fact, something which Amanda was taking very seriously on the journey to and from Folkestone. There was still plenty of evidence of the severity of the flooding. She relished the opportunity to look after her grandmother, at the same time as enjoying their especial rapport.

Lucy certainly seemed in a buoyant mood, and sounded suddenly excited when she asked Amanda to stop almost as soon as they had driven off from her flats.

'What've you forgotten, Gran?'

It was nothing like that. As they drew level and halted beside a tall, white-haired man, Lucy lowered the car window.

'Paul! How nice – but what're you doing here? Thought you'd emigrated.'

Smiling, the man leaned into their car. 'Hello, Lucy. Yes, I'm back far sooner than I expected. Japan didn't work out. Really not for me. A position came up over here, money too good to resist.'

He was giving Amanda a look. Lucy beamed as she introduced them. 'This is my granddaughter, Amanda. She's Caroline's daughter – the senior one now she and Malcolm have the new baby.'

'Ah,' the man said, his expression enigmatic.

'A former resident of the flats, Paul Saunders,' Lucy continued to Amanda.

Amanda's 'Hello' was simply acknowledged by Paul with a nod.

'Ready, Gran?' she enquired, sensing tension, and drove on again.

'Was he awkward with you because of my being there?' she asked as Lucy closed the window. 'He's very attractive. Did you once have a thing about him?'

'Me? Great heavens, no! Paul was just ... a neighbour.'

Lucy made an effort to dismiss thoughts of Paul Saunders, remarked instead on the water still lying in many of the fields they passed, and asked if the torrential rains had caused much of a problem to Malcolm.

'Nothing too awful, I believe. Because of the hillside being so steep there. Though Chris, who's preparing ground for vines, finds digging pretty sticky.'

'And your father's vineyard? Has that suffered?'

'Quite badly. Fortunately, they'd harvested

most of the grapes before the worst of the rains. Now he and Chris are just hoping that the earth dries out without a fresh deluge following on.'

Caroline was feeding Rebecca near an upper window when they arrived at The Sylvan Barn. Lucy ran upstairs to the nursery when Caroline called to her.

'My, but she is a tiny scrap,' Lucy exclaimed, after kissing her daughter. 'But you'll be thankful she is home with you now. And how are you, darling?'

'Surprisingly well, thanks. Must have been that enforced rest during the spell in hospital.'

'That's good, dear. Don't mind admitting I was worried how you'd be, since you're, well...'

'Not as young as I might be?' Caroline finished for her. 'You needn't watch your words, you know. Didn't I tell you I endured being taken for a grandmother rather than a prospective mother during antenatal classes?'

They talked while Rebecca was feeding, then Lucy was given her chance to hold the infant.

'She reminds me of you, Caro, more so than Amanda did. And what do the family think of the new addition? Amanda seems quite enchanted.'

'I feel she is. Bit of a relief, that. According

to Chris, that daughter of mine was afraid at first that she might have to take a back seat. But she's blossoming on the business side, and that's giving her a confidence she never possessed.'

'And Chris, what does he think about his tiny sister?'

'Doesn't say a lot – typical bachelor. I don't believe he feels threatened by changes within the family. He's very much his own man since buying the flat. And having a job away from here has worked for him. No matter how greatly we miss him.'

'And I understand from Amanda there's this new interest, the silver he unearthed from the land here?'

'Right. I'm glad it means he's spending more time around the place. Must admit I'm intrigued to inspect the find properly. Haven't had the opportunity yet to do so thoroughly. And Malcolm's pretty sure most of the silver's family stuff.'

'Have Nick and Bianca seen the baby yet?' Lucy asked, handing the infant back to Caro to be changed.

'Twice, in hospital. I'm just so very thankful that Bianca herself seems about to finally carry a baby to term. After so many disappointments and the boy they lost.'

'She was quite cut up about your becoming pregnant, wasn't she? When she believed she never would have children.'

'Did I tell you that?' Caroline had been so distressed about Bianca's understandable reaction that she hadn't been able to talk about it.

Lucy shook her head. 'Isabel said. Evidently, Bianca confided in her.'

Caroline's eyebrows rose. Her mother-in-law wasn't known for being the most sympathetic of listeners. Although Isabel Parker had been as understanding as anyone when Bianca and Nick lost Baby Malcolm so shortly after he was born.

Lucy smiled. 'As you well know, Isabel never ceases to amaze. *These days*. I gather that whilst you were feeling the effects of pregnancy, she quite often invited Bianca over, sort of took her under her wing.'

Caroline grinned. 'Perhaps the old girl hasn't altered too drastically, after all. Advising and shepherding always were her specialities.'

'And has she done that with you, since Rebecca arrived?'

'As throughout the preceding months. Naturally.'

'I rather gathered that, from Kate.'

'And she's another – that sister of mine grows more like Mother-in-Law by the week! Her being married to Malcolm's brother gives her more access to us than I relish. Plus double entitlement to offer opinions.'

Lucy laughed. 'Opinions which you can ignore.' She understood her own daughters.

'And you'll know that I do just that! Still, despite the drawbacks, it's good to have family around.'

'Even me?' her mother teased.

'You? You're not in their category, not even remotely like our Kate. You're just the person who comes when we need you. And knows when to bite her tongue.'

Ah, yes, thought Lucy. Especially today. She only hoped that Amanda would be equally circumspect. This was not the time for mentioning that Paul Saunders was back in England.

Leaving Lucy in charge of Rebecca the following morning, Caroline went into her office to have Amanda update her on the work situation. Her daughter was on the line to the publishers for one of their clients, a youngish man whose first novel was due to be launched to quite a stir.

Over the years, they had won the interest of several writers, and Amanda was enjoying publicising their books. Caroline listened now to her end of the telephone conversation. She noticed the positive attitude her daughter had acquired, and observed the courtesy and consideration which, in the PR business, sometimes could be lost beneath the need to be thrusting.

'I'm proud of you,' she told her when the receiver was replaced and Amanda smiled across the desk. 'It's marvellous to rely on you as I do, and good to see you happy here.'

'Anything to oblige,' said Amanda lightly, but her brown eyes were gleaming.

Caroline had in mind to offer her a promotion, but she didn't mean to announce that quite yet. She could believe Amanda might see that purely as inducement to work harder still while Caro herself was preoccupied with the new baby. And she didn't wish her daughter to think anything of the kind. By waiting a little she could offer the reward as it was intended: the ultimate acknowledgement of years of excellent progress.

They talked for an hour, mostly concerning the job, and much of that discussing the fees chargeable to certain clients. The nature of their business meant that no two situations were ever alike. Even among the writers they promoted. And naturally they worked for people in all manner of lines: painters, musicians, some politicians who felt their parties were not providing adequate coverage.

'I have kept meticulous records of the time I've put in for each one,' said Amanda. 'You can take a look.'

'I'm not checking up on you, darling. I

know there's no need. We've worked together long enough to assure me on that.'

Her daughter grinned. 'Did wonder. Glad you're OK about how much I'm taking over.'

'Something tells me you were afraid I mightn't be.'

'I'd better come clean. That was my father. He does tend to paint you as preferring a hands-on approach.'

Caroline laughed. 'Really? Now why doesn't that surprise me? I suppose Julian does have a point. As I recall, in the life I had with him there weren't too many occasions when I surrendered will and whims to him.'

'But you do accept each other with good grace now.'

'So long as we don't meet too often!'

'Seriously, I'm glad things haven't soured between you. He says congratulations, by the way, about Rebecca. And he knew you'd cope well.'

Again, Caroline laughed. But she felt pleased that her ex didn't think too badly of her.

'I suspect his mellowing attitude towards me owes a great deal to you, you know.'

'Me?' Amanda was astonished.

'The efficient way you're turning out. Proving I didn't damage you too severely.'

'Mum!' Amanda came round the desk to

hug her. 'You're brilliant. Chris thinks so as well, always has.'

Suddenly, Caroline felt quite emotional. She'd often seemed weepy since the baby was born, and having such assurances from her mature family heightened her feelings. Especially regarding Christopher. She had always had a particular affection for that stepson of hers.

During the past few years she had grown deeply concerned that he had no one special in his life. There had even been one period when Malcolm was afraid that Chris might possibly have some secret leanings that precluded his having a girlfriend. This wasn't a possibility that Caroline had ever entertained, but she was still concerned that Christopher appeared so *alone*.

'Are you going to obtain expert advice about this silver then, Chris?' Lucy enquired.

Rebecca was sleeping in her cot, and Lucy was delighted to find Christopher in the kitchen, still gently cleaning the second of the candlesticks he had found.

'Got someone coming later today, as a matter of fact. Didn't know where to begin, but I found her on the Internet. Diana Frazer, her name is, though Dad's already calling her my "silver lady".'

'Does she have some distance to travel?'

The weather was wretched yet again, so wet that Chris and Malcolm had abandoned all thought of working the ground for those vines.

'Not really, Gran. Her home's in Sussex, not far from me, actually. Near Rye.'

'And if she drives at your pace, that'll take no time at all.'

'Steady – I thought you and I were pals.'

'As we are. And I know you can take a bit of teasing.'

'So long as it's from you. Certainly wouldn't get it from my other gran.'

'Your real one, don't forget.' Deeply delighted though she was that both Chris and his brother treated her as their grandmother, Lucy had always been perturbed that they seemed less affectionate towards Isabel Parker.

'You'll be reminding me next that I'm only Caro's *step*son. You should know by now that the legal relationship makes no difference to the way I feel about you, any more than about my lovely stepmother. But listen to me – going all soft on you. Must be all the sentimentality in the air, new babies and that.'

'Makes you think, doesn't it – new life.'

'Makes me think too much, Gran. And you're not to quote me on that to anyone.'

Lucy reflected on Christopher's admission

when Diana Frazer's car drew up and he went running to greet her. Tall, and quite elegantly proportioned, he was such a personable young man, likeable too – not everyone was both. Especially among career-minded young people.

Chris himself felt rather taken aback, paused just for a second to recover. There was no reason that he should have expected someone around his own age, was there? Yet this woman stepping from her car had silver hair.

My silver lady, he thought, and smiled.

Only as she came near enough for him to grasp her extended hand did he see that Diana Frazer's short, stylish hair wasn't white at all, but a very light blonde. Her serious but lovely face revealed her as being little more than thirty or so. Christopher felt relieved that she appeared to be a contemporary, and not someone whose years might combine with her expertise to make him feel disadvantaged.

Diana Frazer nevertheless seemed forceful, her grip on his hand as firm as her brisk 'Good afternoon' and 'Do lead the way' after he responded to her greeting. The red closely fitted jacket she wore against the rain, black trousers and high-heeled boots reinforced the positive impression.

Walking beside her through the hall to the dining room, Chris sensed Diana glancing about her at the high white walls and dark supporting beams. He felt glad that Caroline and his father had created an impressive house that no one could dismiss as ostentatious.

'You've a lovely home,' she told him with an appreciative glance towards the nicely proportioned staircase.

'Not my home now, actually; I have my own place. But this was a good house to live in – plenty of space.'

'During that period when families irk?' Diana suggested.

He felt warmed by her understanding. 'Especially then. Even brothers who are only a few years younger can seem so infantile that – in their way – they're almost as boring as parents!'

Her smile melted away the sombre lines around her lips, and revealed gleaming teeth. Eyes as blue as his own were glinting with amusement.

'You'll be telling me next that I missed nothing by being an only child!'

Chris shook his head. 'I'd never say that. And our family's still growing: we've a new member – very new, a sister. The first girl, unless you count Amanda, who's no relation, really – my stepmother's daughter from her first marriage.'

They had reached the dining room and its display of silver. He stopped speaking, and recognised that Diana Frazer had generated a rare impulse to talk about his own background.

'Here we are then,' Chris announced. Rather obviously, he reflected.

Drawing out a chair, he invited her to sit, and breathed in her delicate but sophisticated scent. There was a lot to like about Diana Frazer.

She took a pair of cotton gloves from her black leather bag, slipped them on, and reached for one of the candlesticks. Her expression serious again, she turned the object slowly, examining every side. From the square base decorated in relief with a pattern of leaves, it rose in a fluted column which had reminded Christopher of architectural designs. Setting the candlestick down, Diana appraised every angle, checking for any damage, before finally examining the hallmark on the base.

'Any idea how old this is?' she asked him.

'Well, as a matter of fact, I couldn't believe my interpretation of the hallmark.'

'It's from 1765. A column candlestick.'

'I wasn't wrong then. But it's in such good condition.'

'Are these family pieces? Couldn't be sure from what you said over the phone.'

'Dad believes they are. Some are, certainly. They have initials – like those in that sort of crest near the base. He thinks he's identified some great-great-great-whatever. He dug out a family bible, which is sourcing lots of old names. We're all becoming quite intrigued, only there's not been much time yet for researching. And he and Caro are somewhat preoccupied, naturally. The new infant.'

'Quite an exciting time. Well, this is one item where we can fix the date, even without any provenance. Let's see what some of the others tell us.'

Diana placed the first candlestick to one side and reached for what Christopher had identified as a coffee pot. He was proved to be wrong.

'A chocolate pot,' she assured him. 'Probably late eighteenth century, but the mark's almost obliterated by overzealous polishing.'

'I know, I'm trying to be gentle. Not coffee, though? How can you tell?'

'See that aperture in the lid – it's for the *molionet*, used for stirring. Unfortunately, this is one item that's acquired a bit of damage over the years. Not surprising – you did say these things were found buried?'

'Inside a huge bag, then with a massive stone slab over the top. Took both Dad and I to shift it.'

'Wish I'd been here at the time. You did say it was out here somewhere?'

'I'll show you if you want. Perhaps on a

better day.' He glanced sideways to the rain flowing steadily down the window. 'That's if you come here again.'

Diana examined another candlestick, and then a pair, all of which she asserted were Victorian copies of an earlier style. 'Silver, nevertheless, not plated, so worth quite a bit. Do I take it none of this is insured – separately from household contents cover, I mean?'

'That's one of the reasons we need an evaluation. We wouldn't plan on selling unless we became desperate to realise on them.'

'Good, good. I like to hear of things remaining in a home where they're appreciated.'

'While they, in turn, appreciate?' Chris suggested.

Diana smiled. 'With luck, yes. No reason to suppose anything I've examined so far wouldn't do so.'

She had picked up an elegant covered jug with a curved spout that rose to almost the same height as its handle.

'A claret jug, we thought,' said Chris, hoping to be proved right this time.

She shook her head. 'Afraid not, and unless you've an ancestor with a clerical background, this might not be strictly family. I'd need verification, of course, but I'd swear this is ecclesiastical silver. Quite early too – further back than anything I've ever handled.'

'Really? Belonging to the Church?'

'You've no knowledge of any parsons among your forebears then?'

'None. So far as my father knows, Parkers have always been farmers – "gentlemen farmers", he likes to insist.'

He laughed, and Diana smiled, almost conspiratorially. The warmth she generated was delightful and seemed to be enveloping him.

'Well, nonsense like that doesn't hold up too well today, does it,' he said.

Only two or three further items remained to be inspected. Chris caught himself wishing that he'd unearthed more of a hoard. He was enjoying this, felt more at ease than he did with many women, and at the same time more excited.

Grown selective in his choice of female company, he had ceased to expect very much from any chance encounters, was unprepared today for the force of attraction rising right through him to render concentration difficult.

'I'd love to come here again,' Diana was saying. 'See where you found this lot. Are you sure there's nothing else concealed there?'

He was too busy absorbing the fact that she had promised to return to elaborate.

'Couldn't see anything more.'

Diana seemed not to notice his preoccupation, continued just the same. 'These last few things warrant more detailed examination, I believe. In particular, this one here.'

'A wine goblet, isn't it?'

'Could be perhaps. I lean more towards its being a kind of chalice.'

'Something else belonging to a church then.'

'And far older than all the rest, or I'm greatly mistaken. Though there's no mark that I can decipher.'

'How would you set about authenticating objects like that? And wouldn't they have to be returned to the Church?'

'Investigating possible sources and eventually identifying ownership could take ages. There isn't time enough for even discussing all likely avenues today. We might start by enquiring of your local vicar, find out how far back parish records go. There may be inventories of church plate and other valuables.'

'It's a rector locally, and he's very new.'

'Makes no difference. He'll still have access to any records in existence.'

'I could contact him any time. Or ... or would that be venturing into your territory? I really don't understand how much I'm supposed to do.'

Diana smiled. 'Anything that'll help us dig

out the facts. You're keen, which is good. You might wish to consider that whatever you discover will save my time – reduce my fee a bit!'

'What happens if our local church has no knowledge of these items? Where do we go from there?'

'You must have a Roman Catholic church somewhere in the vicinity. Failing that, there are various specialists that I can consult. And we keep an open mind as to who could have been in this area around the relevant period.'

'Or afterwards, I suppose, if they were carrying the stuff with them.'

'There is that, yes. We must bear in mind, though, that people didn't tend to move about anything like so much as they do today.'

'True, of course. Except, our land does adjoin the Pilgrims' Way.'

'Good point, Christopher. I didn't realise we were that close here.'

Her smiling acknowledgement and her use of his name increased his already accelerating pulse. It seemed years since any woman had exhilarated him so swiftly, and to such a dramatic degree.

Chris drew in a long breath, struggling to calm his emotions and hoping that nothing betrayed the effect that she was having upon him. He might have been a lad in his teens experiencing all the power of an urge that had never known fulfilment. Instead of which, he was a fully mature man whose life so far had produced a spectrum of brief relationships with attractive females.

'I'm not boring you, I hope?' Diana was gazing at him, concern shadowing expressive eyes. 'I do tend to go on rather when I'm intrigued by a find. And most of this little collection really is worthy of much closer investigation.'

'You're not boring in the least. I'm just ... overwhelmed.' He hadn't meant to express his reaction in quite that way. The words had somehow tumbled out. Her smile seemed to indicate that she was pleased by his interest. Chris could only be relieved that Diana would be thinking enthusiasm regarding the silver was all that was exciting him. Surely, there was no way that she might guess that *she* was responsible for his elation!

'I'm delighted by our immediate affinity,' Diana announced, making him contain a gasp, while he rationalised again that she was simply referring to their task.

'So am I. I wondered what it would be like to have an expert examine this lot, but I didn't begin to suppose that it'd all be so enjoyable.'

'For me as well,' she assured him. 'So often people are guarded with me, afraid

I'm about to destroy their illusions about precious possessions. Then there are those who believe they know best, waste my time by denying all that I'm telling them.'

'Really? But where's the point – when you call in a specialist, you've got to at least hear them out.'

'You'd be surprised. This has been a real treat. I look forward to continuing our investigation into all this lovely silver. I have a feeling the entire experience is going to prove tremendously rewarding. Fun, too, I suspect!'

They discussed the early tasks each would pursue individually, and a tentative date for their next meeting. Diana also suggested a round sum which should be added to his father's insurance policy to cover the silver at her initial evaluation.

This sounded an enormous amount and Chris reminded himself that if those two pieces were ecclesiastical they could eventually be going elsewhere. Even if that were so, the balance for the family would provide a substantial reserve.

'I can't thank you enough,' he exclaimed, walking through to the front door where her car was waiting.

Diana smiled into his eyes, her hand lingering in his as they said goodbye. 'If you should learn anything ahead of our next get-together, call me,' she said. 'I can't wait to get down to unearthing more with you.'

Christopher smiled. 'Me too.'

He remained at the door and watched while she got into her car, turned it adroitly in the drive and sped off. As Diana reached the end of the drive, she raised one hand in a final wave.

His father, now crossing from the farm office, jolted him back to the reality of what had, after all, been a business meeting.

'A good report from your silver lady?' Malcolm enquired. 'Thought you might have included me in on a part, at least, of the proceedings.'

'Oh ... I didn't really believe you'd spare the time.'

'Fair enough. Just bear that in mind on the next occasion, eh?'

'Sure, Dad. Fine.'

But was that fine? Christopher wondered. He hadn't planned on his father being in on his meetings with Diana Frazer. That wasn't quite the way that he was visualising the agenda.

Three

'You can leave that to me, you know. I'm quite happy to attend,' Amanda assured Caroline firmly.

Of course she was glad her mother and the baby were home from hospital and fine, but that hadn't ended Amanda's unease. She was concerned on her own behalf now, afraid that some of the confidence that seemed so natural during the days when she coped alone was being eroded.

'Wouldn't going up to London interfere with Rebecca's feeds?' she persisted, and watched for Caroline's reaction. This wasn't the first time recently that Amanda had struggled to hang on to challenging aspects of the job.

'I know, but there's always some way round a difficulty.'

Caroline had never intended that having this baby should encroach on her running of the company which she had fought to establish. She was tired, nevertheless – uninterrupted sleep seemed to come harder the older you were. And she must find time from somewhere to organise the christening. Malcolm was so thrilled with Rebecca he was determined she must have everything. As soon as possible. Caroline ran a hand through hair that needed washing.

'I suppose you saw what I did while preparing for last year's Awards.'

Amanda had helped on that day too – literary events were her daughter's speciality. Much of the work for this current function was already completed: press releases had gone out weeks ago with an announcement of the shortlist. Between them, they had already contacted TV and radio book programmes, features editors and regional journalists. This necessary reminder helped to keep the occasion fresh in the minds of the people they relied on for good coverage. Caroline supposed really that they'd done sufficient already to believe the event would run smoothly.

She smiled. 'You'd enjoy taking charge at The Savoy, wouldn't you?'

'I'd love it, of course. I won't let you down, I promise.'

'I didn't think you would, darling. To be honest, it's me being reluctant to let go, even a little.' She hoped the truth would help Amanda understand that she wasn't determined to keep her down.

'You had to fight Malcolm's opposition initially to set the company up, didn't you.'

'You haven't forgotten what I told you – how he only wanted me to continue working in the farm office. For *him*.'

Quite, Amanda reflected, and I suspect that you'll never relinquish enough of the responsibility to satisfy me. Had she been fooling herself while her mother was away, had her own enjoyment of taking charge generated the wishful dream that she would continue to prove her ability?

Thankful that she had at least won consent to tackle this occasion on her own, she smiled. 'You can check all the arrangements I put in place, right up to the time I set out on the day, can't you?'

There'll be no need for that, Caroline recognised. And that fact was at the heart of her own misgivings. It wasn't fear of Amanda's falling short that created this unease.

'I will go through the checklist with you, if you're more comfortable with that, but you'll handle it OK, I'm sure.'

'Thanks. I'm very pleased.'

And she would also be pleased to get away from The Sylvan Barn, just for those few hours. Whatever was wrong with her, she didn't know, but life here seemed less of a delight than she'd anticipated it would be. She had so looked forward to helping with the baby as well as with the running of the office. But, dearly though she loved

Rebecca, the infant created too many disturbing emotions.

Amanda kept telling herself it was insane to long for her own baby when she wasn't even in a steady relationship. She couldn't begin to understand the part of her that seemed obsessed with this yearning for a child. Bringing up a family, surely, depended upon creating a home. And she had never once fallen in love. These days, when women gave their careers priority, settling down with someone was often delayed. But there should be first the desperation of wanting some particular man – the obsession ought to be with one special person.

Was she abnormal? Holding Rebecca generated such powerful feelings. Even the sweet scent of baby powder started up this longing. Amanda hoped it was simply that she'd become too immersed in the family preoccupation with her tiny sister, and only needed to get away and work on something totally different.

The moment she strode in through the riverside entrance of The Savoy to greet and assemble shortlisted authors and journalists, Amanda felt happier. This provided enough of a challenge to distract her from all personal considerations. Early though she was, the room allocated for interviews seemed full already. She crossed briskly to greet the events organiser for the society they were promoting.

A dapper man with white hair and beard, he hurried at her side while she went from group to group, extracting authors from their attendant agents and publishers. It was Amanda's theory that writers made more of an individual impact on the media in an interview conducted without promptings from some 'nanny'. This idea didn't necessarily accord with those of a few people in publishing.

Her PR homework had found for each contender a hook to generate good copy. All six authors were fizzing with the thrill of being nominated – even the more reticent began to enjoy revealing themselves rather than the biographies they had written.

'Don't be afraid to talk about yourself,' Amanda had primed each of them in advance. She felt enormous relief when the room soon began pulsing with elated conversations. Cameras, still and videotape, went into action.

Agents and publishers, many of them former colleagues in a business that thrived on career moves and mergers, sipped their drinks, greeted each other, and waited. Smiles fixed in what they hoped that others would read as satisfaction, they wished away the time leading to the announcement of the winner.

Until after the luncheon in the Lancaster Room, the result would remain known only to the judges – a handful selected by the committee from within the book trade and the media. Amanda checked again that all the writers were being interviewed, watched the press moving from one candidate to another, then slipped away. She needed a word with the president of the society. They were well accustomed to organising these events, but it didn't hurt to take a swift look around the room that was set for the meal, particularly to ensure that no aspect of PR might go amiss.

All in order, Amanda returned to find journalists and authors still animatedly conversing. She began watching the time; this session must not overrun, or seating everyone at tables would be delayed. The timing of the meal and subsequent speeches was finely tuned; announcement of the winner must accommodate final interviews.

The early part of her work completed, Amanda eventually found her table, and relaxed. She gazed around her at the candle-light and chandeliers gleaming back from mirrored walls enhanced by decor which looked quite baroque. Delighted by the ambience, she enjoyed her meal, and the first of the speeches which followed.

It was time then to intervene. She must ensure that the award winner reached the platform and was subsequently conducted away, together with her agent and publisher, to face further interviews.

Amanda was pleased the winner was virtually unknown – not quite a first-time biographer, but hitherto barely recognised. A woman of around forty-five, she seemed astonished to have won, and was shaking as she walked beside her.

'I could do with having you teach me a few tricks for handling media folk,' she admitted. 'Do you take on individual clients like me?'

'We do,' Amanda replied. 'Although I'm afraid lots of writers find that comes too expensive. But maybe after today you won't be counting the pennies!'

'I wish. Anyway, do give me your number, and I'll see how things go.'

Amanda was pleased. Much later, when she was leaving for home, she felt that the winner's desire for their professional assistance – even if it should come to nothing – gave an extra fillip to what had proved a successful day.

'I'm glad we've succeeded in getting together. As I told you over the phone, we rather think these two items were ecclesiastical pieces originally,' said Chris.

Keith Clifton had introduced himself and welcomed him into the rectory. 'And I've brought what records I could find over from the church. It's so cold in there this time of year, even in the vestry. We try not to heat the place on days when it's not being used to the full.'

'Know what you mean. When the farm wasn't doing too well, The Sylvan Barn used to be so cold it'd freeze your balls off...' Chris stopped hastily, shrugged. 'Well, you know what I mean.'

Keith's brown eyes glinted and he grinned. 'Nobody knows better. So, come through then – it's warmer in my study. A bit more comfortable, too, than the rest of the house – haven't got round yet to finding myself a housekeeper.'

'You'd recognise my flat, I suspect,' said Chris, liking the man immediately.

'You don't still live at the farm?'

'Nor do I work there. I manage a vineyard in Sussex – that's why I'm seconded occasionally to help my father prepare a bit of his land for grapes.'

'Hence the unearthing of this silver, yes?'

'Right. As I told you, we got an expert in – she's the one who deemed these likely to be church plate.'

As they sat down Chris extracted the chalice and flagon from his bag and set them in the space Keith had cleared on his leather-topped desk.

The rector picked up the chalice and

began to examine the details of its quite modest ornamentation. He progressed to inspecting the base for hallmarks, then set it down again and looked across at Christopher.

'Nothing conclusive, I'm afraid. You may look through these records, of course, but descriptions of the few pieces that aren't still among the items in our possession bear little resemblance to this.'

'Pity. I'd have enjoyed restoring some long-lost treasure to you. And this other thing ... a kind of flagon?'

After careful examination, that piece also proved to be unidentifiable as belonging to their church.

'Could be RC, though,' Keith suggested. 'Have you contacted them?'

'Not yet, but the expert I saw suggested that. Perhaps because Dad's always been C of E, I naturally supposed the family always were. I'll try them now, though I shan't be as pleased as I would have been if this stuff belonged in the village.'

Christopher asked how Keith was settling into the community.

'Been fortunate in some ways. Anne Newbold has helped to make me feel rather more at home here.' Keith smiled, picturing Anne's friendly hazel eyes.

'She's our doctor. Saved Dad really, when he had his coronary. Did a lot for the village when we were opposing the rail link as well – not that anyone's intervention made much difference, though.'

'So, she's deeply involved here, not solely through her practice?'

'Been on the parish council since for ever. That's how my father first really got to know her. He did a stint on the council, until the powers that be in County Hall got up his nose. Not that we farmers anywhere ever believe enough is done for us, I must admit!'

Keith laughed with him. 'You seem to have a balanced view of family, as well as of the locality.'

'If you don't by my age, you're either thick or an ostrich. I try not to be either.'

Keith offered him a beer, and they sat for an hour or so talking. Chris was interested that Keith had trained in the north of England, and was keen to learn how he reacted to living among southerners.

'Dare I say, it's not easy? Yorkshire folk are forthright, yes. But warm, and you know where you are with them. Here ... but I'd better not say – you will know people among my congregation.'

'Even though you haven't seen me there!' Chris had wondered how Keith might react to someone who never attended church.

The response was another laugh. 'For all I know, you're a regular somewhere near your flat. Since you're not claiming that's the case, I'll adopt my normal policy of not boring friends to sobs by thrusting my beliefs on them. Besides, it's good for me to have acquaintances outside my congregation.' Since arriving in this village Keith suspected that might become even more true.

'And what are your interests beyond your work, then?' Chris enquired.

'Used to be various sports. After leaving the army, the training for this job seemed pretty intensive, so I dropped out of activities like that. The rugby I used to play obviously requires finding a team – must admit I haven't made the effort.'

'Ever tried squash? I played quite a lot at one time.'

'I did give it a go, but never took it very seriously.'

'Want to give it a try? I used to play Anne Newbold's nephew, until he married and moved away. Could be good for us both.'

They agreed to meet up at the club where Chris had been a regular. When Keith saw him to the door they were both feeling pleased by the effect of the evening, if not for the reasons originally anticipated.

'You look great! Been somewhere special?' Chris met Amanda just inside the door of The Sylvan Barn as he was returning those silver items to his father's safe. He couldn't stop looking at her. The softly tailored summer suit was of a blue that enhanced the whites of her eyes, emphasising gleaming brown irises and long, long lashes.

'An awards lunch at The Savoy sound special enough?' Amanda laughed. 'I arrived back on quite a high, to be honest. Went without any hitches, and the winner of the award might even take us on to promote her.'

'So Caroline's even more pleased with you than usual, eh?'

'Seems to reckon I'm doing all right.'

'You'll have to watch it or she'll be afraid you'll make her redundant!'

It was said lightly, meant as a joke, but Amanda glanced over her shoulder to see who was around, and sighed. 'Actually, I wonder sometimes if she does consider that might become a real possibility. She wasn't at all eager for me to tackle today on my own.'

'Want to talk?'

'Aren't you in a hurry to get home?'

'Give me a moment to lock these away, then I'll be with you. Talk in your car, if you like.'

They were accustomed to needing space in which to have a private word without affecting anyone else in the family.

'You smell delicious, too,' Chris remarked, getting into the passenger seat beside her. Today's scent was glamorous, increasing her attractiveness.

Amanda swallowed, steadied her emotions. The compliment made her feel decidedly heady. She had been warmed by his admiration and his willingness to talk through her anxieties.

When Chris prompted her to confide, she sighed again. 'You're going to think I'm out of my skull. I've been so fortunate here, having Mum take me on, train me in such an interesting job. Why am I suddenly sensing that she might be seeing me as, well, as a potential rival within the company?'

'Probably it's largely her reaction to the changes of having Rebecca. If I know Caro, she'll be struggling to keep on top of the work at the same time as giving the baby her best attention. And then she sees you, putting all you've got into the company – and *you* can give it all your time, unlike her.'

'I couldn't bear it if she started to resent me, Chris.'

'Yet you still have your own ambitions, need to prove you can tackle everything that Caroline handles.'

Amanda nodded. 'I thought you'd understand. I don't sound quite paranoid then?'

'Sensitive, that's all – to Caro's feelings as well as your own. No bad thing.'

'I can't help wanting to do better all the time – to, well, to show I have it in me.' It was only at work that she felt in any way mature.

'You don't have to tell me. You didn't see what Dad was like when I was employed by him. Couldn't bear anyone to have any ideas. Even Caroline. That's the worst thing about working with family. Anywhere else, and you scarcely consider whether the other person might be afraid because you're actually learning *too* well.'

'What do I do, Chris?'

'Go for it. Make a bid for whatever you want. If your ambition's stifled you'll be no good. And try not to worry. Know what I think? Long before Caro becomes seriously afraid that you're likely to overtake her, she could be starting to accept that putting Rebecca first equates with handing you greater responsibility.'

Amanda felt better for the talk with Christopher, which was no surprise. He'd always seemed so supportive, yet at the same time encouraged her to stand on her own feet. Not for the first time, she wished he could have turned out to be the right man for her.

That was not to be, as she had recognised for years. Right from the start, any physical involvement had seemed taboo. They might not literally be related, but having her mother become Christopher's stepmother created something too closely resembling kinship.

I do love him, though, thought Amanda, glad he would always be there for her.

The day of Rebecca's christening in November was rare – brighter than many during the previous couple of months. The sun shone brilliantly as they set out in quite a procession of cars immediately after lunch.

Despite Malcolm's concern that Caroline might be attempting too much, she had laid on a roast for all the family. Carefully planned with Florence Dacre, and much of it prepared in advance, the meal seemed to delight everyone. Even Isabel Parker had agreed with Lucy that no one could have produced better.

Amanda smiled to herself, overhearing, made a mental note to tell her mother.

Her Aunt Kate and Uncle Graham seemed out to enjoy the occasion, and Amanda relished the fact that their son and daughter had declined the invitation. She never had felt quite at ease with those cousins.

Christopher's brother Nick was – like him – a good person to have around, fun to be with, especially now that Bianca and he were only weeks away from the birth of their long-awaited baby.

Amanda was travelling in their car to the church, and happy to have a quiet chat with the other girl, away from the general hubbub of family conversation. They had grown so close during that dreadful time when Bianca had endured such a host of miscarriages and the tragic death of her first infant.

Today, Amanda was savouring the fact that she was to be godmother to her tiny sister, and was delighted that Malcolm endorsed her being chosen. He had taken such trouble recently to treat her as part of the Parker family. She smiled to herself over his teasing when she had asked if she would be holding Rebecca in church. 'You'll regret that when she throws up on your glamorous suit!'

'Caroline's looking tired, isn't she?' Bianca remarked as they set out. 'Nick says she's still just as busy on the PR side. Is she one of those people who can't delegate, or something?'

Amanda immediately felt torn between loyalty to her mother and confiding in one of her own contemporaries who might see her point of view. 'She does, in fact. Delegate, I mean.' She told Bianca about the successful event at The Savoy. 'Although I must admit there are times when I sense she's not entirely happy to hand over too much to me.'

'That's Caro,' said Nick. 'Always good at running everything, but not quite sure anyone else should be.'

'Isn't that a bit harsh, darling?' Bianca

suggested. She'd never suspected that Nick might be less than totally enamoured with his stepmother. Bianca adored her.

'I didn't mean to imply she's holding me back,' Amanda put in swiftly. 'She has taught me so much.'

'Use it then,' Nick advised. 'Tell her you think she's not letting you progress. Caro could be looking for an opportunity to shift more on to your shoulders.'

'I couldn't do that,' said Amanda, and wished she'd avoided this conversation.

'Of course you wouldn't – I know you,' said Bianca. 'Wish I knew what to advise. You must feel split between what you wish to achieve and preventing Caro from feeling she's past her best.'

'I'd never make her feel that!' Amanda was appalled by the thought of anything of the kind. 'She's still brilliant, you know.'

'But older,' said Nick. 'Plus mother to a new infant. Makes a difference.'

'Maybe I'm partly at fault,' Amanda suggested. 'Too preoccupied with the job. Never was intentional, that. It's just the way it's happened.'

'Still no one you really fancy then?' asked Bianca. 'When you meet someone you'll wonder how you ever managed to put so much into your work!'

Talking about the subject hadn't helped. By the time they were following the rest of the family up the church path and through the door to assemble around the font, Amanda was wishing that she hadn't risked discussing her misgivings. However nice she was, Bianca made her feel like a misfit. Why did *she* never experience any passion? Over the years, the succession of casual boy-friends had only proved that she wasn't readily swayed by sexual attraction. It wasn't that she'd grown up repressed, rather that she'd matured with a whole spectrum of expectations. Like she needed to be loved more than desired?

Isabel Parker, in traditional matriarchal mode, was scanning the gathering of her extended family, motioning Malcolm and Caroline with Rebecca to one side of her, Graham and Kate to the other. Christopher and Bianca, the other godparents, stood beside Amanda, who nodded approvingly to herself when she intercepted a smile exchanged between Isabel and her own grandmother.

I wish I was more like Gran Lucy, Amanda thought. She might perhaps be happier with less of the ambition to succeed at work and more of Lucy's ability to get along with people.

The rector turned from a brief discussion with Malcolm and Caroline, glanced about checking that Rebecca's godparents were in the right place. Brown eyes met Amanda's, and smiled warmly. He might have recognised some affinity.

Amanda smiled back, began to relax, found she was drawn to this man by his deep, pleasing voice commencing the ceremony. Her determination to concentrate on the full meaning of the baptism was dissipated, altered by the overwhelming need to look again at this tall, striking rector with such dark wavy hair.

Hauling back her attention to the words rather than the man, Amanda prayed and uttered vows on her small sister's behalf, yet still her awareness grew. She was hooked, totally fascinated by Keith Clifton.

Their fingers touched as she handed Rebecca to him; his smile sought her eyes while she gave the names 'Rebecca Lucy Isabel'.

Throughout the remainder of the service, Amanda's feelings went soaring. Only as the family talked softly afterwards did she begin to come down from the high generated by the rector. He had gone off to change, and not a minute too soon for Amanda's composure.

Returning her attention to the family group, she saw afresh the love so evident between her mother and Malcolm, their joy rediscovered since the birth of their infant. All signs of tiredness evaporated, Caroline seemed to glow, hair and eyes alight to compete with the colour of her russet-gold outfit. And as for Malcolm, Amanda wouldn't have believed she'd ever see his grey eyes awash with emotion in public. 'I've never been happier,' she heard him say, and saw the approving nod from his mother Isabel.

As the Reverend Keith Clifton got out of Christopher's car in the drive of the house Amanda felt the surge of another impulse of attraction. When Chris grasped her by the arm, taking her towards him to introduce them, she willed herself not to go all foolish and tremble.

'Don't believe you've met Amanda properly, Keith. She's Caroline's daughter from her first marriage, you know. We're all very fond of her.'

His hands were cool from the November air, but smooth on hers, their grasp firm as her fingers were enclosed, cocooned between both of his palms.

Her strong PR voice emerged as they said 'How do you do?' while inwardly Amanda quivered like a Jane Austen heroine.

'Do come inside,' she said. 'I'm pleased you've got the time to join us here.'

'So am I. Baptism is too short an occasion for getting to know people better.'

Christopher, who'd been prepared to ensure that Keith should feel at ease with everyone, smiled to himself, and turned instead towards Grandmother Isabel. It was years now since he had felt intimidated by her, years during which he'd acquired the self-assurance to cope.

Offering his arm, he led the old lady through into the entrance hall where Florence Dacre had yet again proved an excellent housekeeper. Notwithstanding her earlier efforts at interpreting Caroline's ideas for lunch, she had set out a welcoming array of drinks, together with a finger buffet.

Chris found his grandmother a chair, and suggested that he place it to one end of the long table.

'You might find that more comfortable than trying to juggle a plate and glass while maintaining your usual erudite conversation.'

Isabel laughed as Chris took her coat and she lowered herself on to the chair.

'Wherever did you acquire such a flattering tongue, Christopher? It surely was not inherited from your father!'

Chris grinned. 'Don't tell me I shall become the sole Parker *not* known for straight-speaking.'

'I only know you're a dear – and perhaps someone I've tended to neglect while your brother and Bianca seemed in greater need.'

While well aware of her own reputation as a martinet, Isabel had always tried to be fair in her treatment of the family. Her sons Malcolm and Graham, for instance, different from each other though they were. And Christopher and Nicholas, again not very alike, in her estimation.

Christopher's smile grew serious. 'I've always tried to stand on my own feet. And I do agree that Nick has needed to know he has all the family behind him.'

'And now there's the little one to compete with for your father's attention. There'll be times when other noses are put out of joint, I fear.'

'Not while I have my own place, my own life,' he assured her. 'Though I've enjoyed coming back here to help prepare ground for the vineyard.'

'And that find of silver – don't forget you must show me while I'm here. These days, I don't get around nearly so often as I'd like.'

Isabel straightened her already upright spine, quelled a sigh. All too frequently now she felt tired, exhausted really, but she would admit that to no one. And most certainly not on this day, when everyone must celebrate.

Bianca joined them then, smiling as she began talking about the collection of books which Isabel had entrusted to them.

'One day soon I'm going to read them all, when I'm no longer out at work all day. There are a few I wanted to ask you about, though. They're not published books, you see.'

'The diaries, you mean.'

'You do know they're among the rest, then?'

'Where they're meant to be. If you can't entrust writings to a librarian, who can you trust? Have you read any of those, dear?'

'Just took a look. War things – the one I dipped into was all in the trenches.'

And perhaps not ideal for a pregnant mother, Isabel thought. She was glad, though, to know those diaries would be preserved safely.

Malcolm was opening up the champagne, helped by Nicholas, who began pouring and handing around glasses. He glanced about for Amanda, meaning to ensure that she was grouped with the other godparents and Caro and himself. She was standing a little way off, speaking earnestly with the new rector.

Perhaps he wouldn't disturb them. Everyone present knew who had taken part in the ceremony. He would mention Amanda, of course, along with Bianca and Chris. He might use the opportunity to say a word about his own mother – who would expect that – and Lucy.

Malcolm hadn't forgotten – never would forget – the way that Lucy had come dashing to them years ago when he was rushed to hospital. Always there, always ready to help – that was Lucy. Caroline was very like her mother in so many ways, yet at one time had seemed too busy to simply *be there for him*.

Leaving Nick to hand out the remainder of the glasses, Malcolm strode across to where Lucy was holding Rebecca, smiling as she chatted with Caroline.

'I need you both,' said Malcolm. 'The three of you, I mean. Want you with me while I say a few words. Over here, I think.'

He approached the end of the table where Isabel was seated, motioned to Chris, who moved along a couple of paces.

'Shouldn't you be holding Rebecca?' Lucy suggested to her daughter.

Caroline shook her head. 'It's fine like this, Mother.'

Picking up a glass, Malcolm smiled around at everyone, cleared his throat. He wasn't nervous exactly – emotional perhaps.

'On behalf of Caroline and myself, I want to thank you most sincerely for joining us today to celebrate the naming of our precious daughter, Rebecca. The godparents, Chris, Bianca and Amanda, made a fine job of their part in the proceedings, and we were glad to have the services of Keith, our new rector. Pleased you've made the time to join us here as well, Keith. Family is special throughout our lives, though rare are the occasions when we remark on that fact. In this new century, as during past decades, we're discovering too many values are being eroded.

'However, some of us inherited good standards, the ethics which no matter how frequently deemed old-fashioned give structure to our lives. For such guidance, as well as for their example, I thank both my mother, Isabel and our very dear Lucy.

'And so we come to the main purpose of our gathering today, and I ask you to raise your glasses with me to wish good health and fortune to Rebecca.'

The toasts were followed by applause. As conversation broke out once more Isabel dabbed her eyes with a Brussels lace handkerchief.

'I didn't expect a mention,' she confided to Lucy.

'Nor did I! It's good to be appreciated. But I feel quite guilty – I haven't done nearly so much as I ought these past few months. And today, well, I do feel to be rather hogging my smallest granddaughter. I've had lots of turns with her while I've been staying. It must be time you had a go.'

Isabel smiled up at her as Lucy placed the baby on her lap. An old hand glittering with diamonds went instinctively to support Rebecca's head.

'Your turn soon for being a mother,' Isabel called to Bianca, who was starting to stroll around with Nick, topping up glasses.

The family had barely digested their substantial lunch, so no one was eating very much. Amanda noticed the rector gazing longingly towards the table complete with tiny sandwiches, vol-au-vents, other pastries and snacks.

She smiled at him. 'Don't tell me – you didn't have time to eat before heading for the church!'

'Or am not brilliant, anyway, at making meals,' Keith confessed.

'This way then – come with me. My mother and Mrs Dacre will both be distraught if no one eats a thing!'

Keith still hesitated slightly. 'Don't really wish my first impression here to be as a glutton.' But his dark eyes gleamed eagerly, making his thin face look boyish.

'You're not really such a worrier, are you?' Amanda teased. 'Tell you what – we'll each grab a plate. Then we can go off into the drawing room or somewhere, and find ourselves a corner. Who's to know how much you devour then?'

She would love their having a secret. Keith seemed much more fun than she'd expected a clergyman might be. And, with black jeans and sweater replacing that asexual cassock, amazingly attractive.

The room wasn't unoccupied as Amanda had hoped. Kate and Graham had retreated to a sofa, and switched on the television.

Seeing them, Amanda hesitated, sighed inwardly, but decided regretfully that heading towards one of the other rooms wasn't really on.

'Don't mind us – we're only looking for somewhere to sit,' she called to her Aunt Kate when she turned to see who had come in.

'Bring up the other sofa,' Graham suggested. 'This is quite interesting.'

'It's all right, thanks – we're busy eating.'

Amanda indicated two armchairs, and held both plates while Keith brought over a coffee table.

'Another drink before we settle?' she asked him. 'There's various wines, as well as the champagne. Beer, if you prefer.'

'A red would be nice, but you shouldn't have to wait on me.'

She laughed. 'Fetching a bottle and glasses is nothing compared to some of the tasks my PR work lets me in for.'

'Sounds interesting. You must tell me about it.'

I mean to, thought Amanda, and there's a great deal more to tell, even if my job predominates. And then there's *your* life. I can't wait to learn what makes you tick.

Watching through the doorway from the spacious hall, Lucy smiled. Amanda could look so animated, bless her – glamorous too, now that she was emulating her mother's excellent dress sense. It was her smile that made all the difference, though, lighting her face until she was radiant beneath her golden-brown hair.

Lucy turned, about to say as much to Caroline, and found Malcolm instead at her elbow. 'This has been hugely successful, Malcolm,' she told him. 'Everyone seems at ease, comfortable here, and genuinely delighted for you and Caroline.'

His grey eyes lit appreciatively. 'Think we invited just about the right number of people. Didn't want a big crowd.'

'Thought I might have seen your doctor here – she's been such a friend, hasn't she? I suppose she had another engagement.'

Malcolm swallowed before nodding. He simply had not thought to invite Anne Newbold. The idea hadn't entered his head. And that, he reflected, said it all.

Four

'The christening went well, didn't it?' Malcolm was still on quite a high during the following week.

'Very smoothly,' Caroline agreed. 'Thank goodness.'

None of her fears had materialised. The food had pleased everyone, no family disagreements had surfaced, and Rebecca had been good while they were in church. For Caroline herself the only problem was occurring now, as she tried to get into gear at work. She was late again this morning, partly because she'd been reluctant to go off while Malcolm seemed eager to chat, though more because of her secret ache to prolong the time she spent concentrating on her baby.

'This won't do; I've got to get on. Now that Mother's gone home, I must get back to a routine.'

'Rebecca's good, isn't she, when you have her in the office?'

'Oh, yes. Provided she's been fed and is reasonably dry, she hardly cries at all.'

Malcolm went down on one knee to gaze at his daughter in her carrycot beside the door leading through to the PR office.

'Daddy's little angel, aren't you, my sweet!' he said, kissing her forehead. As he straightened his back, he smiled at his wife. 'If she disturbs you too much, I can have her in the farm office.'

Caroline laughed. 'So you and Hugh Edmonds can drool over her all day? I think not, thanks. We'll manage.'

Malcolm's suggestion had so astonished her that she was still laughing when she went through to join Amanda.

'What's funny?'

'Malcolm really – or actually rather sweet. He's just suggested that he might have Rebecca over in their office with them.'

'You wouldn't let him?' Amanda sounded perturbed.

'I could hardly stop him; she is his baby, too. But I don't believe he'd thought that one through. Still, it's nice to know that's what he'd like.'

'But it's not men's stuff, is it. Baby-minding.'

'Perhaps, these days, we shouldn't argue that point. I thought you were the one who's always updating us.'

'Is Chris due here this week, do you know?' Amanda asked, and hoped she sounded casual.

'No idea – why?'

'Just something I wanted to ask him, nothing special.'

Ever since Sunday she had needed a private word with Chris. He'd met Keith Clifton before the christening, hadn't he?

The last thing Amanda had expected was that the rector would be so stimulating. He had talked such a lot about his army life; he'd travelled a great deal, and had masses of amusing anecdotes. And then he was serious about things that mattered to her, like conservation. When his brown eyes reflected how earnest he was, he seemed magnetic. So attractive. Keith was a good few years older than she was, she guessed, but he certainly treated her like an equal. The biggest problem now was her living so far away from the village.

Of course, if Keith didn't realise her home was nowhere near The Sylvan Barn, he wouldn't be surprised if she turned up at one of his services ... In fact, she might now take up her mother's suggestion that she stay with them while her father and Emma were in Spain.

That, however, was several weeks away yet. Amanda needed to believe that she would see Keith in the near future.

'Come back, Amanda – where are you?' It was Caroline, giving her a strange look. 'It's not like you to be so pensive. Nothing wrong, is there?'

Amanda forced a smile. 'Not in the slightest.'

But concentrating continued to prove difficult. She was glad when her mother suggested she should tackle a batch of invoices – figure work didn't allow for absent-mindedness. And she could have a good think about Keith tonight.

Amanda had the opportunity to exercise her interest in the rector earlier than that, when Christopher arrived at the house just as she was leaving. She lingered before getting into her car, which she'd just unlocked.

'Hi, Chris – can you spare a minute?'

'If you make it quick. I've got to see someone about that silver – the pieces that might belong to a church.'

'Are you picking them up? I'll come back indoors with you.'

Crossing the hall en route to the safe, Chris asked what it was all about.

Amanda cleared her throat, decided to go cautiously. 'You'd met Keith before, hadn't you. Was that at his place?'

'The rectory, yes.'

'What's it like?'

'How do you mean? Typical bachelor home, I suppose.'

Ah, thought Amanda, he isn't married then.

Christopher concealed a smile. Anyone with half an eye would have seen what was going on last Sunday. He was tempted to tease her, but Amanda didn't really deserve that. He came straight out with the required answer instead.

'No woman in his life here, at least that I could see. Want me to ask if there's anyone anywhere, next time I see him?'

'No, no, you mustn't. Promise you won't say anything.' That would be dreadful, the equivalent of kids at school saying their friend fancied someone. But she couldn't leave everything to chance. 'You are seeing him soon, then?'

'Having a game of squash together. And no – you can't tag along. You don't play, do you?'

'I could learn...'

'Mmm. Don't you think he's a shade old, Amanda love?'

She groaned. 'How old do you think *I* am?'

Chris laughed. 'Twenty-six going on seventeen, from the sound of you.'

'I might have known you'd be no use.'

Christopher forgot about Amanda's growing obsession as soon as she had turned and run off towards her car. He was going to be late, and he didn't mean to spend all evening talking silver plate with that Roman Catholic priest.

The meeting proved to be brief enough, and fruitless. The church, in the next village along the Kentish downs to the east, was built during the 1950s. A direct hit by a flying bomb during World War II had destroyed the original building.

'Including all the church records,' Chris was told. 'I should have explained when you rang, but I did wonder if there might be some way I could assist.'

A swift examination of both the chalice and the flagon convinced the priest that neither were likely to have belonged to the Catholic Church. 'Certainly, because of being less elaborate, this seems to be an Anglican Communion cup rather than a chalice. I think you'll find that such plainer vessels were adopted after Queen Elizabeth the First's proclamation restored the cup to the laity. Sorry I can't help.'

'Don't worry,' Chris assured him. 'Now I've learned this bit more I'll have another word with the expert I consulted.'

Chris wasted no time chatting in the church. After saying goodbye to the priest he was on his mobile to Diana before he drove away. Her voice sounded reassuringly warm when she listened to his news.

'I'll try this end then, as promised, assuming you agree,' she told him. 'That does mean you'll have to entrust those pieces to me.'

'No problem. I have them in the car, anyway. That's if it's convenient for me to drop them off sometime? What about this evening?'

'Fine with me. Where are you now, Chris? I'll give you directions.'

Diana's cottage was just off the main road between Playden and Rye. Chris smiled to himself, pleased. That could be useful; it wasn't any distance at all from his own flat in a Georgian house near Northiam.

'Do come in, nice to see you again.'

Smiling at the door of her home, she looked radiant. Her pale hair contrasted with the rather dark interior, while a blue sweater and matching skirt enhanced the shade of her eyes. Lots of silver rings gleamed from her graceful hands.

Diana took his coat, and Chris followed through the tiny entrance hall into an exquisite living room where a log fire crackled and flared, glinting back from a brass fender, matching fire-irons and scuttle. The walls were painted a warm apricot shade which combined more effectively than he'd have expected with red curtains and carpet.

As he sank into the armchair she indicated, he smiled to himself, noting on the sideboard a George III silver tea set, and a candelabra which he failed to date.

Seeing his gaze, Diana smiled again. 'Well,

I would collect, wouldn't I?'

He laughed. 'Sorry – is my expression giving me away?'

'Perhaps I'd be perturbed if you *didn't* show any interest. But come on – let's have another look at the stuff you've brought with you.'

As Christopher handed across the pieces, Diana glanced at him from beneath long, fair lashes. 'Must confess I wasn't sorry to learn that the Catholic priest knew nothing about the history of these. Gives me the opportunity to try and track down their provenance. It's not often that I get to handle something that could prove to be sixteenth century, with potential to be extremely interesting.'

'The priest did say he thought these too plain to be Catholic pieces.'

Diana nodded, then went on to outline the next steps her research would take, and promised to phone him the moment she had any news, although that could well take several weeks, at least.

Sensing that, for the present, their time together was drawing to a close, Chris suddenly felt deflated, wished he could find some means of remaining.

'And tonight?' Diana enquired. 'Are you eager to dash off somewhere?'

'Not at all.'

He felt so comfortable in this room, which

he was beginning to recognise was designed to flatter several items of Regency period furniture. The only discomfort was personal, and one which he could not regret. As she had during their previous encounter, Diana Frazer was affecting him quite forcefully.

'Fancy a glass of wine?' she suggested.

'Just one glass would be lovely, thanks. I try to restrict myself when I'm driving. Wouldn't help, work-wise, if I lost my licence. Being in the wine business doesn't excuse over-indulgence.'

'Good to meet someone so self-disciplined.' Diana had reasons for deploring reckless disregard for laws.

Chris wondered if she might be teasing, but her expression as she crossed to the sideboard and opened a bottle of claret revealed no more than concentration on her task. Which was just as well, he reflected; if Diana Frazer slipped into a teasing mode, he would have difficulty maintaining that reputed self-discipline!

The wine certainly did not help, swiftly relaxing his guard until he grew even more aware of the desire coursing through him. Somehow, he must suppress that, try to ignore it and string a few sentences together. Returning to the chair which she'd occupied since his arrival, Diana was prompting him to talk.

'How did you become involved in viticulture, Christopher? Did you feel that you'd been concerned in growing other fruit for too long, or something?'

He smiled. 'Have I said I worked for Dad for a time after agricultural college? Only the farm wasn't doing too well. He ... he had to let me go.'

'Oh, dear.'

'Quite. Not a good time for anyone. However, being vineyard manager has always worked well for me, and I keep being given greater responsibility. Then there's the way I've been helping Dad prepare to devote a few of his acres to grapes.'

'So, any breach has healed.'

'Years ago, I think. And it is good to avoid being totally involved at the farm.'

'More opportunity for extending yourself?'

'And less for creating tension!'

They laughed together, and their glances held. She had such beautiful, powerful eyes, which seemed to read his soul. His glass was empty; she crossed to take it from him. Their fingers touched. Every nerve, every pulse was screaming that he must draw her down into the chair with him. To ease this enormous ache.

He could do nothing of the kind, of course. But Diana seemed intent on building on the rapport they were developing.

Returning to her chair, she smiled.

'There's a lot to be said, isn't there, for being left to create for yourself the life you want. Provided there are people around for the times when self-sufficiency begins to pall.'

She understands, thought Chris, and felt the attraction between them gaining a further dimension, where recognition of each other included something far deeper than desire. Their talk became general, of areas of Kent and Sussex which they both knew and loved. When he eventually had to leave, the steady gaze of her eyes again conveyed an unmistakable affinity that promised increasing friendship.

Had he been a fool to play squash again, following such an age with scarcely any sporting activity? Whatever the wisdom of taking Christopher up on that suggestion of a game, Keith was suffering.

After so long confining exercise to nothing more demanding than a brisk walk, he had forgotten the old knee injury. He'd tried at first to ignore the pain, but had been compelled to admit to Chris that he really wasn't able to play on to the end of the period booked.

Chris had ribbed him, naturally, after the initial concern, while Keith hoped that his own failure at squash wouldn't preclude their continuing friendship. He had liked the young man from their earlier meeting, liked the whole family since the Parker christening.

'I did this in while trying to prove I *am* as young as I used to be!' he exclaimed now, smiling at Anne Newbold across her desk. 'Chris would tell you I didn't come up to scratch.'

'Chris Parker? Let me guess – did he have you playing squash?'

'Abysmally, yes! Overlooked the fact that this knee tends to demand I give it respect.'

'You'd better show me.'

The knee was grossly swollen, so sore that Keith flinched as she began to examine it.

'You've taken painkillers, I suppose?' Anne enquired.

'Last night – only way I could sleep.'

'Not today, though?'

'Thought I'd endure it till I learned your verdict.'

'It's very inflamed; I'll prescribe something for that. Give it a few days, then come in again, I'll take another look. We might have to arrange x-rays, but that will take time, I'm afraid. You've heard of the waiting lists. So, you've made a friend of Chris – that's good.'

'The whole family, since the baptism. A great bunch, very hospitable.'

Anne kept her head down, preventing him

from reading her expression. She was an utter fool to feel upset because she hadn't been invited, to hate not even having known that the christening was taking place. Why on earth should she feel distressed, *neglected*? Only the other week she had turned down the suggestion that she should join Malcolm and his family for drinks.

'Have I said something wrong? Blundered in feet first again?' Keith was perturbed. From this angle he couldn't see her face, but her entire attitude had changed. He was growing fond of Anne Newbold, would never upset her.

She shook her head. 'Not at all. It seems you're becoming well integrated into the village. Good.'

'I still need people I can confide in. I had hoped that you and I, well, I did say we might prove to be a bit of use to each other in that way.'

'Why not?' said Anne, sitting back in her chair. She felt tired, in need of fresh stimulation. She had been in the village for years; her local council work had ceased to excite, yet she often felt too exhausted to search out different interests.

'A meal out, perhaps?' Keith suggested. 'Needn't choose anywhere too far away if we both happened to feel too tired to put much effort into an outing.'

Anne's laugh was rueful. 'Fine with me,

even though it sounds like we're seeking to be comfortable rather than exhilarated.'

'I'm not implying you're past having a good time,' Keith exclaimed hastily. 'I didn't mean...'

She laughed again. 'Stop fussing, Keith, or you'll endanger the comfortable aspect of being friends!'

And she would regret that, Anne realised when the rector left. They had arranged to eat out together on the first evening when she wasn't on call, and she was looking forward already to seeing him again. Despite that absence of excitement.

Trying to prevent her emotions from surfacing, Anne was walking along the Pilgrims' Way. She needed to clear her head before afternoon surgery. She was determined to adapt to this new turn her life was taking, needed finally to make room for Keith by ceasing to cling to a close friendship which had run its course.

She had been shaken by her own feelings when Keith mentioned the Parker christening. Hadn't she believed herself cured of any last fondness for Malcolm? It was months since she'd reasoned that whatever had once existed was relinquished.

While she was struggling to suppress memories, he was the last person she wished to encounter. Yet there Malcolm was. His vigorous stride as he headed uphill towards her reminded Anne again of how healthy he'd become. And of her own part in ensuring that he remained no worse for that heart attack seven years ago.

His warm smile lighting those beautiful grey eyes didn't help, nor did his evident satisfaction with life in general. And the spot where they met couldn't have been more appropriate. Hadn't their years of friendship deepened after the affinity discovered while walking the Pilgrims' Way together?

'Nice to see you, Anne. Just taking a breather. Caro had a dental appointment, Amanda's in charge of Rebecca, so I thought why don't I seize the opportunity to meet my wife, have a chat while we stroll back to the house together.'

'Good idea,' said Anne, and concealed a wry smile. So, she might have guessed! Malcolm himself was providing evidence that she must, indeed, understand that whatever the two of them once had shared truly was supplanted. As it should be, she added grimly within her head.

And now Caroline was in sight and, despite any dental work, looked stunning. Her heavy russet coat, tailored in a military style, fitted perfectly to a figure which appeared fully restored after the effects of pregnancy.

Her smile for Anne was friendly enough as

she said hello, but she gave her only a hasty glance. The gaze she fixed on Malcolm lingered, lovingly. No one could doubt that his arrival delighted Caroline.

She continued to smile up at her husband. 'Darling, what a lovely surprise. It's so rarely that you leave the farm midweek except on business.'

They paused for a few minutes to chat while Anne enquired how the baby was progressing.

Watching as they walked away, hand in hand, Anne recognised afresh that an era surely was ending. She could have accepted that without any such proof that this was so, she decided. And hurried onwards.

Further along the hillside, where construction work for the rail link was gouging out wide swathes of their Kentish countryside, she could believe her own past was interred. Beneath those bridges of concrete, amid the upturned soil lay her personal history. The hours which she, and Malcolm too, had devoted to opposing this wretched scheme or mitigating its impact were buried there, lost. They would never again combine in a common cause, never would know the joy of finding someone so closely attuned.

Christopher arrived at The Sylvan Barn at around seven that evening, just as Caroline was serving their meal. Nick and Bianca had come over, and Caro swiftly invited Chris to eat with them.

'Florence Dacre has cooked masses too much, as always when there isn't just the two of us. You're more than welcome.'

Chris smiled at his stepmother. 'I'm fine, thanks. Julian and I had lunch with one of our distributors – a meal that threatened to continue throughout the afternoon. And I'm only here to meet Diana.'

'Frazer, the silver lady?' his father enquired. 'You'd better count me in – don't forget you haven't yet introduced us.'

Chris chatted for a time with Nick and Bianca, who was very heavily pregnant now, counting the last few weeks to what they hoped would be a prompt delivery. Always pale, she was looking exhausted, and particularly fragile, despite the large bump. But she was cheerful enough and eager to have Chris tell more about the possible source of that silver.

When Diana arrived the others were still eating. Malcolm left the table briefly to be introduced, but before she could meet the rest of the family Diana was frowning as she handed over the items she had brought with her.

'Haven't much to report, but I've photographed these, especially the markings. Sorry to be a pain, but I can't linger. Got a cab outside, clocking up by the minute. The car wouldn't start this morning, so I've been using trains. Had to visit, er, *someone*,' she ended hastily.

'Forget the taxi, I'll run you home – it's no distance from my place,' Christopher assured her.

As Diana went to pay the driver off, he did some hurried thinking. Having his father determined to muscle in on meetings with Diana was bad enough – he didn't mean to include his stepmother, Bianca and Nick as well. Especially when he'd noticed how his brother sat upright with interest the moment that Diana appeared. Within minutes he was hustling her out of the house.

The darkness surrounding his tiny car seemed to enfold them more closely, clamping side against side. Was that her pulse, or his own, expressing this delicious yearning? Chris wished he might believe that Diana too experienced this intense pull of attraction.

The drive to her house felt all too short, entirely tantalising in the excitement her scent, her warmth, her *nearness* generated. Wondering despairingly how he might avoid saying goodnight this soon, Christopher sighed.

Diana leaned across. Her lips were cool from the wintry air, their touch delicate at first against his heated face. And then she was in his arms, their mouths searching, tongues exploring, bodies pressing. The surprise was intense; its impact delivered joy to rage right through him.

'Come into the house.' Her voice sounded husky with longing.

The staircase was shadowed, lit by a single gold-toned lamp, their footfalls silent over the green carpeted steps. Her bedroom was furnished more spartanly than Chris had expected, but with good antique pieces. And a bed enhanced by an elaborate frame of brass. Diana's beautiful eyes seemed charged with love.

Discarding outdoor coats, they came to each other, embraced clumsily, their eagerness too urgent for refinement. Laughing softly, she sought his mouth again, clinging, her breasts pushing at him through layers of clothing.

'I want you,' Chris murmured, his fingers at the nape of her neck, her hair cool on his hands, the only coolness anywhere.

He couldn't say who initiated the move towards her bed; in mutual consent they arrived to lie there, limbs entwining. His hand found her breast. Her long fingers began to search, to caress.

'I've needed you from that first day,' he admitted, and stirred to her touch.

'I've hoped I was right to believe so.' Diana's voice was smiling.

He was loosening his belt, wishing she

would begin to remove her own clothing. He wouldn't be swift enough, dreaded fumbling with female fastenings.

Leaning slightly away to tackle his zip Chris saw the framed picture. A photograph – Diana unmistakable in bridal gown, and the man, whoever...

'Tell me you're divorced.'

Miserably, all passion fleeing, she shook her head. 'Oh, God!'

'You're not a widow?' Chris could not wish that on her, but wished it true for his own sake.

'No. Vernon isn't living here, though. It's all very complicated; don't ask me to explain.'

'Just as well I discovered in time.' His own voice was a snarl, bitter.

Chris swung his legs off the bed, shrugged off Diana's hand, and strode away to snatch up his coat.

'Christopher, please...' At the top of the staircase she grasped him by the arm.

'We're not living together, I said.'

Very slowly, he turned to face her, searching his agitated brain and coming up with the only acceptable explanation.

'You're legally separated? Is that it?'

'No.'

He spun away from her, hurtled down the steps on legs as unsteady as during severe illness. Flinging himself into the car Chris was hit by the scent of her. He couldn't escape that, but was compelled to drive as rapidly as he could away from her home.

Chris reached his flat in minutes, sighed grimly at the irony of only recently relishing the proximity of Diana's place to his own. Only one good thing remained – the privacy of living alone, possessing this space where he need share with no one this massive, aching distress.

He hadn't known. Was sure she wore no wedding ring. He'd had no inkling that Diana was married; he had never in his life encouraged any woman who was committed to someone else. But *she* had known, all along had been well aware that she had a husband. Vernon. Wherever he was.

What did the man do? Was he in some line that took him away on business, abroad perhaps? And what of *Diana?* Chris wondered if he'd totally misread her. Had he chosen to ignore some intuition of his own? For he surely had not suspected even for a moment that their shared glances, those kisses, all nearness should have been forbidden.

He need not see her again, he must not. Never prepared to fool anyone, least of all himself, Christopher knew that he could not trust his emotions in her company. That was it then, the end.

'I suppose I can't quite believe that this

won't continue for evermore.'

Isabel was sitting almost as upright as ever on her chair, but Caroline couldn't ignore the uncharacteristic wistfulness in her voice.

The telephone call asking her to visit, and to come alone, was a surprise. With Kate and Graham in this house where Isabel had her own apartment, Caroline had never felt that her presence was required there very frequently. Or desired!

'Is something wrong?' she enquired carefully, uncertain how to proceed, especially now that her indomitable mother-in-law appeared disturbed.

'I decided that someone ought to be told,' the old lady went on. 'I've a lot of respect for you, Caroline, and I believe I can trust you to respect my wish that this should remain confidential, kept from the rest of the family.'

Caro stilled her alarm as it began to rise, tried to speak evenly. 'Anything you say will be treated in that way, for as long as you feel that is necessary.'

'I wouldn't expect anything less of you.' Isabel paused, sighed. 'I didn't believe I was this foolish, that I would be so taken aback to learn that I am not quite so indestructible as I supposed. Common sense should perhaps have cautioned me that I have survived quite a span, that I must reflect on the fact that I am heading towards ninety.'

'What is it, Mother?' Even while feeling this sudden tenderness Caroline wondered if she'd previously addressed Isabel as Mother.

'I am faced with a shock, a grossly undignified illness that threatens to culminate in a ... in a demise which will be totally unacceptable to my fastidious nature. The consultants' diagnosis is bowel cancer.'

'Oh, no. Oh, God! I am so sorry.' Instinctively, Caroline rushed to hold her mother-in-law.

For the first time that she recalled, she felt Isabel leaning into their embrace, permitting herself to be hugged. Fingers heavy with diamonds clung to her arm.

'But what do they really say? Isn't there some treatment? Something they can do?'

Straightening her back so that Caroline drew away, Isabel shook her head.

'When I demanded a second opinion, I began to understand why the first consultant offered nothing more than palliative treatment. Were I younger, they might have attempted chemotherapy, but I am not. And nor am I prepared to sacrifice my final weeks or months to drug-induced wretchedness.'

I don't blame you, thought Caroline, but that wasn't an opinion she should express.

Isabel managed to smile. 'The drugs I will accept should help me to endure, and in the end may, I hope, enable me to display some illusion of retaining a little of my self-possession.'

'I'm sure that will be so.' Caroline felt tears on her cheeks.

'Oh, dear. I chose you as my confidante for your outward composure as much as your common sense.'

'I'm sorry, I, well, you did say this news was a shock.'

'And maybe if you hadn't shown some distress I might now be thinking less of you. You see, Caroline, while needing one family member who can be relied upon in a crisis, I also need assurance of our belonging together. Without fussing. That would be Kate's reaction, were she in the picture. And she does always know what one ought to be doing! As for Graham and Malcolm ... Sadly, I suspect that both of my sons inherited the tendency to prefer to assume that all will be well – until catastrophe proves otherwise. False optimism is not something I choose to contend with.'

'I can't tell you how sorry I am about your news. And I'll do anything you wish to help make ... make it more bearable.'

Caroline wondered how long Isabel would survive, didn't know how to ask if the specialists had given her any indication.

Her mother-in-law confided what she'd been told. 'They say I might see Christmas.

I mean to live to share in the joy when Nicholas and Bianca have their baby.'

Caroline dried her eyes. 'I was trying to find a tactful way of asking that one.'

Isabel smiled. 'Don't worry too much about tactful approaches, my dear. It is going to be such a relief to have you around for frank exchanges.'

Caroline was deeply moved that her mother-in-law had chosen her to share this dreadful news with; so often over the years she had felt intimidated by the old lady. Keeping Isabel's secret from Malcolm and the rest of the family nevertheless became an enormous weight. And with each day Caroline foresaw further implications of Isabel's terminal illness. By the end of a week she was so perturbed that she was hardly sleeping. How on earth would she herself function properly while concealing this tragic prognosis?

By the end of another troubled week she had concluded that she would have to speak to someone. Isabel had insisted that her illness be concealed from the family; she had been less concerned that the news should be withheld from others. And Caroline knew just the person who would listen and understand.

Only as she drove into Folkestone did she begin to wonder if she would be wrong to tell even her own mother about Isabel's condition. Was her need to share the burden making her entirely selfish, willing to overlook the meaning of Isabel's request for confidentiality, if not her actual wording?

Instead of driving straight to Lucy's flat, she parked a short distance away, placed Rebecca in her folding pram and began to walk. It wasn't so much that she was afraid her mother might be unable to keep the news to herself – she knew Lucy Forbes, and could trust her to guard her tongue. It was more that Caroline mistrusted her own judgement, and would somehow compromise her conscience by failing to remain totally silent. But she still came back to the fact that she felt ill-equipped for coping with this situation.

Lucy's quiet wisdom and inherent good sense might do far more than make Caroline herself see the way ahead clearly. Together, they could be better able to ease the remainder of the old lady's life.

'Caroline...?'

The voice a few paces behind her was familiar, too dear for her to feel other than exultant as she swung round.

'It is! I was sure I couldn't be mistaken. And this must be your new daughter – do let me see.' Paul Saunders sounded as delighted that she'd had the baby as he was to see her. But he didn't appear surprised that her family had increased.

'Hello, Paul. Didn't know you were back in this country. Taking a holiday?' Somehow, she'd made the words tumble out. Her pulse was racing while it ought to do nothing of the kind, and she should not be feeling thankful that he appeared so much better than during their last meeting months ago, at the airport.

Leaning over to gaze into the pram, he smiled. 'You must be very happy to have this young lady to complete your family.' He straightened his back, looked her in the eyes. 'Your mother hasn't told you that Japan didn't work out? Not quite my scene, as the saying goes.'

'So this isn't just a break over here.'

'Indeed not. I'm settled happily into a new position, and finding a lot of satisfaction in looking up old friends. In-laws too – my late wife's younger sister is taking me in hand.'

The warmth in his voice told her that his sister-in-law was becoming an important factor in his new life back in England. Caroline felt pleased for Paul, and greatly relieved for herself. No possible opening now existed for them to renew any aspect of the feelings he'd once aroused in her. She wouldn't even need to exert any will power to keep out of his life. But she would have appreciated a word of warning that he was living over here again.

'You didn't tell me Paul was back in Folkestone,' she challenged her mother as soon as they had settled Rebecca comfortably and were looking out to sea from the sun room. Caro needed to have this matter out of the way.

'Ah.' Lucy shrugged, looked slightly uneasy. 'To be frank, I'd no wish to disturb you by reminders of him. Your recent happiness is evident to us all; there was nothing to gain from unearthing the past.'

'Oh, I suppose now I'm over the surprise, you needn't be uncomfortable about keeping his arrival to yourself. I am past wanting to know what Paul is doing. Come to that, he seems to have enough to interest him without ... without raking up anything that's best left interred.'

Lucy's frown waned. 'Glad that's sorted between us, darling – I thought you were going to be cross. But you are still looking anxious. Nothing wrong with Malcolm is there, or any of the others – Bianca *is* fine still, isn't she?'

'Very well, especially for a slender girl with an enormous bump to lug around. No, it's not the young people, nor Malcolm. Maybe I should be glad you've kept so quiet about Paul. I've been trying to decide whether or not to confide in you.'

'You will, of course.'

'You mustn't tell Kate – I'm afraid I'm

going to have to insist on that, Mother. It's Isabel, you see, and it's serious...'

'Oh, no. And I have become really quite fond of the old lady over the years.'

Lucy listened most concernedly, and had tears in her eyes when Caroline finished relating the extent of Isabel's illness.

'You can rely on me to hold my tongue, naturally. Especially where Kate is concerned. But I'm glad you've confided in me, Caro dear – it was too much weight for you to shoulder alone. You need to feel free to do for Isabel whatever she will permit.'

'Which won't be much.'

'Quite. But it really is a tremendous compliment, you know, that she has turned to you. That's the only good thing to come out of this terrible news.'

Five

Caroline felt scarcely any better for her visit to Folke stone. Although she was thankful that Lucy seemed to believe she'd been right to share Isabel's news, the immediate relief had waned during her drive back to The Sylvan Barn.

Against her inclination and certainly against her intention, she couldn't help recalling too many earlier occasions when meeting Paul Saunders there had created such excitement within her. No matter how contented she was now – and she was utterly contented – memories of high elation evidently weren't eradicated readily.

As they arrived at home Rebecca was demanding attention, crying for her feed and lying in a sodden napkin. Holding the baby to her breast, Caro recognised afresh that *this was her reality*. And more, the culmination of all her dearest hopes.

Whatever she and Paul had shared belonged in the past, a past where her marriage to Malcolm had been uneasy. And that marriage, stronger than ever now, was cemented daily by this child they both loved so dearly.

Sitting in the nursery, Caroline thought about the strength of the bond between herself and Malcolm, and with all their family. Suddenly scared by what might have been, she was infinitely thankful she'd never permitted any unfaithfulness to tarnish the good relationships among all the people who meant so much to her.

Even Isabel's cancer seemed less overwhelmingly sad when set against the background of all the support available. *If* her mother-in-law would only accept support. Knowing her as she had for years, Caroline understood that it was not in Isabel's nature to relinquish self-sufficiency.

Thinking about the surrounding family began to restore her feeling that she would cope, even created a certain quiet to withstand the shock of Isabel's illness.

Below them in one of the downstairs rooms a sudden exclamation from one end of a telephone conversation startled her into noticing the fragments she could hear. The voice was Christopher's, sounding hurt more than angry, perturbed enough to be shouting.

'I've said all I have to say. I'm not going to see you again ... The silver's not that important ... All right then, I'll get someone else in. You can't be the only one who's capable...' His voice ceased; evidently he was listening to whoever was on the line. But suddenly he was shouting again. 'Well, I'm sorry about that – I know you were relying on the fee. Naturally, I shall settle for any time you've put in to date ... But that *is* the point, because I've decided this is the end of your commitment to investigating our silver...'

Even from the room above Caroline heard the clatter as Chris replaced the receiver. So much for believing I'd recovered some sort of peace, she thought. But she supposed that this was a condition of being a part of this dear family of hers. Troubles arose daily – one of her roles should be to help alleviate them.

Without meaning to overhear, she'd gathered that Chris was going to need a bit of understanding in what was clearly a disagreement with Diana. Caroline hadn't known he was in the house; from his car in the drive she'd assumed that he was out somewhere on the site for those vines.

Christopher knew well enough that Caroline was there. From his old room, where he still had a desk, he had seen her drive up. Already depressed following the upsetting visit to Diana's, he had come to tell his father he was relinquishing all interest in the silver they had found, and would take no further part in its eventual assessment.

Malcolm had proved less than amenable

to taking over from him. 'Sorry, old son – there's a difference between wishing to have some involvement and taking on the whole lot to handle. Gone are the days when I wished to fill every minute to the full. Everything changed with Rebecca's arrival – more than ever, I'm determined to make time for my wife and family.'

'But this stuff's a family concern – and belongs way back in the past. More yours than mine, I'd say.'

His father refused to listen. 'Don't know what's got into you – someone your age ought to be over the moon to be working with a woman that attractive!'

No one could see it, no one comprehended that Diana's desirability was the whole difficulty. Unless...

Chris had been contemplating talking things through with his stepmother when he decided instead to phone Diana herself and end any indecision. She refused to listen, urged him to stop being so wary, to give their friendship a chance or, failing that, to continue working together to identify the origins of that silver.

Hearing her voice was sufficient to arouse him, and inflame along with the desire the longing to know her better. Torn apart between feeling that they should be able to work together and awareness of this passion, control had deserted him.

Of course he had shouted – against Diana's insistence that two adults might make a success of the matter which had caused them to meet. She'd apologised for not admitting she was married. He couldn't accept that. Any reminders of the awkwardness of that night only made him adamant about refusing to see her.

And now he was bereft, devoid of hope, just as surely as visiting that bedroom had destroyed the elation which had been soaring throughout that evening.

Chris went striding across the entrance hall to get to his car and escape to his own home. He reached the outer door as Caroline called him from the staircase.

With Rebecca held over her shoulder, she came running down to join him.

'Hi, Caro. Just on my way...' Even while he spoke he half-hoped that she would prevent him from leaving.

'What's wrong, Chris? Haven't heard you shout like that since, well, since you and Nick were still at home, still at each other's throats.'

'No, well, guess nobody's made me that mad since then.'

'Sure you don't want to talk? Was it Diana?'

Chris couldn't pretend it was anyone else's fault that his phone conversation had been fully audible. Maybe he had rather needed there to be some witness to his distress.

He followed his stepmother into the drawing room, waited until she was seated with the baby more comfortably arranged on her shoulder.

'It was Diana, of course. And I was severing all contact. Father is determined not to take over from me. Seems unable to understand – not sure you will either.'

'Try me.' Caroline nodded towards the other end of her sofa.

He'd always said that if Caro were his real mother she couldn't have known him better. Sitting, Chris hoped she wouldn't be too appalled to learn what a fool he'd made of himself with the first woman in years who'd really mattered to him.

'I didn't know she was married.' His blue eyes were earnest. 'It all started through business – it wasn't like a date or something, when you need to find out.'

'And she is a very attractive woman.'

'It's not like me to go after someone I don't know more about.' He needed to emphasise to her that he wasn't only motivated by desire.

'I know that, Chris.' He looked so miserable that Caroline longed to hug him. He might be a mature male, but at the moment this stepson of hers had all the appeal of a perplexed boy.

'Couldn't tell anyone now just when or

how it all started to develop swiftly into something quite serious. On my part.'

'These things happen to the best of us, quite often simply because of our current situation – life seeming a bit dull perhaps, or us feeling neglected.'

'But it wasn't, I wasn't.'

'And not in need of one special person to take an interest? That so often is the key.'

'Particularly when you somehow gain the impression that they might be equally in need of someone who cares?'

Even more so then, she thought, remembering how greatly Paul had been distressed by his wife's suicide. But Diana Frazer had a husband around. So why did she get this strong feeling that the woman could be as much a loner as Chris himself?

'She wouldn't explain where he is, or anything. Why he's not living with her. I wanted to understand – what's gone wrong between them, why he's left her alone.'

'Sometimes,' Caroline began carefully, recollecting. 'Sometimes, the reason's too painful to be mentioned. You need to have long enough knowing a person to be able to tell them something deeply traumatic.'

'You think I shouldn't have dumped her so swiftly.'

Caroline shook her head. 'More that you had acceptable reasons for continuing to see her. As someone you consulted, in a situation where feelings could be regulated.' She saw the colour flood her stepson's cheeks. 'Or not...?'

'Got it in one. Now you'll think I've let things get out of hand. Actually, I didn't.'

'You don't have to tell me.'

'I just don't remember being this drawn to somebody this swiftly. Couldn't help feeling overwhelmed. By everything about her.'

'Yet you possess the qualities which would have enabled you to work with her, and withstand the obvious, well, *temptations*.'

'You reckon?'

Caroline smiled slightly. Her special feelings towards Christopher had always sprung from sensing that, even without being truly related, they couldn't be more alike in attitude.

'Where your deeper emotions are involved, you've never been one for getting into a girl's knickers regardless. No longer a fashionable attitude, perhaps. But one that bestows the strength to tackle difficult situations.'

'Meaning I should continue to see her?'

'Your decision, Chris. We can only ever weigh the good against the bad, assess who might be harmed.'

'Sounds easy when it's not you that's involved.'

'And it's anything but. I do know that.'

Chris gave her a look.

Caroline did not mean to confide. 'Would Diana be hurt by your friendship's continuing? Would her husband, wherever he is? Or would you be the only one to suffer if, say, you took a chance and it all came to nothing?'

'I'll give her another call later, from home.'

Keith looked different without his dog collar, younger, Anne thought when he called for her after evening surgery. It was also touching that he seemed like a youthful escort trying to distract from the shabbiness of his vehicle when he opened its door for her.

'At least it's on the road again,' he exclaimed while they fastened seat belts. 'Might have marred my image if I'd had to ask you to pick me up.'

'That's one thing about a GP – got to have reliable transport for emergencies.' Anne considered for a moment. 'You must have emergency calls too, though.'

'I also have a bike – nearly as old as the car, but it has fewer sources of potential trouble.'

They laughed, once again remarkably easy with each other, despite their relatively short acquaintance.

'But can you always ride? How's that knee – improving?'

'Thanks to your medication, it's heaps

better.'

'And how are things going? Are your ideas becoming more acceptable to your parishioners?'

'To some of the younger element perhaps. We're setting up a youth fellowship; those involved seem prepared to at least listen. I've got them to agree to a sort of, well, course of instruction. On different services, their history, where the various forms of worship are coming from – that kind of thing. They surprised me by their willingness to take that on board. I stressed that they'll still be free to cling to their preferences afterwards.'

'Sounds good – their choices will be informed ones.'

'Wish some older members of the congregation were more open-minded. Did my predecessor always accept that there should be so little variety in village worship?'

'As you know, I've never been involved to that degree. But he was getting on in years – I rather suspect that once he was indoctrinated into adopting their style of service he didn't bother to make changes.'

Keith nodded pensively as he negotiated the curves of the darkened country lanes.

'And how's life treating you?' he asked. 'I suspect that alongside an NHS doctor's difficulties my problems should seem minor!'

Anne smiled. 'Certainly not the best of

times, these days. Too many patients are waiting for the referral that you're afraid they won't receive before it's too late.'

'Meanwhile, they're not being spared the pain they might avoid?'

'Worse than that. The situation's so bad that treatment sometimes doesn't become available until an illness is terminal.'

'Oh, God. Must be dreadful for patients and their relatives.'

'Exactly. People would scarcely believe that we were trained to recognise the need for prevention as much as cure! We barely get from one day to the next coping with crises that arise. Merely doing our best to help patients to endure, where we yearn to provide the life-enhancing treatment that ought to be there.'

'Depressing.' His brown eyes were reflecting his concern.

'For them – for us as well. No wonder there exists this massive shortfall within our profession. However, Keith, I did promise myself not to spend this evening moaning...'

'I'll bear that in mind. No more shop-talk, on either part.'

Anne caught herself wondering where on earth their conversation might lead – she knew so little about Keith Clifton. But she did like what she knew.

They had chosen the restaurant of a country inn, high on the hillside above

Smeeth and Brabourne, nicely furnished without any pretence of ostentation. The warm interior and a comfortable number of diners created an easy atmosphere. Discussing the menu and selecting a wine to suit both their tastes led Keith to reminisce about other places he loved, many in Anne's native Yorkshire.

'Where you surely would receive more generous helpings than anywhere else in England,' she exclaimed, hazel eyes smiling.

'And necessarily so while I was training for the priesthood – no one there was going to endanger our souls by inducing gluttony!'

'You were allowed out to replenish your strength then?'

He laughed. 'Mirfield wasn't a prison. Nor even, I suppose, so strict a community as many. Let's just say the restrictions while I was in the army had been of a different nature.'

'And you'd been an officer, didn't you say?'

Keith laughed again. 'Where did you get the impression that officers have a better time of it than their men?'

Learning a bit about his army experiences gave Anne an insight into the man who had relished the travel synonymous with that life. But it was of Yorkshire again that Keith spoke, and with great affection, after she asked about favourite areas he had visited.

'The North York moors and harbours on the nearby shores; then there are all the Dales, quiet valleys, spectacular escarpments, limestone, sandstone, waterfalls and peaks. Farmsteads and ruined castles, abbeys, churches built of millstone grit.'

'And the grittiness of the folk there?'

'Never sure that as a newcomer I should use that expression of the people. Not sure it was a compliment.'

'It is, it is – or I believe so. The grit that means endurance, the ability to be stoical beyond what folk expect of you.'

'As many in that part of the world have been required to endure, through catastrophes, wars, years of financial depression. Is that why you began to fight here, against the injustice you saw in the planning of the rail route?'

Anne was taken aback. 'That had never occurred to me. I only saw, through the council work I was doing, that too many people here seemed to be failing to voice their feelings adequately. And I live that small distance from the worst of the upheaval that the rail link was to create. I could protest on their behalf, rather than irately in my own interests.'

'And you have the intellect and the position to lend weight to whatever cause you're supporting.'

Anne smiled, a little embarrassed. 'I like to

think so.'

She wasn't sorry to receive Keith's estimate of her. Being taken for granted was part of a doctor's life, some indication of why they had trained to serve in that way. Recognition of what they were about did no one any harm. Exhausted as she so often felt, Anne really appreciated this acknowledgement.

'You've learned a bit more about me tonight,' Keith continued. 'What of you – how did you come to settle in Kent?'

'By chance, in a way, as with so many big moves. Have I said that I did some of my training in the south? And so it was around here that I began looking for general practice work. I came to the village as a very junior partner, liked the people and the area, couldn't refuse to take over when the old doctor retired.'

'And you've never longed to return to your home county?'

'Yes, Yorkshire pulls quite frequently. A well-loved location on television is enough to set me off. But I'm beginning to wonder if I've been away so long that I'd be disappointed if I moved back there.'

'I'm sure *I* wouldn't. My first curacy was in Halifax – not the most picturesque of towns, but surrounded by countryside that is. And I loved the people.'

'Yet you came about as far south as you

could in this country.' Anne was puzzled.

'Between ourselves, that wasn't solely for my own benefit. My mother was a widow who suffered terribly from chest troubles. I believed a warmer, drier climate would help her. Unfortunately, she didn't survive to come with me.'

'Oh, I'm sorry.'

'Mercifully, the first stroke she had proved final. It was severe, and she would have loathed becoming dependent. Naturally, the shock was great. But by the time I stopped asking why, I realised that if the faith I represent means anything, she has only moved to a better place, somewhere.'

After a moment's silence Keith grinned across the table. 'And who can say there might not have been greater difficulties had she survived? Differing generations – especially when each has experienced independence – don't always sit comfortably together, do they?'

'Surely someone of your vocation has the ability to get along with everyone.'

Keith's laugh was loud. 'I won't rise to that one!'

Their food arrived and he poured wine into her glass and then into his own, which he raised to her. 'Here's to an agreeable evening, and the start of a firm alliance to strengthen us through the traumas.'

Smiling, Anne sipped her wine, nodded

approvingly. 'You expect traumas then?'

'Don't you?'

'To be honest, I don't really consider the problems patients bring me in that light. Most times I'm too busy weighing possible solutions.'

'And the really bad things that happen, like death?'

'You'd go under if you didn't learn to steel yourself against the horror of failing to save someone. It does still hurt, but being there for those whom the loss hurts most does concentrate the mind.' She gave him a look. 'However did we fall into such a morbid discussion?'

Keith shook his head. 'I don't know, and didn't mean us to either. Still, a few minutes' conversation on the realities can only firm up a friendship.'

By the time they were heading back to the village Anne was beginning to sense that, for whatever reason, their friendship *was* becoming cemented. And she could feel already that she would be thankful to have Keith Clifton around.

Well though they were getting along, she was surprised to be kissed when he saw her to her door. Hazel eyes widening, she gazed into his face. Keith raised one eyebrow, his own eyes rather uneasy. She gave him a reassuring hug, returned the kiss but without lingering, and said goodnight.

'Sleep well,' he called back as he returned to his car.

And I might very well find that I do just that, thought Anne, unlocking her door.

Her second surprise of the night came later, when she found that sleep was, in fact, evading her. No matter how innocent those kisses were, they were generating an unmistakable longing. And I once believed there would be no excitement in knowing our rector! she thought ruefully. She only hoped the sudden appearance of this additional dimension to their relationship wouldn't cause its demise.

Amanda wasn't at all happy. Her father and Emma had postponed their visit to Spain. Instead of counting the days to their departure, as she had, she now was trying not to mind that her freedom was delayed. She'd planned everything so well – staying at The Sylvan Barn each weekend, she'd have good reason to meet Keith in church. Most of all, though, she was determined to use coming home alone to the bungalow during the week as a rehearsal for getting her own place. It could be ideal, and if she hit a problem, Chris was always around the vineyard.

Learning he and Diana were no longer fast becoming an item had pleased Amanda more than she would have admitted to anyone. She had never felt that Diana was quite right for Christopher. The woman seemed to her to be containing altogether too much, as though she had another life elsewhere. Caroline had said no more than that the friendship appeared to be cooling, but Amanda wouldn't be surprised if there was some barrier to prevent anything more developing.

This was just the time when she'd show Chris he could rely on *her*. He didn't deserve indifferent treatment from anybody; no one could have been more encouraging to Amanda herself. He used to be fun; she would make sure they enjoyed some time together. Her own life needed brightening. When she went for a drink or to the cinema with friends it didn't really help. She felt she was simply marking time, waiting.

Much of her working life felt like that, too. Her mother appeared determined to prove that she could put in just as many hours now as she had before Rebecca's arrival, and only occasionally was Amanda given the opportunity to tackle a really interesting challenge.

Every major event since The Savoy luncheon had been handled either by Caroline on her own or the two of them together. Amanda regularly tried to convince her that she needed further experience in organising PR for such occasions. Inevitably, the most she gained was the promise that she would be given such opportunities later on.

It would soon be Christmas, another prospect that filled Amanda with less excitement than she felt it ought. A year ago she would have been delighted that her mother suggested she spend half the holiday at The Sylvan Barn. These days, she admitted privately that Parker family gatherings were rather beginning to pall. Although infinitely preferable to lazing around at home with her father and Emma and their friends, life geared to a new baby and a heavily pregnant daughter-in-law didn't offer much exhilaration.

When Christmas finally came Amanda decided that by paying special attention to Grandmother Lucy, the few days she spent with her mother's family would pass more cheerfully.

Freeing Caroline to continue preparations for Christmas, Amanda drove down to Folkestone on Saturday December the twenty-third, and immediately felt better while she and Lucy chatted away the drive back to The Sylvan Barn.

Mrs Dacre had left by the time they arrived and Caroline seemed satisfied that everything that could be prepared in advance had been completed.

Kate and Graham were bringing Isabel over on Christmas Day; meanwhile Nick and Bianca would be spending the Saturday with his parents before going on to join hers.

By Christmas Day Amanda was happier, quite elated. She and Lucy had gone to church at midnight, and she had relished the long service in which to listen to Keith Clifton's beautiful voice. Afterwards, leaving the church, her hand had been grasped firmly in his while he wished her a happy Christmas. His brown eyes had been smiling again, straight into her own.

The feeling that Keith had been especially pleased to see her in his church coloured her emotions throughout the following twenty-four hours, and Amanda found them passing more enjoyably than she'd anticipated.

She was still feeling quite euphoric later that night, until trouble flaring between her mother and Malcolm ended in a row that no one could help overhearing. Amanda realised then that she had suspected earlier that something was wrong.

During the prolonged Christmas lunch she had noticed that Isabel Parker appeared extremely tired. The old lady's normally ramrod-straight back was sagging and more than once she supported one elbow on the table. She would notice then what she was doing, sit up in her chair, and force a smile on to her narrow lips.

Amanda watched Caroline watching Isabel, and followed her out to the kitchen to help with the next course.

'Is old Mrs Parker all right?'

The reply was hesitant, not the immediate reassurance Amanda hoped to hear. Her mother was known for always trying to ease family concern.

'Er ... yes. We must remember how old she is, though. And she's never looked exactly robust, has she?'

'Hasn't she? She's always seemed quite steely to me. I've admired her for being so upright, and, well, strong, I guess.'

Caroline glanced beyond her daughter as Malcolm came to the doorway.

'Something wrong?' he asked, quite sharply. 'Kate's just suggested you might need a hand...'

'No, no, we're fine. I'm just about to set light to the pudding. You can carry it in, since you've left the table. We'll bring the sauce and brandy butter.'

After the meal was finished everyone helped to clear away before the whole family adjourned to the drawing room. Malcolm offered round drinks and they settled to listen to the Queen's speech.

Again, Amanda noticed that Isabel seemed to doze, which wasn't at all like her. She appeared rather unresponsive when Lucy began chatting from the sofa beside her after the television was switched off.

Chris was making an effort, trying to organise charades, a family tradition and normally a game in which his grandmother joined enthusiastically. This time, though, Isabel surprised them by rising slowly from her chair.

'I'm sorry, everyone, but I'm afraid I simply do not have the energy for joining in. In fact, if you will forgive me, Caroline, I really feel I ought to be taken home. I need to rest.'

Caroline hastened across the room to Isabel's side, and leaned over to murmur into her ear. The old lady nodded, then Caroline spoke again, quite loudly: 'It's the heavy meal, I'm afraid – my fault. Of course you must rest, Mother. We quite understand if you wish to do so in your own home.'

'You don't have to leave so soon,' said Malcolm from his chair. 'There are enough bedrooms here, or if you prefer there's a comfortable sofa in one of the other rooms.'

Isabel gazed up at Caroline, her eyes pleading for an escape route.

'Someone will drive you home, and see you settled.'

'I don't need anyone to "settle" me,' the old lady asserted with her normal spirit. 'Delivering me to my door will be quite sufficient.'

'I'll do that,' said Malcolm when his

brother made no offer. He was growing uneasy about his mother, and wondered why no one else was experiencing similar concern.

During the short drive to Isabel's apartment she appeared her usual sharp-witted self, discussing the Queen's speech and the meal they'd all enjoyed, and sounding quite forceful.

'Caroline's a fine provider, a good homemaker,' she reminded her son. 'I hope you'll always appreciate that. She has a wealth of good sense, and more compassion than most businesswomen today. Come to that, more than many who do no more than run a home.'

Malcolm agreed, of course, but wondered what had triggered his mother's unusual praise of Caroline. So far as he knew, his wife had done no more than lay on a good spread for Christmas, something she had been managing for years.

Giving a hand as his mother got out of the car and walked, unsteadily for her, up the path, Malcolm couldn't avoid noticing how thin her arm felt through the cloth of her winter coat. Reluctant though he was to admit it, Isabel Parker appeared to have become very frail.

He knew better than to ask if she was all right, and was glad to find that her living room was well warmed by the log fire blazing beyond the fireguard. He stoked it for her, added a further couple of logs.

Glancing towards his mother, who had removed her coat, he saw that the sofa she was approaching already had a pile of cushions to one end, plus a sort of blanket, folded neatly. He was surprised. Isabel Parker was the last person he expected to see indulging in lounging before the fire.

'You are all right, aren't you?' he was compelled to enquire.

'Merely in need of a little quiet,' she assured him firmly.

He noted her swift glance towards the sofa, then read in her eyes the subsequent decision to cross instead to her favourite straight-backed chair.

'Thank you, Malcolm, for driving me home. Do close the door properly as you leave.'

He was still feeling somewhat bemused when he arrived back at the house. Charades appeared to have been postponed. Chris was in the kitchen, where he and Amanda had finished unloading the first batch from the dishwasher and were stacking it again. Amanda was disappearing off with Lucy to select some CDs and Chris was beginning to set out the silver they'd found for his Uncle Graham to inspect.

'Is Caro upstairs?' Malcolm enquired.

His son nodded. 'In the nursery, I believe.

Rebecca wakened needing a feed.'

Malcolm glanced into the drawing room to check that his brother and Kate weren't feeling neglected. Both were drowsing on one of the sofas while Lucy was following Amanda to another room where they could play their music. No one needed entertaining for the present.

Running upstairs, Malcolm felt the soaring of his customary delight about their tiny daughter, as it always did when he saw her. It might lighten the concern he felt for his mother.

He walked into the nursery and found Caroline looking no less perturbed than he had been feeling.

'How was your mother, darling? Did she say anything?'

Her question shook him. 'That she needed a bit of quiet in order to rest. Why?'

'No reason, just, well, not really *her*, is it?'

He continued staring at his wife. He knew Caroline so well, he could recognise all the signs when she was concealing something.

'You know something, don't you, about her?'

'She just seems under the weather. Her age, I suppose.'

Malcolm raised an eyebrow, feeling positive now that there was more than he'd suspected to Isabel's sudden departure. But then he heard Lucy moving around, and

Graham's voice as he went to join Christopher and look at the silver.

'Got to go back to playing host. We'll talk later.'

'Later' proved to be at eleven that night, after his brother and Kate had driven home, and Chris and Amanda were watching a video movie. When Caroline went into the kitchen to prepare hot drinks, Malcolm followed.

'I need to get to the bottom of this business with Mother. You know something, don't you?'

Caroline sighed. 'She's not quite up to par, yes. Not unexpected at her age, is it? I suppose we'll have to prepare ourselves for facing the fact that she won't always be with us.'

'Tell me what you really know.' He didn't doubt now that Caroline had been the recipient of some information that should have been given to *him*, directly. 'I'm not going to be fobbed off – I shan't let this alone until I get at the truth. The entire truth.'

'I think we've got to respect your mother's wishes, darling. *If* I've been told anything – and I'm not saying that I have – it was in the strictest confidence–'

'For God's sake,' Malcolm interrupted, shouting. 'I'm her son; I've a right to know if something's wrong. You've got to tell me.'

Caroline frowned, torn between her promise to her mother-in-law and her own instinct that at least one of Isabel's sons should be in the picture.

'I ask you again,' Malcolm persisted, 'and I'll go on asking until you tell me – what is wrong with my mother?'

'Oh, this is so difficult. She confided in *me*, darling. And asked for my promise that I would respect her wish to—'

'To keep this from everyone else? That what you're saying? Brilliant! My mother tells you – what, that she's ill? How serious is it? And you don't think to mention it!'

'If I tell you now, you must give me your word you won't pass on any hint of this to the others. Not until they have to know.'

'And who's to decide that, for heaven's sake? You?' Malcolm swallowed, trying to contain his fury and frustration. 'Never mind that, for now. You've got to tell me everything – you must see that.'

'I only hope you'll explain if she learns the news is out. You'd better sit down, darling.'

He ignored her suggestion. 'Get on with it,' he said wearily.

'I'm afraid she has cancer. I am so sorry, Malcolm.'

She watched him pale, waited while he seemed to take the news on board.

'Where is it, and how far advanced?'

Caroline told him everything that Isabel

had confided to her, along with all the reasons behind the old lady's determination to keep the news quiet.

'Graham must be told immediately; being the eldest he has every right.'

'No, Malcolm, no. She's old and she's ill – can't you at least do one thing to make her feel easier?'

'The family have got to stand by her, for God's sake – discover what may be done for her. There must be some treatment.'

'Your mother said not.' Caroline paused. 'Maybe this is part of the reason for her wish to keep it from you all.'

'And Kate should be in the picture – she's the one to hand day by day, after all. The senior daughter-in-law. Can't think why Mother confided in you.'

Mention of her sister reawakened Caroline's consciousness of how fervently Kate might try to manage Isabel's remaining days for her. Not that she'd needed any reminder of Kate's usual approach! But she wouldn't mention this to Malcolm; he knew well enough what the situation was.

He was already using that against her. 'No doubt you've relished having information that neither your sister nor my brother shared. To say nothing of your decision to keep it from me!'

He hadn't felt so distressed in years. His mother was ill, gravely ill from the sound of it, and he had not known. His own mother, whom he loved – and admired, despite her determined ways. And she had chosen to talk to Caroline. Not to him – to his wife. The sensation of being left out, *deliberately left out*, seemed familiar. Memories flooded to him of the years when Christopher and Nicholas had been growing up.

'You've won her over, haven't you,' he snarled, strode to the door, and swung round to face her. 'Not content with winning the boys away from me, you've taken on Mother as well, haven't you? Made her turn to you instead. That's unforgivable.'

Six

The rest of Christmas was ruined for Caroline by Malcolm's reaction to learning of his mother's illness. Determined to avoid making relations between them worse, she resolved not to ask him whether he was respecting Isabel's wish to keep the news from Graham. Since he was hardly speaking to her, the matter didn't arise between them – the only thing for which she could feel thankful.

'At least it's not my sole responsibility to

cope with whatever happens in the future,' she said to Lucy as she drove her home to Folkestone after the New Year. 'It's up to Malcolm now, whether the others are to be told, and if Isabel is to be pestered regarding possible treatment.'

'That's how you view it? That she wishes to avoid contention over her not having an operation or drug therapy?' Lucy asked.

'What would *you* want, Mother – if, heaven forbid, you were in her situation?'

'Time and peace in which to order my affairs, enough medication to deaden the pain so that I might retain some dignity.'

'Which seems to be what Isabel wishes in the light of their gloomy diagnosis.'

'As she will assure Malcolm, or anyone else prepared to offer an opinion. Who knows, it may do her some good to be able to reiterate her own thoughts – make her feel she's in control of the situation, that kind of thing.'

'And she is still capable of asserting her will.'

'Quite. Meanwhile, Caro darling, you should still feel good about her original choice of confiding in you. A compliment, if ever there was one. And something that isn't altered by Malcolm's being able to force the truth out of you.'

Despite Lucy's words, Caroline remained unhappy about the whole business, no less so because the unease between herself and Malcolm was preventing her from offering her understanding of the inevitable distress his mother's illness must be causing him.

The evening that Malcolm took a call from Adrian Lomax, Bianca's father, the uncomfortable atmosphere at The Sylvan Barn began to ease. Bianca and Nick had been visiting her family when she went into labour. Frances Lomax had rushed to the hospital with Bianca and her son-in-law, and had just called Adrian to announce the arrival of their grandchild.

'A boy, and he's fine,' he told Malcolm. 'Great, isn't it, at last. Especially as it's a boy.'

Telling Caroline, Malcolm sighed. 'Adrian Lomax went a bit over the top, I thought. Can't believe having a boy will ever make up to them for the baby they lost.'

'Nor for all those wretched miscarriages,' Caroline agreed. 'They won't forget. But they will soon find they have less time for remembering!'

She herself was still learning that new babies were far more time- and energy-consuming than ever she recalled.

Malcolm grinned. 'Said with feeling? Certainly, Rebecca keeps you pretty busy.'

'Just as well – prevents my interfering too frequently in Parker family business.'

He hesitated, thinking. 'I suppose, in a way, I'm glad that Mother did choose you to confide in. Shows she appreciates your strengths, and that you're to be relied on. And I haven't passed on the news to Graham yet. Time enough for that when the illness grows self-evident.'

'Your mother will be delighted about the new baby, that's for sure – she was determined to live to see it.'

Malcolm turned pale, gave her a look. 'Is the time she has left so uncertain? I didn't realise...'

'You know doctors. They won't give a close indication of how long people may survive. And you know your mother – she's likely to confound everyone by outliving all expectations.'

'Only hope she doesn't suffer too badly, mentally or physically.'

There was no evidence of Isabel's ill health on the day when she arrived with Kate at The Sylvan Barn to meet her great-grandchild. She came striding through to the drawing room with all her old vigour, and went down on one knee beside the carrycot where the infant was sleeping.

Smiling, Isabel touched his head of pale gold hair, looked up at Bianca, who was in a nearby chair.

'He's going to have your lovely colouring,

my dear. And how well he looks! I told you, didn't I, that you'd have a healthy baby one day.'

Bianca smiled back at her, blue eyes gleaming with tears. 'You did indeed, just when believing anything would come right seemed impossible.'

'And what are you naming him? No one's told me.'

'Mark – it's my father's second name. Actually, though, we'd like him to have a middle name, too. I wanted to ask you, do you have names that mean a lot in your family?'

'Parkers tend to always have a Graham.'

'I know that,' said Nick, coming into the room. 'We meant your side of the family.'

Straightening her back as she slowly got to her feet, Isabel beamed at the surprise which so delighted her. 'George – the eldest son of every generation always was George.'

'There we are then,' said Bianca.

The two of them went to hug the old lady. 'Let's hope he inherits some of your splendid spirit,' Nick went on. 'That ought to see him through any difficulties.'

'You foresee difficulties, then,' Isabel teased. 'Not the proverbial bed of roses?'

'As if!' Bianca exclaimed. 'Unless the problems that led up to his being here could mean his share of problems are already experienced.'

Late that afternoon Amanda joined them after finishing work for the day. She had seen the baby already in hospital, but again was struck by how tiny he appeared. Rebecca had grown so swiftly that Amanda had virtually forgotten that her young sister had been even smaller at birth.

'Aren't you frightened of holding him?' she asked Bianca, who was taking Mark from the cot.

'I'm the one who's scared of that,' Nick told her. 'Bianca's brilliant with him.'

'Must be all the coaching we had at the classes,' said his wife. 'And having plenty of time for getting used to the idea of having him around.'

She had revelled in the few weeks prior to going into labour when, no longer working in the library each day, she could indulge her skills as a housewife. Now that Mark was actually here, her happiness seemed boundless.

Sharply aware of Bianca's joy, Amanda experienced a tumult of emotions. She was delighted for Nick and his wife, of course – no one better understood the agonies they'd endured in the past. But she couldn't help wondering if it ever would be *her* turn for a family, for a home of her own.

I'm beginning to bore myself with feeling this way, she acknowledged. It was only a matter of months since Rebecca's arrival had produced a similar reaction. This time, it seemed to hit all the harder, and she noticed that whenever she experienced that longing it was for a son.

She could picture him quite clearly, and there could be no doubting who he would resemble, with his friendly brown eyes and dark hair. This Christmas she had sat in church, listening to Keith's sermon, acutely conscious of the near-hypnotic effect of those magnificent eyes. Hadn't she willed him afterwards to say something to indicate that he was pleased to see her?

He had said just that, along with 'Happy Christmas'. He had smiled into her eyes while shaking her hand. The trouble was that, fool though she was about him, Amanda had the sense to recognise that was no more than the greeting he used for everyone attending the service.

She was hoping for an opportunity to continue getting to know Keith better during the christening of Nick's baby. She could never forget how well they had got along following the similar service for her own tiny sister.

Stupidly, she hadn't foreseen that they would choose the church near their own home. Suddenly Nick had begun telling Isabel Parker about their plans, and Amanda felt deflation overwhelm her. Another opportunity that wouldn't materialise. She could visualise no likely prospect of meeting Keith ever again.

But Chris might be able to help, she thought, smiling as she recognised the distinctive sound of his MG in the drive. It had to be significant that he'd arrived just when she was despairing. Chris did know Keith pretty well now. Just believing that he might suggest some solution was cheering her up.

She heard his voice in the hall, left the others, and ran through to meet him. A pace or so beyond the drawing room doorway, Amanda halted. Christopher was there all right, but following him into the house was Diana Frazer.

'Hi, Amanda. Just leaving?' Chris called cheerfully.

'Right. Time I did,' she responded sharply. She glanced towards Diana again, tossed a casual 'Hello' in her direction, and strode through the hall to the outer door.

Getting into her own car, Amanda sighed. And then she smiled ruefully. No good depending on Chris either, she thought. Not even as a friend. If that Frazer woman was back in the frame, he would be too busy to notice anyone else existed. Today she certainly didn't want to know what brought Chris and Diana together again.

Admiring the new baby and asking how Bianca was, Diana was smiling easily, making Chris smile, too. Despite the awkwardness that until recently had kept them apart she seemed so eager to integrate with his family. He had contacted her before Christmas, after talking things over with his stepmother. For a time, though, both he and Diana had remained distant and uneasy with each other.

Matters had improved at last only the other day. Diana had telephoned to confirm that further investigation of the church silver he'd discovered dated the Communion cup for sure as 1572.

'That was following Elizabeth the First's proclamation of 1559, when the cup was restored to the laity. Instead of the more ornate chalice of the Roman rite, these cups were of simpler design, as we supposed. Do you remember our discussion?'

'And it is really that old?' Christopher still could hardly credit the date.

'So the experts say – I've consulted more than one of the top people.'

'If the stuff's C of E, do I show it to Keith again?'

Diana had suggested waiting a while, during which she would make further enquiries in various areas.

'I mentioned this to Vernon the other day, and he was explaining how silver during that period often was made within the region where it would be used. For instance, in

Norfolk there were masses of sixteenth-century silversmiths. If we continue on trying to identify who created these pieces, we ought to discover something to point us towards where they truly belong.'

Chris was only too happy to continue on and on, trying to learn more. So long as he remained in contact with Diana. He'd have expected that hearing of her discussing things with her husband would be disturbing. To his surprise, he'd felt curious more than anything about Diana's situation. Perhaps he was beginning to accept that she did have Vernon in her life, *somewhere*. Even though she wasn't prepared to explain how seeing him while he seemed to be absent from her home was possible.

Diana's interest in Bianca's baby was generating a feeling of well-being that became sheer delight when she agreed to Christopher's suggestion that they eat at the village pub that evening. He was playing this cool, as he was obliged to play it, but they were together. That counted for a lot to him.

The restaurant side of the pub was quiet that night, which seemed to please them both. Choosing a table near the open fire, Diana slipped off her coat, smiling her thanks when Chris took it from her.

It felt like a fresh beginning, an opportunity, the second chance, one which he did not mean to spoil by permitting desire to slide into their relationship.

They ordered, and talked about the place itself – the warm interior was welcoming after the chill February breeze that had accompanied them from his car to the inn door. Neither ultra-modern nor antique, the style was pleasingly subdued, with the fire itself providing the brightest focus, and wall lights a foil for oak panelling.

'A good place for this late in the day,' Diana announced. 'Not so brilliantly lit that it reveals every work-weary line.'

'Does that mean researching my silver find is wearing you out?'

She laughed. 'On the contrary, that's the light relief. I'm amassing information for a book. A sort of "how-to" on collecting silver for the amateur. Ought to be simple to write, but isn't. Mainly because of trying to find the right line between daunting with too much information and patronising by not providing enough. Vernon thinks I should throw everything in, and let the reader select what they need.'

'Could prove indigestible perhaps?' Chris suggested.

'Quite. And the last thing I want. There are enough books for experts.'

'How would you interest me in your subject? If I wasn't fascinated already?'

'In your case, by describing then identifying your find. In a way, that should apply for each individual. So, I'm dealing first with the most commonly found items of silver. The kind you'd unearth in a good junk shop or a modest antiques place. Then there's stuff you encounter elsewhere – like ecclesiastical silver. Your discovery has aroused my interest in that particular line. And although it shouldn't be collected by individuals perhaps, it does enlighten us about history in addition to providing examples of hallmarks and so on.'

'Sounds great to me. You will let me have a copy when it's completed?'

Diana laughed again. 'Provided we both survive that long.'

'Vernon isn't helping you with it then?'

'He's not in a position to, I'm afraid.' Her tone was cold, dismissive.

'OK. Forget I asked.'

Diana looked across the table towards him, sighed. 'Oh, what the hell ... It's not something I usually talk about, mainly because, initially, I was determined that what he'd done was not going to affect my career. So far, it doesn't seem to have done so to any great degree.' She paused, swallowed. 'Vernon's in jail – an antiques scam, I'm afraid. It went horribly wrong.'

Chris struggled to find something to say while he took the news on board. 'You must miss him terribly.'

Diana shook her head. 'Only because of

having no one around at home. Actually, you're the person I've really missed these past several weeks. That's rather beside the point, unfortunately.' She sighed. 'I can't forget what Vernon did – we were business associates as well as married – but I'm trying to forgive.'

'How long is he inside for?' Any satisfaction that her husband was out of range must be weighed against the man's eventual release.

'Barring problems that delay the date, he'll be out later this year. And he'll rely on me then, to keep us afloat. With his integrity in doubt, he'll not find any further clients.'

'So you'll stand by him, naturally.' Chris knew enough about Diana now to feel sure she wouldn't desert anyone in such need.

'Can't kick him when he's down, can I? Whatever I feel.'

Minutes ago he'd have been delighted to hear Diana suggesting that her chosen loyalty would be towards himself. As things were, amid the mass of emotions aroused by Vernon's imprisonment, he only felt acutely conscious that the man had this massive claim upon Diana.

Their meal together began to seem quite ordinary, and the inn itself dreary rather than cosy. Christopher was gradually feeling pole-axed by the truth of Diana's situation, totally confused.

He avoided looking across at her, yet still he remained aware of how lovely she was. And how vulnerable she appeared that night. Some impulse incited him to make the most of the time they had left together. But between them stood the knowledge that whatever they shared could lead nowhere.

It didn't help when Diana invited him in after he drove her home, and turned the desire generated inside his car to a yammering of all his senses.

'I'd better be getting home.'

'Then kiss me here,' she persisted. 'I can't keep pretending I don't need you.'

Christopher shook his head, leaned across Diana to open the door for her to leave. He would have to think carefully before they went down that road again.

'There are too many people with needs, aren't there,' he reminded her grimly.

'No farmers needed a crisis like this. Thank God we haven't any livestock,' Malcolm exclaimed. 'We've had our bad times, I know, but lots of people are losing all their animals.'

Hugh Edmonds, who assisted him so ably, had heard from his former employer. Only a few years previously the man had grubbed out all his fruit trees in favour of sheep rearing. Today, his entire flock had been destroyed because of the outbreak of foot-

and-mouth disease.

'Where does he farm – is that in Kent?' Caroline asked when Malcolm began telling her.

'Think so. Hugh didn't say exactly. I offered him time off to go over there and help, but they're discouraging all visitors, of course.'

'Must be diabolical to lose the lot in one fell swoop. And I gather it's far worse in other parts of the country.'

'Quite. Not that our locality's unaffected. I noticed driving back from Graham's that most of the woods are out of bounds to walkers, with footpaths over farm land closed as a precaution.'

'From what I heard on the television news, some of the European ports are becoming reluctant to welcome English tourists.'

'That's overreacting if they're not from a heavily infected area, I'd have thought. After all, they can soon have everyone disinfect their feet and so on as they enter the country.'

'I wonder if that will affect Julian and Emma's extended visit to Spain?'

'Shouldn't imagine so. If the airport authorities over there are worried, they'll arrange disinfection for arrivals from the UK.'

Amanda had entertained similar concern

regarding her father's trip abroad. She was looking forward to the freedom of having the house to herself for a while, and was greatly relieved when Julian received confirmation that his travel plans were going ahead as scheduled.

Caroline had been pressing Amanda to stay at The Sylvan Barn during the whole of Julian and Emma's absence; so far Amanda herself was delaying a firm decision. She was eager to try living on her own – for years she had been very conscious that most of her contemporaries had long since become independent of their parents. So many times she felt smothered by the older generation.

During every weekday she spent hours with her mother, and well though they worked together there were all those occasions when she longed to be allowed her head. Discovering how effectively she handled living alone might provide just the opportunity to suggest to her father that she should have her own home. If she could make a success of a solitary life, the work situation might seem less limiting.

There was another reason also for not leaping at the chance of staying with Caroline and Malcolm. The christening of Bianca and Nick's infant had seemed a pale echo of Rebecca's but, even without her own active participation as a godparent, the ceremony had renewed her aching for a child. The longing seemed to be becoming a constant physical pain.

The prospect of staying at The Sylvan Barn had lost most of its appeal. Seeing Rebecca during some part of every working day was enough to trigger emotions which were becoming hard to disguise. Being around the place full time, plus having Bianca visit with her baby at frequent intervals, would make hiding her own feelings even more difficult.

Why am I such a mess? Amanda wondered wearily, arriving home to the empty bungalow on the first evening after her father and Emma had left for Spain. Forcing herself to do something to relieve her dissatisfaction, she went through to the kitchen. Ignoring the masses of ready-made meals that her stepmother had bought for her, she took from her bag the steak that she had purchased en route.

There were vegetables in the freezer, and she had bought a few potatoes; she would enjoy cooking everything just the way she liked. For pudding she was having yoghurt – Caroline's influence, she supposed. No one familiar with life in the Parker family home remained unaware of the healthy eating regime existing since Malcolm's heart problems.

Thinking about Malcolm Parker as she gazed through the window, Amanda was surprised to see his son, and to recognise how like his father Christopher was becoming. Seeing her, he waved, and she opened the kitchen door as he approached through the gathering darkness.

'Didn't know you were still around, Chris.' She was so accustomed to his car being parked near the vineyard that its presence hadn't registered with her.

'Suddenly less keen than normal to get off home,' he admitted. Even working alone, as he often did here out of season, seemed preferable to spending time in the flat mulling over difficulties.

'Want to talk?' Amanda enquired, and wondered if the likeness to his father which she'd noticed could be due to the weariness in his eyes and the uncharacteristic slump to his shoulders.

'Why should you listen to me going over all the problems in my love life?'

Amanda grinned. 'Because you've always had time for *my* moans? Mates, aren't we, Chris?'

He came to sit at the kitchen table, watched as she prepared vegetables.

'The steak might stretch for two,' she suggested.

Chris shook his head. 'Thanks, but no. Got something defrosting ready for tonight; mustn't waste it. No – just a bit fed up. Usual thing. Diana, not being available.

Trouble is, she never will be.'

'She's married then?' Amanda had long suspected that this must be the case, and had considered privately that Christopher was an idiot for letting himself fall for the woman.

'Unfortunately, yes.'

'And they're still living together?'

'Not exactly. It's ... complicated.' He sighed, yearning to have Amanda know what the problem was, to understand how he was feeling. But the truth was Diana's secret – he wouldn't betray it.

'You'll have to free yourself, won't you, old love? I can see how this is eating into you. It's, well, all such a waste. You're so attractive, and time's—'

'Rushing on?' His expressive eyes rueful, he shrugged. 'Doesn't seem to matter.'

'I don't like to see you this disturbed. Can I do anything to help?'

'Listen from time to time, I guess. When I can't take much more.'

'I will, of course. But I can't help thinking you're wrong to cling to ... to whatever it is you feel for Diana. Can you really not let go?'

'Too late.'

After Chris had left her, Amanda wondered why on earth he had become so besotted with a woman he could not have, a married woman. And what did Diana herself think she was playing at? Why wasn't she giving all her attention to that husband of hers, instead of playing up to Chris until he thought he couldn't live without her? It was obvious today that he was seriously involved there.

Although she began to enjoy returning each evening to her own company in the bungalow, Amanda gradually became preoccupied with Christopher's problem. Pondering over his apparent obsession with Diana Frazer soon was making *her* feel dejected. Chris had been such fun, always encouraging her to make more of her life, yet now he seemed imprisoned within his desire for a woman he could not have.

I wonder if Caroline knows what Chris is going through, Amanda wondered, but refrained from mentioning him at all. The office was no place for such a discussion. More seriously, she owed Chris the silence that had always rendered their shared confidences special.

Chris was waiting beside his car outside the bungalow on a wet Monday evening. Amanda thought he must have some news about Diana that he couldn't wait to share. Getting out of her car, though, she saw how grave his blue eyes were, and that he seemed almost to be leaning against the MG for support.

'Let's go into the house, Amanda. There's ... there's something I've got to tell you.'

'Tell me now.' He looked so upset, she mustn't make him delay.

Christopher shook his head. 'Waited out here to make sure I caught you. Come on indoors...'

As soon as she unlocked the door, he propelled her through into the sitting room, ushered her towards a chair.

'What is it, Chris? You ... you're not going away or something, are you? With *her*?'

'Nothing like that. It's bad news, I'm afraid, Amanda. Very bad. I took a call just before locking up the office. It was Emma. I am so sorry, little love. There's been a terrible accident. Your father—'

'No, no – not that!' she screamed. 'Is ... is he badly hurt? Where are they exactly? Take me to him, please, Chris – take me there.'

'I will, of course, if that's what you wish. But I'm afraid ... afraid that'll do no good. You see, Amanda, sadly ... he died. Instantly. At the scene.'

'But he can't have. I'd have known. Not my father. It can't be true – no, no, no! I want him, I want Daddy.'

She was shrieking hysterically. Numbed with shock himself, Christopher tried to hug her to him. Amanda fought him off, pushing him away with such force that he went sprawling.

'It can't be true,' she sobbed. 'It isn't. There's some mistake. Emma's got it wrong.'

'I'm sorry, but she hasn't – she's badly shaken herself.'

'But not hurt – is that what you're saying? Why did it have to be Daddy who's been ... been killed?'

'I don't know, no one will – until the accident is investigated.'

'Where did it happen?'

'Somewhere in the mountains, I think. Your stepmother said the roads were quite treacherous, up above the snowline or something.'

'The Sierra Nevada – that was one place *she* wanted to visit. Why did he ever have to meet her, why marry that ... that cow?'

'You're only saying that because of the shock. You know really that Emma has made Julian happy.'

'But for her, he'd not have wanted this trip. He never went off like this before.'

'While you were too young to be left, perhaps. But we shouldn't really consider that he ought to have restricted his life in that way for ever.'

Christopher poured brandy and made Amanda drink, then stood over her while she threw overnight things and a change of clothing into a bag. He insisted on taking her to The Sylvan Barn. Caroline would know how to cope, would by now have recovered from the shock of this news, which he had phoned through to her. He had hoped that Amanda might still have been in the office with her mother. Caro would have been better able to convey the dreadful news of Julian's accident.

Waiting in the dark outside the bungalow, Chris had wondered how on earth he would manage to tell the poor girl what had happened. Strangely, though, he felt a certain relief now because he *was* the one who'd been obliged to tackle that awful task. He couldn't feel that he'd said the right things at all, but he had done his best, while all he knew was this great yearning to do something for Amanda.

At The Sylvan Barn Caroline was distressed, badly shaken, and scarcely believing that her ex-husband was dead. Malcolm had been his stalwart self, sympathising, and immediately offering any assistance that they might need.

'If necessary, I could leave Hugh in charge here, fly out to Spain – either with you or on my own – to bring Emma back.'

'With the ... the body.'

'Er ... yes. Naturally.'

'There's nothing natural about any of this, is there? Is there?' Caroline was weeping, and angry with herself for letting the tears come. She'd told Chris to bring Amanda home. Not that he hadn't already thought of doing just that himself. When her daughter arrived she must be composed, ready to give, well, whatever was needed from her. Support, strength – though God knew where she would find that! For herself, Julian was a part of the past, yet the shock was enormous, draining. For Amanda he was – and always had been – an enduring presence. Her anchor.

'It will be up to me now to help her to survive,' Caroline told Malcolm.

'There's Chris as well, don't forget. The pair of them have always been close.'

That seemed to be the case when Chris stopped the MG in the drive and helped Amanda out. An arm around her, he walked slowly with her to the door that Caroline opened to them.

'Come on in, Amanda darling,' Caroline said, then felt her own tears rushing down her cheeks as she held her daughter to her.

They wept together, huddled on one of the drawing room sofas, their grief making Chris feel helpless. He wasn't sorry when Malcolm called him into one of the other rooms.

'Caro's taking this badly – more upset than I'd have expected.'

Chris was surprised to see how troubled his father's grey eyes appeared. 'I suppose that's largely on Amanda's behalf – the girl has relied on Julian for a very long time.'

'And Caroline always knew that Amanda leaned towards her father.'

'They were very close. She's going to find sudden independence comes hard.'

'Did Emma say what her ideas were on funeral arrangements?'

'Gracious, no. Much too soon to be even thinking of that. She'd only just left the hospital A&E when she rang through.'

'Poor woman will need someone to see her over the worst, being abroad like that. I've told Caro that I'll fly out there to assist, if need be.'

'I think Amanda will want to rush out to Spain as well. She asked me to take her, but that was her immediate reaction. Didn't like to say, but I don't see how I could, anyway – there's only me to organise the business side.'

'God, yes. Hadn't thought. Did ... did his widow have any say on that front? Has she a seat on the board or anything?'

Chris shook his head. 'Never been involved at all. She didn't want that.'

Much later that night when Amanda was about to go to bed, Malcolm again offered to fly out to Spain. Caroline smiled her thanks, and glanced towards Amanda.

'The two of us are going anyway, aren't we, Amanda love. We both feel it's something we've got to do.'

'And Chris – you said you'd take me to Daddy, didn't you?'

Chris sighed, ran a finger around the inside of his shirt collar. 'Actually, Amanda, that might not be possible. I wasn't thinking straight earlier. I've got to look after the vineyard now; your father would want—'

He was interrupted by the ringing of his mobile phone. They heard him speaking into it from the hall, where he was seeking a bit of privacy.

'Yes, Diana, but we've got a crisis here as well, I'm afraid.' There was a pause while he was listening, and then he spoke again. 'Well, OK then – I'll drive over and either get your car started or run you home.'

He came back into the room. 'Something of a problem – got herself stranded. I'll be back, I promise. As quick as I can.'

Caroline watched Amanda's newly composed face crumple, saw her swallow, twice. Eventually, she faced her mother, straightened her shoulders.

'We'll cope somehow, won't we, Mum.' But Amanda flinched as they heard Chris drive away.

Seven

On the following day Chris drove them to Gatwick for the flight to Malaga, which had been easy to book because of being out of season. All the way to the airport Amanda was composed but naturally subdued.

Everything felt so unreal; she could not believe that her father wouldn't be rushing to greet her when they touched down in Spain. She had spoken to Emma that morning, and had cried over her stepmother's very evident distress. Whilst accepting their marriage, she had never until now really acknowledged that Julian and Emma were in love.

'The poor woman sounds devastated,' Caroline had remarked after Amanda handed the phone to her when she was unable to continue speaking.

'Yes, I wonder what she'll do – afterwards, I mean.' Amanda couldn't visualise Emma remaining at the bungalow.

At the airport Chris stayed with them, seeing them booked in for their flight and only then admitting that he was anxious to get back to the vineyard. 'People to notify about what's happened, that sort of thing.'

Caroline thanked him sincerely for all he had done. Amanda had grown quiet, merely murmured, 'Yes, thanks, Chris.'

'He has been very good,' her mother reminded her after he had left them. 'Helping to arrange our flights after you were in bed last night.'

'We could have done that ourselves,' Amanda stated baldly, thinking that from now on they would manage quite well without his help. Would have to manage, so long as he remained subject to Diana Frazer's requests!

Neither she nor her mother paid much attention during their time in the air. Both dozed intermittently. No one had slept well the previous night, burdened with sadness plus the mass of thoughts whirring through exhausted brains. Even this short trip to Spain needed some planning. And Amanda had then been unable to check the eye of her mind as it flicked this way and that trying to envisage what must be done about the funeral.

Emma was waiting for them in the room she had shared with Julian in a tourist hotel in Malaga. The Mediterranean warmth felt stifling compared with the chill March winds of Kent, and Emma herself looked drained.

'Were you hurt at all?' asked Caroline concernedly when they were all seated after the initial surge of hugging.

Emma shook her head. 'Shaken, that's all, but that was nothing to discovering Julian was out cold beside me.'

Caroline reached out and grasped the woman's arm. 'You don't have to tell us yet, you know, if you're not up to it.'

'Got to talk – suppose I've had too long just thinking. The hotel people are very good, bringing meals up here, that sort of thing. But they have their work, and don't seem to be overstaffed. Maybe because it's not high season.'

'We're here now,' Amanda stated, then thought how obvious and banal her words had been. She wanted to help. A part of her understood how Emma would be feeling, but that was only a small portion of her own senses – the rest was one massive inescapable *soreness*. She had never ached so completely, never felt so entirely raw.

'Was the car badly damaged?' Caroline was asking.

Amanda frowned. What did that matter? Daddy is dead! she cried, but only within her own head. Perhaps the other two needed to discuss these practicalities in order to avoid raising more hurtful issues. Like where was Julian's body?

Evidently, the car was likely to be a write-off, and needn't concern them for the present. The traffic police, which Emma knew as the 'Guardia Civil', had been most helpful at the site of the accident.

'They were still with us when we reached the hospital, and seemed to know who would help us through all the formalities. There are such a lot of formalities,' Emma sighed.

'That's why we're here, to see they're all sorted,' Caroline assured her.

Amanda stared beyond her through the window. The hotel was situated in a pleasant avenue, and although this room faced away from the sea the view was quite spectacular. Against a steep hillside stood large houses, all looking relatively new, their cream- or white-painted exteriors elegant as they gleamed in sunlight that seemed much too bright this early in the year. At any other time she would have loved it here, would have yearned to explore.

'We may see him this evening,' Emma told them quietly, her voice witnessing to the strain of not giving in to emotion. 'I've explained that you will be with me. Amanda, of course, will spend as long as she wishes there.'

Hearing her name, her stepdaughter nodded. 'Thank you. I do need that.' She also needed to do something practical towards the arrangements that must be made for taking her father home. For the funeral. If only she didn't feel so overwhelmed. By sadness, by this enormous abyss that was loss. By dread.

Remember, O man, that dust thou art...

The words were coming from nowhere to awe her by the finality of death, to terrify.

'I've got to make a phone call,' she announced abruptly. 'I can, can't I, to England?'

'Why, yes.' Emma sounded astonished.

Amanda didn't care. She listened while the procedure was explained, and began dialling. No one knew she'd ever made a note of the number; she couldn't have been more thankful that she'd indulged that whim. Nobody would understand how much having this contact mattered.

'Must be calling Chris,' Caroline murmured to Emma.

Keith answered almost immediately, sounded slightly puzzled when she gave her name. Amanda rushed on desperately.

'Can't take long over this – I'm calling from Spain – but I had to talk to you. It's my father – he's dead. There's been a terrible accident out here...'

'Malcolm, you mean?'

'No, no – not him. He's my mother's second husband. You don't know my father...'

'Oh, oh – well, Amanda, I'm most

dreadfully sorry to hear of your bereavement. Wish there was something I could...' His voice trailed off while at the other end Amanda began picturing his brown eyes, and the sympathy darkening them. 'In Spain, you say?' Keith went on. 'Look, if there's any way I can advise, or anything, ring me again. That's if there isn't something specific now...?'

'I just ... just wanted to talk to you.'

'Look, keep in touch, let me know if there is anything. Otherwise, give me a call when you arrive back in England. Meanwhile, you'll be in my thoughts, my special prayers.'

'Keith – Keith Clifton, our rector,' she told the others as she hung up.

Caroline was staring across, amazed. Today, Amanda seemed quite unlike her recent self and more like the rather fey individual she had been in her teens. How strange that her daughter should ring the rector; they'd scarcely seen the man since the day of Rebecca's christening.

'And I'll have to ring Malcolm, just to check,' Caroline told Emma. 'We asked Bianca to come to the house and look after both babies. And fortunately, Mrs Dacre is proving to be remarkably unflappable with little ones around.'

'She's your housekeeper, isn't she?' asked Emma. 'I got Julian to pension off the woman he'd had at the bungalow – I much prefer to do things my own way.'

You would, thought Amanda, without reflecting on the occasions when she and their housekeeper had disagreed, in the old days.

'Daddy's very easygoing,' Amanda remarked.

'Amanda...' Caroline reproved, then stopped herself. The girl was too upset to consider the likely effect of her words upon other people's feelings.

Emma shook her head, waved a hand dismissively. Nothing counted any longer. Julian had gone, and along with him all purpose, all emotions that weren't directly generated by his passing. She had cried for so long yesterday that her head felt stuffed with wool, or wood – certainly everything about her felt wooden.

Caroline and Amanda were allocated their own room for the night, and went thankfully from the one which seemed to alert them to reminders of Julian's recent presence. Did Emma not notice that his swimming trunks still hung – long since dry – on the balcony; did she not see his shaver beside the mirror, favourite cufflinks on that tiny china tray?

Darkness was gathering in the tree-lined streets beyond their taxi as they were driven off to see him. If anyone had said why they must wait so long, Amanda had not heard them. Thank God her mother was here, she thought; this great numb feeling overtaking her was preventing her from being of much practical use. And she would have helped Emma, sensed now that empathy should deepen the relationship between them.

He looked so *alone*, but physically not as different from his normal self as she had expected. But it wasn't like her daddy to be totally immobile, so passive. For as long as Amanda could recall Julian had been extremely busy, always active. Years ago, when he was the editor of that glossy countryside magazine, she'd found his dynamism quite intimidating.

Not that he'd ever been anything but indulgent towards her, she thought fondly. Even when she'd been so set on taking up the violin professionally he'd allowed her all the time in the world to try and make the grade.

Walking nearer to the silk-lined coffin, she reached out, touched his cold forehead.

You must have known I'd never be more than a competent violinist, she thought, yet you never tried to compel me to be more realistic. I wasted so much time, while you were working long hours to achieve your ambitions.

The flourishing vineyard had been no more than a dream he wished to realise when Julian began studying in order to locate suitable land and begin planting. In those early days he had dug the ground and inserted every vine himself while seeing Amanda through her teenaged years, helped only by their housekeeper.

'You never let me down,' she murmured aloud, understanding how difficult that task must have seemed to a lone parent, a father. There had always been time for hearing her woes or rationalising her schemes, for shrugging off exhaustion to entertain her schoolfriends. Never until this day had she known how much she owed to him.

I must have hurt you so many times, thought Amanda, especially since I renewed the relationship with my mother. How did it feel to have me work with Caroline, and to expect you to spend hours listening while I enthused about the life she'd created away from you?

Worst of all, though, was her own reluctance to fully understand his fresh life with Emma. Seeing her stepmother as the intruder need not have been so entirely inevitable, should not have precluded some effort to take Emma to her heart. Might treating her more kindly now help to compensate? wondered Amanda. Would that also be too late?

Too late. Would she find some way to undo those months of small unkindnesses which must have contributed an element of hell for the poor woman? The woman for whom the bliss of new-found companionship ought to have reigned untainted.

Amanda could believe today that some premonition of this tragic loss might have created the unease with which she had witnessed his and Emma's plans for the journey carrying them away from her. Intuitive or not, such feelings were not to be excused, and now may remain unforgiven.

Leaning forward, she kissed his cheek, the frozen lips, eyelids lowered for ever.

'Dad, I am so sorry.'

This time there could be no reassuring smile, no hand reaching out, no words however sharp to confirm their relationship was enduring.

Amanda yearned to say that she had done her best. But Julian had infected her with his own brand of honesty. Even the kind that hurt.

In the ante-room her mother and stepmother waited, seated on identical straight-backed chairs, Caroline's hand on Emma's, two women little more than strangers, by grief united.

'He might have been a good husband,' Caroline was admitting ruefully, 'if I'd been better as his wife.'

'You were young,' Emma reminded her. 'Tolerance grows with the years, doesn't it, while we learn from earlier marriages.

Mostly not to expect perfection.'

Amanda walked slowly towards her stepmother's side, but Emma was speaking, squeezing Caroline's hand before releasing it.

'Your turn now. You'll want time alone with him.'

'Not sure that I do.' Caroline surprised them both. 'Confronted by Julian like this, I suspect I'll feel more than inadequate.'

Emma's quiet laugh made them both gaze at her. 'You? And I truly believed you possessed no reservations about yourself!'

Amanda slipped into Caroline's place, grasped the hand still warm from her mother's.

'Will you be all right?' she asked.

Emma's eyes were glossy with tears; she tried to shrug and Amanda felt her tremble.

'Who can tell?' Emma responded. 'I surely do not know. But I survived yesterday. Today I have you beside me.'

Their lives would never be the same. Whether or not those lives would get better, they would be different. There could be no going back. Pressing forward seemed an unwelcome alternative.

Caroline anticipated having to take charge, but it was Emma who had matters in hand, Emma who already seemed aware of each stage they must face in arrangements to bring this man they loved home to England.

For Amanda, the succession of episodes continued to feel unreal, a jumble of impressions. The uniformed men of the Guardia Civil, then officials in further rooms, clearly accustomed to dealing with death. And through it all was Emma's competent Spanish, which seemed to flow more readily than any local attempts at translating into her own language.

Long journeys with hired car and driver took them high into the mountains where Amanda tried not to notice the splendour any more than the precarious nature of the roads which, somewhere here, had killed her father. The life where once such wooded slopes, spectacular escarpments and snow-capped mountains would have thrilled her, was now grown remote. There felt to be no part of her free to indulge such love of beauty.

They passed through towns, pausing in some where another stage of the necessary process must be negotiated. She saw their colourful streets, animated inhabitants, picturesque houses, was hurt by their attractiveness.

'There's Granada.'

Emma's exclamation compelled them to look. It was dusk of another day; the Alhambra on its hilltop shone golden, magnificent against a sky darkening to purple. Amanda wept. Even before her stepmother continued speaking.

'We spent our last day there.'

Their last. This was all too much. How soon could they go home? However swiftly the arrangements in Spain might be concluded it would be too long. And they felt to be never-ending, exhausted as the three of them were, all but too weary to eat of a night, stumbling thankfully into strange beds and hoping for oblivion.

The day came at last when they stood on airport tarmac, respectful of the casket which none of them quite believed held Julian. Bringing him home brought lumps to their throats, tears that – although contained – prevented words between them as, some time later, their plane circled over the English countryside and landed.

Just as their endurance faltered, there was Malcolm; at his side were people who had handled a homecoming coffin before, and the Reverend Keith Clifton.

Amanda ran, fell into Keith's outstretched arms, felt them holding her while his black cassock brushing her legs increased the feeling of being enfolded completely.

And then she remembered Emma, her new-found appreciation of the woman, and her own need to be of use to her.

Leaning slightly away from Keith, she

half-turned, extended a hand for her step-mother.

'You don't know my stepmother Emma, do you? She was with my father when ... when it happened. Emma, this is Keith, who's been so good to me.'

The rector was startled to learn her estimation of his worth, Amanda noticed, his surprise evident in the momentary hesitation before grasping Emma's hand.

'You've all had a dreadful shock,' he said. 'I hope what little I can do may help to ease things for you.'

Malcolm had practicalities in hand; the accompanying funeral directors soon ensured they were starting out on the final part of this journey which felt endless.

Amanda had expected that coming home would restore a little sense of familiarity, some point of recognition that might link her old life with the one now forced upon her. Numbed by grief, she'd totally overlooked the facts: Emma had been absent in Spain, the house securely locked since the evening Amanda herself had left so hastily. Sealed within its walls, in every room, were all the tangible *things* that witnessed to Julian's existence. Unbearable reminders.

She could not take this, would never endure one day or night surrounded by everything *he* had loved, seared by all these memories.

Amanda locked herself in the bathroom, splashed cold water on cheeks and forehead, stared at the gaunt face and wild hair reflecting back at her. 'This is where you grow up,' she said aloud, wishing from the depth of her being that had been achieved long years previously.

'Your mother's leaving now, and Malcolm,' Emma called to her.

Straightening her shoulders, smoothing her hair with a hand as she went, Amanda walked towards them.

'I can never thank you enough,' she heard herself saying, without consciously forming the words.

Emma was smiling a little. 'Exactly what I've been saying. But we'll both be all right now, won't we, Amanda?'

She tried to smile, nodded, restrained her true emotions. 'Oh, yes.' Linking an arm through her stepmother's seemed right.

Keith Clifton was there with them, but about to ride back to the village with her mother and Malcolm. In front of everyone she couldn't cling to him as she needed to cling, could do no more than offer her hand and fervent thanks for being with them.

His smile was kind, understanding of her loss, and seemed regretful that they were parting now. 'You know where to find me,' he said. 'You mustn't hesitate. Oh, and I've been asked to join the local vicar here for the interment.'

The door shut out the rest of the world after they'd waved off the others. And felt to be walling Amanda in with the horror of what had happened. Everything was wrong, and never could be put right.

Emma appeared composed, was walking through to the kitchen. 'I must make some tea; there's always long-life milk in here somewhere. Not the same, I know, but we need something. Presently, I'll see what the freezer yields, rustle up some meal or other.'

How *could* she? Amanda felt she should be on her knees, beseeching God for merciful relief. Not only for her father's soul, but also for release from this unrelenting anguish.

'Whatever you cook will be fine.' Amanda supposed Emma needed to be busy with some action she might recognise. The least she should give was token agreement.

If Keith could have remained even for a short while, perhaps she might have been eased through these first testing hours. His departure left her even more bereft, yet despising herself for giving Emma too little consideration.

While drinking tea they opened the mail discovered in the hall. Amanda pounced on one, a note without envelope. She recognised Christopher's writing. Dated the previous day, it was brief, quite informal.

> Afraid I haven't a key for the house, couldn't check that everything indoors was OK or prepare for your return. Externally, everything seems all right, and I have kept an eye on the place.
>
> See you as usual when I report for work. If you should need to contact me earlier my home number's in Julian's book. Failing that try...

Amanda didn't read further than the number. Diana Frazer's telephone. If he was with *her*, she was the last person who'd disturb them!

Her attitude softened as soon as she saw Chris the following morning. Unable to stop herself dashing out to his car as he parked, Amanda began to believe that there might be some parts of her life which hadn't altered too devastatingly.

'I won't ask how it went,' he said at once. 'I can see from your face that it's been totally harrowing. Now you're home, though, there should be ways I can help – I hope you know I'll do anything.'

'Thanks. Emma'll be grateful too. She's in the kitchen – want to have a word?'

'Later, if that's OK. Got to get on – there's masses of things to do. Left a pile of work in the office, and there'll be today's mail any minute, if it's not here already.'

That made sense, Amanda knew, just as she knew that Chris would do his best now to continue running the vineyard and winery along the lines that her father had taught him. At least, *here*, he wasn't spending time with the Frazer woman.

Amanda would have forgiven Chris a lot, but not his suggestion to Emma later that day that he might be accompanied by Diana for Julian's funeral.

'We've grown very close,' Amanda heard him say. 'And she understands that Julian meant more to me than I realised, lets me talk out how much I miss him.'

'Of course, of course,' Emma responded. She had suffered so much that she neither knew nor really cared who was to join the many people who would attend her husband's interment.

Amanda could not understand the reason why Chris must have that woman at his side, and why he seemed so unaware that she herself needed to have him beside her. Had all their years of friendship, of being mates, evaporated before the strength of the desire he felt for that Frazer woman?

And then she remembered. Keith would be there for her – Keith, who fully recognised all the feelings which would be generated on that dreadful day.

A few hours after the funeral Amanda

realised that Keith in no way disappointed her, in fact provided more support than she could have anticipated. During the service, in church and at the graveside, he naturally deferred to their local vicar, taking only a small part in proceedings. But the few words he said before the funeral began were reassuring. And started Amanda thinking. Whereas all she had done so far had been to shudder beneath this massive dread.

'I know nothing about his spiritual life,' Keith admitted when Amanda was worrying because she'd never been sure what Julian believed. 'But I do feel certain that you'll be reunited one day. There's one thought which I like – especially for people who don't seem staunchly church going. We may all be surprised to discover who is in heaven awaiting us.' He hoped she didn't know the version ending 'and who is *not*'!

Afterwards at the house, when she most needed him, Keith drew Amanda aside.

'You've done very well today, love, and in many ways you are the person most vulnerable at this terrible time. Emma may have been Julian's wife, but I gather that their marriage was comparatively recent.'

Amanda tried to smile, gulped, and swallowed hard. Her eyes were awash with tears. Keith placed a hand on each of her shoulders, noticed that she was shaking, and steadied her against him. 'As I was saying, your father's been there for you throughout the whole of your life. I know how I felt when I lost my dad – no one ever fills the gap they leave.'

'Trouble is, I don't know what to do, not really – not what I should be doing now. I ought to be supporting Emma, but she seems more able to cope than I am.'

His arms felt to be tightening around her. When he spoke again Amanda heard a smile in his voice.

'She's much older, isn't she, has had previous experience of loss, of subsequently managing on her own. The first close bereavement always strikes more forcibly. And you *are* permitted to just let go and cry, you know. In fact, grief is good for you, better than bottling it up.'

'If I start, I might never stop. I can't just go weeping about the place for ever.'

'And you won't. There'll be things to attend to here, then you've your work – when are you going back there?'

'Mummy says I'm to take off as long as I need, so it's up to me really. Later today, Mr Longbridge, our solicitor, is coming to talk about the will. After that it's a matter of sorting out my father's things, and so on.'

'Presumably you and Emma will tackle that together...'

'I don't know. Didn't like to mention it yet. I was upset in Spain seeing his stuff around. Remembering that I shan't see him again, and that.'

'Yes, well, some people find it's best to go through everything straight away – they're so upset, anyway, that they couldn't feel that much worse. Other people need time to accept what has happened, can't bear to touch anything.'

'I'd prefer to get the worst over as quickly as we can. But I can't put that to my stepmother, I just can't.'

Keith gave her a gentle squeeze; she felt his fingers stroking her hair.

'Then you don't have to, love. Would you like me to try and find out how she would like things done?'

Amanda was thankful that she hadn't been the one to ask Emma about disposing of Julian's belongings. Keith reported back that his widow had no intention of letting anything go for some long while.

Grimly, Amanda sighed. 'Then I'll just have to live with his stuff reminding me all the time of the way things used to be.'

'You may discover there will be some benefits in having his possessions around.'

'You reckon?'

Strangely, though, Keith was proved to be right only a short while after she and Emma had thanked him and waved him off from the door.

On her way through the hall Amanda

noticed a notebook of Julian's on the telephone table, left there casually before he went abroad. Mostly daily jottings of matters concerning the vineyard, but with a few older entries relating to herself. She whisked it away to her room. Today, her emotions might be too raw for even reading his handwriting, but one day she could treasure this link with the everyday life of the father who meant so much to her.

Not long after Keith had left, Caroline set out for The Sylvan Barn. The three days of separation from Rebecca while she was in Spain had hurt; she could hardly bear now to be away from home for more than a few hours.

Diana Frazer drove off at the same time. The only non-family member who remained was Chris – he was expected to be present when the solicitor arrived. Some business acquaintances from the days when Julian had edited the magazine had departed immediately after the interment was concluded. None of the rest had stayed very long at the house; few of them knew Emma, who had come into Julian's life only after he had severed virtually all his links with publishing.

'I'm going to our room for a short time,' Emma told Amanda suddenly. 'My head is pounding.'

'Shall I find you some tablets?'

'I've taken a couple, thank you, dear. Just give me a call when Mr Longbridge arrives.'

Emma was allowed very little time for resting. The solicitor drew up outside the bungalow fifteen minutes later. Amanda wasn't sorry. The reading of her father's will was yet another matter that she needed to have over. And she was feeling abnormally uneasy with Christopher. The fault, she suspected, was her own. He seemed prepared to sympathise and to chat, just as he would have in the old days. *She* was the one who was letting the existence of Diana Frazer insert itself between them. Why couldn't she simply let go, be thankful that the woman had gone off to her own home?

After fetching Emma from the master bedroom, Amanda followed her into the dining room, where Christopher was seated already. Mr Longbridge, a small, dapper, grey-haired man, was standing behind the carver to one end of the long polished table. Chris rose as the two women entered and were gestured towards chairs to either side of the solicitor.

Brisk in manner, Mr Longbridge barely waited until the three were seated before beginning to speak.

'Firstly, I must offer my condolences on the very sad and sudden nature of Julian's, er, demise. We'd been on first-name terms from studying together at grammar school, and were at Cambridge during the same period, although reading different subjects. I can't apologise enough for not attending the funeral today; by a very unfortunate coincidence, a member of my family was cremated at about the same time.' He took a deep breath and continued. 'So you see, I do understand how you must be feeling. I shall, therefore, with your consent, be as brief as I may and then leave you in peace...'

Amanda had never in the past even contemplated what the contents of her father's will might stipulate, and since the accident had been far too distressed to want to guess what the position might be regarding Julian's estate.

There was no surprise in learning that she and Emma jointly were left the bungalow and its contents. And her stepmother appeared either to have been aware of this already, or to have anticipated that it would be so. Various shares and other investments were, likewise, to be divided equally between the two of them.

The astonishing clause, pleasing Amanda and evoking a gasp from Emma, was the legacy of ten thousand pounds to Caroline Parker 'in recognition of the years of marriage once shared by us, and of our continuing friendship'.

Delighted as well as amazed, Christopher

grinned across at Amanda. Emma was looking stunned, and not in the least pleased. She might have been grateful for Caroline Parker's assistance in Spain, but that did not mean she condoned her husband's outrageously large bequest to the woman.

'She must have known,' Emma muttered.

Mr Longbridge gazed over the top of gold-rimmed spectacles towards her.

'I shall be on my way to call upon Mrs Parker and inform her of this when I leave here. I must assert that I have always abided by my client's wish to conceal this matter until after his death.'

Emma sniffed. Glancing sideways, Amanda expected to see that her stepmother was weeping. There was no sign of a tear, only tautly clamped lips and a furious expression in eyes that were hardening.

'I merely wonder what justification there might be for such a generous gesture towards someone who so evidently runs her own business and has a husband to support her.'

The solicitor tried a quiet smile. 'From my documentation, it is apparent that this decision was made by Julian years ago, around 1993, in fact. From memory, that was a period when Mr Parker's farming business suffered a setback, and his wife was working alongside him.'

'If that were so, then surely there would

have been some amendment more recently, when the Parkers' situation improved?' Emma protested sharply.

She was informed, equally sharply, that no such amendment had ever been applied.

Mr Longbridge glanced at his watch. 'If we might move on, perhaps...' He outlined a few, smaller bequests to the local church, a handful of charities, and token amounts to former colleagues now retired from the magazine.

'The vineyard then – I trust that I shall at least benefit from its continuing good business?' Emma suggested.

Amanda could understand that the poor woman might be feeling alarmed about her future prospects, and sympathised with the insecurity she must be experiencing.

She herself had never really understood how the vineyard was run, nor even if it had a board of directors. So far as she knew, her father had made all decisions, in consultation with Chris during the years since he'd been made manager.

The solicitor quickly confirmed that the vineyard and the relatively new bottling plant were very profitable. He smiled encouragingly towards Emma.

'Your share in the business should – these figures assure me – keep you well provided for during the rest of your life.'

'My *share*?' Emma murmured.

Amanda sensed that her stepmother carefully avoided looking her way, and quelled her own sigh. She herself wanted no part of the vineyard; couldn't her father have left it all to his wife, to provide her security, and the satisfaction Emma evidently needed?

But Amanda was not the other beneficiary.

'Fifty per cent,' Mr Longbridge told them. 'The rest is to go to Christopher Parker, and I quote, "for the sterling efforts he has put into the vineyard, from that first day and throughout the whole time that he has been working with me".'

'Good Lord,' said Chris, reddening with surprise while he absorbed his late employer's assessment of him. 'Well, certainly great to learn you're appreciated.'

'It must be,' muttered Emma.

'You will be very comfortable,' the solicitor began to reassure her.

'Well financially maybe – if not with the arrangements Julian has thrust upon me!'

Amanda had smiled to hear that Chris was to benefit, but her smile waned. She was beginning to understand that her already tricky life with Emma was likely to come under the greatest pressure yet.

Eight

'I can't take it. I cannot accept anything from Julian. Whatever he left should be Emma's. Hers by right.' Caroline was adamant as she discussed the startling news with Malcolm following the solicitor's visit.

She had tried to tell Mr Longbridge how she felt about the whole matter, but he had remained inflexible about Julian's decision.

'I must execute my client's wishes by every means available to me. You must know that, Mrs Parker.'

Although she had protested, and tried to argue against taking a penny from the estate, Mr Longbridge had been uncompromising.

'Much as I appreciate your wish to seem anything but grasping, I cannot help feeling that Julian would have been happier if he could have learned that you were accepting his generosity graciously.'

There he had left the matter, if Caroline was not prepared to do so. 'I could pass it on to Emma, I suppose,' she reflected that night.

'Or to Amanda,' Malcolm suggested. 'That might be more suitable. And since it seems the two will share a home now, anything that benefits the girl will relieve any financial pressure on the household.'

'You believe there might be some threat of financial pressure there then?'

Malcolm shook his head. 'From reports, and from the good screw Chris has always earned there, I'd say that the vineyard's doing very nicely. And word has it that since Julian started bottling on site it has boosted profits.'

'It's just ... there was no need for him to do this.'

'He's always had a soft spot for you, darling. And he did know about that bad patch we went through. Must admit the prospect of my gaining from a handout from him sticks in my gullet. But *I'd* not be using the cash.'

'Nor me. What you say about investing it for Amanda could be a solution. I'd speak to Emma first, though...'

Speaking to Julian's widow was not the best idea Caroline had ever had. On the day they'd arranged for her to drive over to the bungalow, Emma was already in a prickly mood.

She had requested and been granted a private interview with Julian's solicitor, and had come away no more contented than she had been on the occasion when details of the will were first revealed. Her opposition to Christopher's holding an equal share in the vineyard was the matter for contention, and Mr Longbridge had confirmed that there were no means open for negotiation.

'Further, I would suggest, with respect, that it would be in your own best interests to work with Mr Parker as he continues to run the business to such good advantage. He has been there long enough, I am sure, to have proved his capabilities. You will have a steady income, year on year, and need do no more than you have in the past. Unless you wish to participate in its running, of course.'

'No, no.'

Emma wanted to sell. It was all she could think of as a solution. She couldn't bear the prospect of living there, alongside the vineyard which Julian had created, now that he was gone. Lost to her, as surely as if he had chosen to desert her.

She didn't want to see Chris Parker arriving daily, and to know full well that he would be taking Julian's place. That he was the one now tending the vines, ensuring full production of their wines, marketing to good effect. That vineyard had been as much a part of her husband as their personal lives had been. How could Julian have given such a large proportion of it away?

'I'm vexed, Caroline,' Emma admitted,

showing her through to the sitting room. 'I hope you're not about to distress me further. I thought I knew my husband, understood him, but I'm beginning to believe that never was so.'

Caroline quelled the impulse to turn and quit before more damage was incurred. This matter must be sorted, and delaying would merely exacerbate the already troubled situation.

'I'm sorry, Emma,' she responded. 'My heart went out to you at the time of the accident; you shouldn't be having to face additional upset at this dreadful time. And that's why I'm here. I'll come straight to the point. I don't need Julian's bequest, I don't understand why it was made, and I can't touch it.'

Emma shrugged wearily. 'Oh, just take it, can't you? I'm told the interest on it will make little difference to my position. I'm well provided for, as the saying goes. And I really cannot be doing with any more discussions of this nature.'

'But I thought ... Hasn't the amount he left me perturbed you?'

'Initially, perhaps. But that seemed insignificant beside Julian's wretched decision that Christopher should inherit a half-share of the vineyard. Where does that leave me? He'll never agree to selling.'

'And that's what you want?' Caroline was

shaken; Chris would be shattered.

'I did – yesterday, it was all I could think of. Being rid of it all, no more reminders of the life we had loved.'

'Oh, dear.' Caroline paused, then continued. 'Chris will always see you're all right, you know. That's the way he is. He'll neither make rash decisions without consulting your wishes, nor would he ever neglect the business.'

'I know all that.' Suddenly, Emma was weeping. 'I can't help resenting him – because he's the one that's here, not Julian. I'm not going to like this at all.'

After a time Emma recovered some composure. 'What did you come here for? You didn't finish telling me, did you?'

'I'd like to suggest investing the money Julian left me – for Amanda's future.'

'But she already has a half-share of the house, and any capital not invested in the business is divided between us.'

'Even so. And *I* know that she's earning good money, don't I? I still think she's the one who should benefit. Look to the future, Emma – you ought to be free from any worry that Amanda might ever become an added responsibility.'

Emma groaned. 'What future? I've just seen mine wiped out, haven't I? Through one appalling incident in what should have been a brilliant holiday.'

'Which was terrible. I don't really know what to say.' Hadn't she said it all already? She was handling this so badly.

'No matter. Nothing would help.' Emma managed to smile. 'I do appreciate your suggestion, though, regarding that money. However little Amanda and I seem to be in any real need of it.'

'Well, it just looked like a good solution to me.'

'Do I take it that you've mentioned this to me before putting it to her?'

'Oh, yes.'

'Maybe it will help Amanda to lighten up a little, enjoy herself more. I am quite anxious about her, you know.'

'Oh?' Caroline wasn't at all pleased. Was Emma implying that her treatment of her daughter was still inept? Or did she perhaps believe that Amanda was made to work too hard, for too long? 'I don't hold her nose to the grindstone.'

'Caroline, I'm not suggesting that you do. It's only that she's always appeared to be a serious girl, who doesn't have enough young friends.'

Caroline sighed, shook her head ruefully. 'True enough, I guess. But you should have seen...' Again, she shook her head, this time against her own inclination to confide more.

Revealing what a fey girl her daughter had been throughout her teens would do no one any good now. The bright, frequently animated businesswoman who was great on PR work was such a vast improvement that Caroline quite often rated her own success as a mother far higher than she'd once believed.

'She seemed delighted when your Rebecca was born – perhaps she'll really come into her own when she meets the right man and starts a family.'

Caroline nodded. 'She certainly loves babies – I've watched her watching them, especially since Bianca and Nick produced a healthy son. Trouble is, as you say, Amanda rarely makes the effort to meet other young people.'

'Can I ask you something?' Emma began after a brief hesitation.

'Why not? I'll see if I can answer.'

'Has Amanda always been quite keen on your stepson?'

'Christopher?' Caroline's smile was wry. 'We used to be rather concerned – they were very close. And although there's no blood relationship, of course, Malcolm worried that our family was complex enough already. Recently, however, Chris has widened his circle.'

'To include this Diana, er, *Frazer*, isn't it? The one who came with him.'

'She's around quite a lot, yes. I don't think that will lead anywhere, though. It just began through her being an expert on silver, you know.'

Emma nodded, retreated into her own thoughts. She was relieved if Christopher Parker truly was unlikely to wish his friendship with Amanda to turn into anything more permanent. With his owning half the vineyard and Amanda possessing a similar share of everything else, she herself might indeed be in a vulnerable situation.

'You're tired, Emma. I must leave you to get some rest. I hope I haven't added to your problems.'

'I don't suppose so. I'm sleeping badly, naturally. And anticipating that visit to Julian's solicitor didn't help.'

Leaving her, Caroline recognised how lost Emma must feel now. She didn't envy Amanda coming home to this every evening. And yet she knew she must, for a time at least, quell her own impulse to persuade her daughter to stay at The Sylvan Barn.

Only on the way home did Caroline begin to wonder where Amanda had spent the past few hours. She hadn't yet returned to work, and there had been no sign of her around her own home. Caro hoped she had more friends than they believed.

Keith had been surprised to see who his visitor was when he opened the rectory door. Dressed very smartly in a navy blue suit and cream blouse, and with her brown hair gleaming golden in the sunlight, she'd obviously taken great care over her appearance.

'On your way to somewhere special?' he asked, after inviting her inside.

Amanda's laugh was light. 'Just smartened myself up to come here. Had enough of looking drab by the time I got through the funeral.'

'Was there some, er, reason why you've called?' he enquired, somewhat nonplussed by her sudden arrival. Amanda was looking so cheerful today, he could hardly believe she was so distraught that she needed his counselling.

She followed him through into the sparsely furnished sitting room, hastened towards the one low armchair, straightened her skirt, and sat down.

Keith suddenly seemed quite awkward with her. He looked as if he wasn't really accustomed to having girls visit. Well, he needn't worry – she'd make herself at home. No trouble.

'How have you been?' he asked, still wondering why she needed to see him again when he'd been there for her and her stepmother only a short time ago.

'Today, fine. I know all the trauma of losing Daddy is going to keep surging over me, but I mean to emerge on the other side of all that.'

'Good, good.'

'Staying in doesn't help at all, and my mother didn't think I was quite ready for going back to work. That's why I'm using this time to do something about the rest of my life.'

'And...?'

'Well, here I am. You can't have had time yet to get to know too many people around here. Except for your congregation, I mean...'

Amanda paused; Keith was frowning, but she'd been determined nothing must deter her. She had worked everything out before driving off from home. He was always busy, caring for everyone but himself, not allowing time for striking up friendships, *forming relationships*. They got along so well together, neither of them should waste any of that. Just seeing this room was confirming her intuition that he needed a woman around. Needed *her*.

'You've been so good, so understanding. I ... just wanted to ... to give a bit in return...'

As her voice trailed off Amanda read in Keith's eyes that the impression she had gleaned from his kindness was mistaken. Coming here was a mistake. A big one.

He cleared his throat, resisted the impulse to run a finger inside the clerical collar. He hadn't thought it was a size too small...

'We can always use volunteers,' he said, after a moment. 'I could put you in touch with the ladies who do the church flowers, or perhaps the verger could use help somewhere around here. Is that the kind of thing you had in mind?'

It was not, of course, and Amanda sensed that Keith knew that. She could not fault him on his skill in dealing with an unwanted offer. Containing a sigh, praying that the flush in her cheeks wasn't too evident, she stood up. The action was less graceful than she might have hoped – the sagging springs and clinging arms of his chair seemed to detain her – but on her feet she regained some composure, and smiled.

'I'll bear in mind what you've suggested,' she told him, and willed the quiver out of her voice. 'I'll ask you for further details when Emma and I have completed all the masses of tasks needing our attention at home.'

She was heading smartly towards the hall when the doorbell rang.

'Excuse me,' Keith said and passed her en route to opening the door.

'Hello there – hope I'm not late,' said Anne Newbold. 'Last-minute patients don't allow for their GP's social life! What time did you say you'd booked the table for, love?'

Love? Amanda was shocked. Surely the

doctor was too old? For *him*. For having a date even?

Keith glanced from Anne to Amanda, and beamed. 'You're not too late, Anne. And as you see I've been delayed too. Amanda's just leaving.'

Noticing who his visitor was, Anne crossed the hall to grasp the girl's shoulder. 'I was so very sorry to hear about your father, dear. A terrible shock for you.'

'Yes, it was. Thanks. But people are very kind.'

She was going to cry. She wouldn't be fit to drive, and they would both see her go to pieces. Keith might even think that making such a fool of herself here was turning her into an even greater emotional wreck.

'Got to go,' she said firmly, and ran towards her car.

The Sylvan Barn wasn't all that far away. She could just about make it there before giving in completely to tears.

'You look bewildered, Keith.'

He grinned, drew Anne to him and kissed her. 'Just never thought I was the sort of man who evoked such ... such...'

'Potential affection?' Anne suggested.

He laughed. 'Goes with the job, I guess. Though I thought that came to an end when I left my first curacy.'

'Not that long ago, was it?' she teased.

'You can't have aged so drastically.'

'Almost wish I had! Was beginning to wonder just now how to evade what so evidently was coming my way. But without crushing her too completely.'

'What is there about doctors and priests, I wonder? Something must make us peculiarly desirable!'

'We're obliged to offer kindness and we try to understand, I suppose.'

'Well, people certainly can't get enough of that. What did you say, though? Amanda seemed intent on leaving, even without my sudden appearance.'

'I assumed her offer of *help* was to be taken as meaning to do the flowers, clean silver and brasses, sweep the church...'

'Poor Amanda. She must be dreadfully lost with her father dead, and so suddenly. She did seem to cling to him rather. Afraid we're wrong to laugh.'

'Got to, haven't you, though. Weep with folk while they're there, but you couldn't carry all their sorrows with you throughout each day. You'd not keep your own sanity.'

'Such as it is.'

Amanda made it dry-eyed to The Sylvan Barn, and strode towards the PR office. She had one hand outstretched to open the door when somebody spoke behind her.

'Didn't expect to see you here quite yet.'

It was Malcolm; the warmth in his tone made her smile as she turned to face him.

'Any more than I expected to be here this soon. I was just, well, needing someplace where I felt I belonged.'

'Ah.' Malcolm smiled and placed a hand on one of her shoulders while he gazed down into her troubled eyes. 'That brings me to something I've been meaning to say. Or were you urgently needing a word with your mother?'

She shook her head.

'I hope you won't take this the wrong way, Amanda – I'm well aware that nobody will ever take the place of your father. But I do want you to know that I shall always be here for you. For several years now you've seemed to be one of my extended family – I hope you'll feel you're a part of everything that goes on here. You must never hesitate to turn to me if there's anything I can do.'

The tears that had been threatening began to spill over. Amanda blinked them away, smiled at Malcolm, and hugged him.

'Thank you, thank you! That's brilliant. These past few days I've felt like a little girl again – it will be so good to know you're around for me.'

Finally entering the office, Amanda leaned back against its door, and gazed towards her mother.

'You have one fantastic husband – I hope

you know that.'

Caroline smiled. 'Malcolm said he wanted a word with you. I'm glad it's today – you'll be needing plenty of people around to provide a bit of anchorage.'

'No kidding.' She walked slowly across to take a client's chair facing her mother. 'It isn't as if Emma and I hit it off terrifically well. I don't mean there's any real trouble between us, it's just...'

'Things have never quite "gelled" between you?' Caroline suggested.

'Afraid that's so. No particular reason. I'll have to live with that now.'

'She is very concerned for you, especially since, well, you know.'

'Dad and I were such pals. Most of the time. When I grew out of being a slob. I only hope Emma takes up some outside interests – then I'll feel justified in going out more.'

'That reminds me,' Caroline began. 'An idea I've had.'

'Don't ask me to come and stay. I'd jump at that, and I mustn't. Not before Emma's started to create some sort of life for herself.'

'I wasn't going to say anything of the kind. But you know you've your own room here, always will have. Actually, this is to do with your future lifestyle, in a way.'

Amanda gave her a look. Was she about to be offered more responsibility here, a substantial salary increase?

'It's unconnected with your job, as a matter of fact,' Caroline went on. 'You know your father left me a legacy. It was totally unexpected, and rather unnecessary, however nice of him. I've decided to invest that money for you, darling. To give you an amount that's quite separate from everything else. I hope you'll use it for enjoyment.'

Amanda smiled wryly. 'What a time to suggest that! When I feel as if going anywhere would be an ordeal rather than fun.'

'But that will pass with time, and then you can treat yourself to a bit of sheer pleasure.'

Her daughter was nodding, her expression serious but not displeased. 'Thank you, anyway, Mummy. Could be good to have something else to think about, to make plans around. When I feel like holidays, and stuff. If I tell Emma, she'll realise that I shan't ever want more than my share of Daddy's money.'

'Emma knows already. Thought I'd put her in the picture about my intentions. I don't want her ever to think that you and I are excluding her.'

'Bit of a tall order, isn't it? You know me – once we're over the first awful shock, I'll be back to treating her as though we don't really belong together.'

'Will you? I rather believe you'll continue

to consider that she's going to feel terribly isolated. However, that's in the future. More immediately, there's something else I've got to tell you. And this is to do with the job.'

'I hope it's good.' Amanda couldn't face any more unpleasant changes in her life.

'I trust you'll think so. Ever since you coped so well while I was having Rebecca, I've been meaning to give you the recognition you deserve. Over the months, and especially since I had to leave her behind when we went dashing off to Spain, I have hated spending so little time with my new baby. I hope you are willing to shoulder more responsibility?'

'Need you ask? I'm itching to handle everything clients throw at us.'

'Excellent. Just as I wished. And you're to be well rewarded. I want you to be a partner in the company, Amanda.'

'That is great! Thanks so much, Mum.' Her brown eyes were gleaming.

'We'll go into the figures before long. Didn't know you'd be in today, so I haven't worked anything out. But naturally you'll be better off financially.'

'As if that mattered. It's like you said – the recognition is what counts. Most of all, the opportunity to really show what I'm made of. And this couldn't have come at a better time.'

They talked for a while longer until they

were interrupted by Bianca, carrying a baby in each arm and looking slightly harassed.

'Hello, Amanda,' she said. 'Didn't know you were here. I was so sorry to hear about your father. You must be devastated. And what about your stepmother – how's she taken it?'

'Not too badly, considering that she was in the accident with him, and had to tackle all the early arrangements on her own. She just seems tired now, and lost, poor soul.'

Bianca nodded. 'Understandably.' She turned to Caroline. 'Do you mind awfully if I leave Rebecca with you now? This young man here's finding it a long day. And he's used every nappy I brought with me.'

'You could take some of Rebecca's – you shouldn't need to ask.'

'Hers are massive for his tiny bottom. And I really do believe I ought to get him home.'

Caroline smiled. 'No problem, Bianca. You've been a star, taking over for yet another day to let me catch up on the backlog. Can't thank you enough.'

Bianca grinned. 'I'll find a way for you to reciprocate! Just wait till Mark is a bit older, perhaps when he's getting around and into everything. That'll be a good time to have you baby-minding.'

Amanda offered Bianca a lift, which was accepted gratefully. Nick had dropped her at the house that morning, and couldn't say what time he would be heading home.

In the car Bianca asked how Amanda really was feeling. 'You look exhausted, poor love.'

'Dare I say ready for a break? The sadness has been so intense, and I don't quite know how to evade any of it – without seeming heartless.'

'You're anything but that. Has your stepmother got no one, no relatives to rally round her? Is that why you're reluctant to get out, or is it that you're not ready for company?'

'Not sure. Bit of both, I guess.' She couldn't bear to recall her ghastly attempt at ensuring she might have more of the company she most wanted.

'Well, whenever you feel like it, you must come to us. Just ring to check I'm in. I've never forgotten how good you were when we lost Baby Malcolm, and after all those wretched miscarriages.'

'I will come over, soon,' Amanda promised. She wasn't quite ready yet.

Spending time with Bianca and Nick was a good idea. She had lots of friends through her job at the library, and he knew loads of people because of teaching locally.

Later that night Amanda was feeling prepared to be philosophical about revising her plans for socialising more, embarrassed though she had been by Keith Clifton's reaction. Perhaps she hadn't quite ruined everything there, but had simply chosen the wrong time to approach him. And as for his going somewhere with Anne Newbold, that might be no more than business, the need to confer about something or someone who mattered to them both.

'Has that girl, er, *Amanda*, upset you?' Anne asked as they finished their main course and studied the list of puddings. He had been rather subdued throughout their meal.

Keith shook his head. 'Not really, no. Although she did leave me feeling rather inept, yet another illustration of my mishandling of a situation. I never for a moment supposed that she'd have inferred that I was interested in her – not in that way.'

'Then what is it? Do you want to talk?'

He sighed. 'Does it sound terrible to admit that I believe I've come to the wrong place? That this bit of Kent's not right for me? I was indoctrinated with the idea that, once trained, a priest should live and practise his religion anywhere. Effectively. And without yearning to belong.'

'You don't feel you belong in our village?' Anne was shaken, dreaded the prospect of his deciding to leave. She was only just getting to know Keith. To really know him. And to like everything she knew about him.

'I was spoiled in Yorkshire, I suppose. Relished the straightforwardness and gritty reality of the people there. Dare I say too many folk around here seem to be becoming image-conscious, or too heavily influenced by material wealth?'

'You're sounding like a parson now!' Anne chided him.

'Perhaps I don't possess your tolerance.'

She laughed. 'Doctors aren't expected to be so "nice" all the time. Must be quite a strain, living up to that collar you wear.'

'Now you're laughing at me.'

'I'm not, I'm not. Only don't you think that you may be giving this too little time? You've scarcely allowed your parishioners the opportunity to contemplate accepting some of your ideas.'

'Or to accept *me*?'

'There are some lovely people in and around our village, Keith. And they do possess the grit to fight their corner. You should have heard them during meetings to try and prevent this rail link route from ruining their lives. It was all quite, well, inspirational. And even when that made little difference, they still battled to limit the damage to the countryside, to properties.'

He sighed. 'Maybe I'm foolish, feeling sort of homesick for somewhere that is, after all, just another part of this same country.'

'You could test that out – you must be due

some holiday.'

A slight smile played about his lips, brightened his dark eyes. 'Come with me – show me the parts of Yorkshire you know, and I'll do likewise.'

Anne was startled. She hadn't been back there for years, not since the time she had headed north alone, desperate to rationalise a forbidden relationship. And she had this feeling that Keith had been weighing up making this suggestion, rather than bringing it up spontaneously.

'Why not?' he persisted.

She laughed. 'If I thought you were serious, I might...'

'I am. Anne, I really am. It's a sort of dream I had, though I didn't know how to begin to put it across. Yorkshire, and you. Just think – you'd have no cause to worry. You couldn't be safer than with a parson!'

She gave him a look. 'It's been years since I worried about the "safety" aspect of any friendship. You'd better believe I'm well equipped to take care of myself.'

'Pity!' said Keith. 'But you will come?'

'I'll give it some thought.'

'I'm not at all sure Julian would be happy about this.' Emma was talking to her cousin Dick, who'd always been the brains of the family.

She had written first of all in reply to his

letter expressing his shock and sadness about Julian's death. Now Dick was ringing to try and reassure her. She had been distraught again, this time because of Christopher Parker's plans for the business. She and Chris had had a disagreement.

Within days of the funeral he had said they must discuss where the business was going. He'd upheld Julian's thoughts on avoiding too much diversification in the past, but that was *then*. He was determined now to go ahead with some of his own ideas.

'The sooner we get together on this, Emma, the better it will be.'

'But I don't want to become involved in any of it. Julian would understand that I know too little about the business to make the right decisions.'

'You'll leave that to me then?' Chris suggested hopefully. 'Trust me to have our best interests at heart? You can rely on my judgement, you know.'

But alarm bells were sounding in Emma's head. They wouldn't need to talk if he meant things to remain as they stood.

'I'm not at all sure about the wisdom of making too many changes, Christopher, not this soon. Shouldn't you wait a while, adapt to running the vineyard without Julian's experience? To say nothing of keeping the winery going?'

'Procrastinate, you mean? That's not my

way, and it's not the route to success. Development is the key these days, staying ahead of the market.'

'What do you have in mind?' she asked warily. She couldn't help resenting this early determination to alter everything that Julian had worked to create.

'I've always kept my eye on current trends. There are fashions in wines, you know.'

'As in everything else, yes, yes.'

Chris gave her a look. Her tone was saying it all. Emma wasn't prepared to allow him carte blanche. She might profess to have no intention of being involved in the business, but she seemed determined to wield the power that her half-share gave her. And without listening properly to his considerations.

'We've got to have a discussion on this one, if only to clarify what must be done. You must realise that we can't simply stand still.'

'I realise that you're determined already to alter what Julian was doing here. I won't risk your ruining everything for the sake of introducing newfangled ideas.'

'But, initially, all I want is for us to talk, make plans.' Chris was becoming irritated beyond endurance. 'I can't understand why you're being so obstinate about keeping things as they are. Especially when, days ago, you were willing to sell your share of the business.'

'I changed my mind. And that would have been different.' She would have moved right away. A very different prospect from remaining here in the home adjacent to Julian's vineyard. She would have remembered the whole place as it was, just as she would remember him.

Chris went striding towards the outer door. 'I don't know how the hell you expect us to work together when you won't enter into a reasonable discussion.'

'I can't believe he used to speak to Julian in that manner,' Emma said to her cousin now. 'Where we go from here, I certainly cannot tell. I surely do not mean to let him have his head. I'd no idea he could be so arrogant.'

'You don't need any upset after the shock you've just had,' Dick remarked. 'Are you sure it wouldn't, after all, be better to sell your share of the vineyard?'

'And play into Christopher Parker's hands? Nothing would induce me now. And that's another thing – how did he know I'd once had that in mind?'

'You'd never mentioned that to him?'

'Absolutely not.'

'Then you must have told someone else. Amanda?'

'No, I wouldn't distress her with suggesting such drastic changes. The only person I told – other than our solicitor – was Caroline.'

'Julian's ex? And she married into the Parker family, didn't she?'

'And has a rosy opinion of her precious stepson. I like her more than I ever expected I would, but I can't help feeling all the Parkers are lining up against me.'

'Isn't that a little over the top, Emma? Perhaps a result of all the recent traumas. Now why don't you come down to us for a long weekend. We can talk this through.'

She accepted immediately. 'Thanks, Dick, I will. I'm going to need somebody's clear thinking to back me up if I'm to prevent Christopher Parker from doing everything his way. And I don't mean to give in without a fight.'

Nine

'I couldn't believe it when Emma said she was going away for a few days. Gives me a break, one I'm desperate for.'

'And you will stay here, won't you, Amanda? Unless you've somewhere livelier in mind?' Ever since Julian's death Caroline had felt this longing to look after their daughter.

Amanda's smile was rueful. 'Lively isn't on my agenda quite yet. I feel so exhausted all the time.'

'I know, darling. It's still that dreadful shock, and you did come back to work very early.'

Amanda shook her head. 'It's not that.' The job was saving her sanity, providing the need to concentrate all her attention, which was quite healing. In the office she only occasionally thought about her father. Whereas at home...

Initially, she and Emma had got along far more comfortably than she could have anticipated. Her own efforts to show understanding seemed reciprocated fully. Despite the inevitable low-key atmosphere, they ate together quite amiably each evening, then either listened to classical CDs or watched television. The situation had suddenly turned fraught in recent days, and Chris had revealed the reason.

All the insecurity, that sense of nearing a precipice, had been resurrected to the full when he'd confided the extent to which he and Emma had disagreed.

'I wish to God she'd stuck to her original idea of selling her share of the vineyard. I could have found somebody to invest capital with me, and then run it in the only way that it should be run.'

For once in her life, Amanda was furious with Chris. How could he even contemplate going against her father's ideas? How could he believe it would be right to deny Julian's widow a half of this business that, to her at least, *was* her husband?

'Don't you think it's a bit soon, Chris, for wanting her out? The poor woman's trying to come to terms with losing everything. You could surely indulge her for a little while by sticking to Daddy's wishes, his *priorities* for the vineyard.'

'I might have known you'd still be clinging to notions that belong in the last century.'

'Thank you very much. Just the time for having my morale boosted.'

Amanda didn't mean to tell Caroline the

reasons behind her conflict with Chris; all she wanted was to get right away from any contention arising in the bungalow. If she wasn't spending every evening in her step-mother's company there would be fewer reminders of all the problems that followed on her father's death.

And as for the difficulty between herself and Chris, he could be right to have ideas of his own. If she bumped into him on neutral ground at The Sylvan Barn there should be opportunity for healing the breach. She needed old friends more than ever now, and wouldn't let any difference of opinion keep them apart.

Amanda was particularly pleased that her grandmother had arranged to come over from Folkestone at the same time as she herself would be staying at The Sylvan Barn. For years now the two of them had got on especially well; they soon were planning to make the most of each other's company whenever Amanda wasn't busy in the office.

She hadn't reckoned on Lucy's suggesting they attend church on the Sunday morning. Amanda felt torn apart, unable to decide between longing to see Keith in order to put right the awkwardness between them, and her dread of being as horribly embarrassed as she'd felt during her impromptu visit to the rectory.

When Malcolm offered to drive them to

church, Amanda couldn't easily refuse to attend. Less than ten minutes after the three of them went in through the heavy door and settled into one of pews quite near to the front, she was experiencing all the familiar attraction that Keith Clifton always seemed to generate in her. Amanda willed herself to resist his charisma, carefully avoided focusing all her attention on his magnetic eyes which always seemed to draw her, but when his sermon began she couldn't help becoming riveted.

Keith was speaking of the fellowship which enhanced life when things were good, and helped people through the bad times. He's aiming this at me, thought Amanda, reassuring me that he does appreciate having me around. I didn't ruin our friendship. Everything between us is fine. Good.

Immense relief surged through her; she leaned back against the hard wood of the pew, and listened even more intently.

As she stood up to follow her grandmother and Malcolm towards the altar for Communion, Amanda noticed how weak her knees felt, and smiled. She couldn't deny that Keith really did have such a devastating effect on her. She felt glad that he could not know. This was neither the time nor the place for such distractions.

But she herself was distracted, acutely conscious of his fingers pressing the

Communion wafer into her palm, and then his breath on her head while he leaned forward to offer the silver cup.

Throughout the final prayers Amanda was struggling to recover some composure. Whatever else, she wasn't going to make a fool of herself again. She would be friendly, but self-contained; that way she wouldn't risk destroying any of the warmth of that sermon, which she was still sure was directed towards her.

Despite her resolve, Amanda felt exhilarated as they moved slowly towards the church porch, where Keith was shaking hands with his parishioners. Behind her she could hear Malcolm talking with some woman whose voice sounded vaguely familiar. Lucy was a pace ahead, her white hair gleaming above a cream-coloured coat which fitted perfectly, enhancing her tall, slender figure. I should be more like her, Amanda resolved, and impress people by being poised.

Keith was telling her grandmother how lovely it was to meet her again, and then it was Amanda's turn to have her hand shaken by his.

'Nice to see you again,' he said, and withdrew his fingers. Hastily? she wondered. Determined to put that right by saying something, Amanda found her ideas submerged beneath the intrusion of Malcolm's words to his companion.

'Have a great time then, Anne. You deserve it.' He was urging Amanda on ahead now, seizing the rector's hand hurriedly. 'You too, of course,' he added.

'Didn't you see that was our doctor, Anne Newbold?' Malcolm asked as he smartly marshalled Lucy and Amanda in the direction of the Jaguar. 'Off on holiday to Yorkshire tomorrow, with the rector.'

'Ah, yes,' said Lucy. 'Caroline was telling me they seem to be an "item", as the saying goes.'

'That's right,' Amanda heard herself confirm. 'I saw her arriving at the rectory the other day.'

Getting into the car, Amanda sank on to the seat. She needed its support. Her worst fears were realised. She had been altogether wrong to believe that Keith's sermon held any significant message for her. Just as she had been wrong to tell herself that any relationship between him and Dr Newbold was by nature professional.

If she hadn't been weakened by these realisations, Amanda might have noticed that Malcolm was especially stony-faced as he sat at the wheel.

His shock was great. How had he never learned any hint of the deepening friendship between Anne and that parson? Evidently, his wife knew, and Amanda seemed aware that something was going on there. Why was he – the one who'd once been a great friend of Anne's – the only person who was kept in the dark?

Caroline used to resent Anne – had she chosen to keep the information from him in case it resurrected old emotions? As it did, to some degree, he admitted silently. But much as he'd never forget Anne Newbold, he would never again need to look outside his marriage. For anything. Didn't Caroline feel as he did – that the relationship renewed between them since Rebecca's birth was great?

Being blessed with a daughter this late in their lives transformed everything. Rebecca brought so much delight and interest into their family, each day was filled with excitement. Recovering now from the surprise, Malcolm realised it was time he wished Anne well in her relationship with Keith Clifton.

Christopher had arrived at The Sylvan Barn, partly to discuss further progress concerning the new vineyard, but also because nothing more had been done since Diana had confirmed the information about their find of church silver.

During lunch he began explaining what she had learned. 'As we already supposed, those two older items are ecclesiastical pieces. The Communion cup has been verified as dating back to 1572. There's no firm confirmation, as yet, regarding the item we're calling a flagon. But, again, its styling suggests it is likely to be from around that date.'

'And we're duty-bound to restore both to their true owners, yes?' said Malcolm. 'Are you any closer to discovering which church they do belong to?'

Chris shook his head. 'Tracing that's going to be far from easy, since we've already tried the obvious local ones.'

'Shouldn't you simply advertise for the rightful owners?' Amanda suggested.

'Not our wisest course, according to Diana,' Chris contradicted her. 'Even people connected with churches aren't immune to temptation – there'd have to be some means of verifying any claims.'

'And don't you have that?' Lucy enquired.

'Afraid not, Gran. We wouldn't have been stumped for this long if there'd been any means of identifying their source satisfactorily.'

'So, what will you do?' asked Caroline. She couldn't believe that Chris would have a great deal of free time for pursuing this now. He had full responsibility for Julian's vineyard, to say nothing of acting as advisor on viticulture to his father.

Christopher shrugged. 'Diana has one more contact who might enlighten us further – if he comes up with nothing we shall just have to explore different avenues. Clearly, those particular pieces are not family ones – we're obliged to locate their real home.'

'I could help perhaps,' Amanda suggested. She had been keen to do something from the start, although that had materialised into no more than being given the task of helping gently to clean some of the stuff.

'Don't see what you could do,' Chris responded. 'A matter for the experts now, isn't it?'

He wasn't looking for assistance from anyone here. While questions regarding these two items continued, he still had good reason for remaining in contact with Diana. And that reason was precious to him. All too soon her husband would be free, and that was a situation which he had no desire to contemplate.

'But the remainder of the silver is ours?' Caroline checked. She had been so occupied by trying to look after a new baby while running her company that she hadn't kept abreast with any developments.

'We're assuming so,' Malcolm told her. 'Not that there's any proof as to how it came to be buried out there. Any more than there is confirmation that we're correct to take the engraved initials on several of the pieces as proof of ownership. Have to admit that it seems strange to me that family records, meticulous as some are, make no mention of its existence.'

'You've discussed this with your brother, I suppose,' said Lucy.

'Several times. Graham's come up with no more than we ourselves.'

And at present Malcolm was reluctant to spend very much time with his brother. Graham was as busy as ever, while Kate was becoming increasingly concerned about her mother-in-law's poor health. Very conscious of how hurt and annoyed he had been when Caroline had kept him ignorant of Isabel's serious illness, Malcolm hated deceiving the other two about its nature. He was also acutely aware of how strong-willed his mother could be, and how furious she'd be if the truth about her cancer became known throughout the family.

'I shall be obliged to put Graham in the picture before too long,' he had told Caroline quite recently. She had agreed this must be so, but hoped for some means by which the old lady might be pacified. Meanwhile, the two of them were left feeling uncomfortable about the deception, as well as terribly anxious about Isabel.

With her own sister married to Graham, and bearing the brunt of Isabel's poor health, Caroline was the uneasier of the two. Kate, who'd always known what action everyone ought to take, was unlikely to understand their silence on the subject.

Her own mother was proving an excellent go-between, visiting their part of Kent more frequently, and calling regularly on Isabel. This was something that Lucy had tended to do in the past, and would evoke less curiosity than if Caroline herself were to begin to become a frequent visitor. Kate had soon remarked on her sister's sudden arrivals at their house during those early days when Isabel's news compelled Caro to call there more often.

Setting out for Yorkshire with Keith at the wheel of her new Alfa 147, Anne was elated, reflecting on how much better this felt than her last holiday spent in her home county. And Keith couldn't have been happier. Accustomed to his old, unpredictable Ford Escort, he was relishing this car's performance. The chief source of his delight, though, was the woman beside him.

Anne Newbold had been the first person to make him feel really welcome in Kent, and had quickly become the one he could confide in. The first parish entrusted to him following his initial curacy was proving such a disappointment, yet he had to guard his words whenever he was surrounded by parishioners. Their early reluctance to co-operate and at least try different services had become symbolic of the attitude of most of his congregation on several matters. Whatever he might suggest, the majority seemed determined to cling to their own method of doing things. Was it his fault that he often felt he was only in the way there?

'You've borne with me a lot, Anne – I want you to know how much that means to me,' he said as they headed towards the Dartford Tunnel. Being aware that she was adept at keeping confidences had freed him to be honest about his misgivings.

'We all need one good listener,' she said lightly, a smile in her voice.

He glanced sideways at her as they drove slowly into line at the tunnel approach. 'You've helped me rationalise my thinking, and that's no mean feat!'

'Really?' she teased. 'I'd have said your training was about harnessing thoughts and ideas.'

'And ideals?' Keith suggested, smiling to himself. 'Even when you discover a situation far from ideal, just where you're establishing your career? Got to admit that has set me back. But not any longer.'

'That sounds decisive,' she prompted him.

'I believe it is. This trip could turn out to be more than pure recreation. Only the other day I learned there's a parish coming vacant near Halifax. I hope you'll understand when I take off for a day to learn more about the place.'

'Fine with me,' said Anne swiftly. But would it be fine if he decided to move back to Yorkshire? She was growing accustomed to having Keith around, wouldn't like being obliged to accept her old life again. The life without him.

'It's very early days, of course,' he went on. 'But you know how uneasy I've been in this parish.'

'I wouldn't blame you for seeking a change. Although I would miss you.'

'Mmm.'

Anne wondered what he was thinking. They'd always got along, but hadn't yet acquired the total affinity where each other's reactions could easily be gauged.

'I don't mean this to undermine our ability to just enjoy this break, you know,' Keith reassured her. 'You wouldn't believe how happy I am that you've agreed to take this holiday with me.' He'd never met anyone else who so quickly made him rely on them.

Life in his own parish was very different from any previous existence. Even as a curate, he'd had the friendship of his vicar, an elderly man who took the trouble to ensure that his assistant became deeply integrated there. Before that, while training, he'd experienced the companionship of his fellow ordinands, a situation which in many ways reminded him of his army life.

'You're finding your position a little isolating, aren't you?' said Anne. 'Much like my own, but perhaps with less substantial evidence of the good one might be doing for people. Can't be easy.'

'Maybe it shouldn't be. Isn't it only through the tough times that we acquire the necessary understanding?'

She laughed. 'Enough! I should have extracted a promise that you wouldn't threaten to dig up all the philosophy!'

'That bad, am I?' Keith grimaced. 'I'll try to do better.'

Perhaps because of having unburdened himself to that extent, he immediately lightened up. Before they'd completed half of their journey they were laughing and talking inconsequentially, beginning to make it a true holiday.

Anne was surprised by her own reaction. Being entrusted with his troubles created a warm feeling that she was needed. These days, she felt glad that this extended beyond her surgery. But what would an analyst say of her need to prove she was necessary?

However, she was in the mood to simply let go, had none of the lingering concern that often made her reluctant to leave her practice to a locum. Dr Thomas Hannah was young, had only recently completed a spell assisting in a busy London practice, and couldn't have had a great deal of experience since qualifying. Something about him, though, instilled confidence, making Anne happy to have him serve her patients.

Amanda was finding her stay at The Sylvan Barn slightly disappointing. Had her stepmother intended spending longer than that weekend away from home, she might have gone back to the bungalow before Emma's return. As the arrangements stood, she had to endure her conflicting emotions that seemed to escalate while she was with her mother and Malcolm.

They really were such besotted parents that Amanda felt quite uncomfortable about being unable to enthuse over Rebecca to quite that same degree. She loved her tiny sister, of course, admitting privately that she longed to have a baby like her. But she'd already said all that she could about the infant. Countless times.

The worst of it was the very real pain she felt whenever she considered her own childlessness. At present, the fool she'd made of herself by indulging in dreams about a possible relationship with Keith Clifton was crushing her. She felt such a mess that she couldn't begin to look ahead and hope for better times. She couldn't even settle to enjoying anything.

On Sunday afternoon she had driven Lucy

over to visit Kate, Graham, and Isabel Parker. Normally, she would have stayed there for a while; she'd never been intimidated by Isabel, perhaps because she wasn't her grandmother. On this occasion, however, the old lady had seemed too tired to exert herself and talk. When Amanda found that both of her cousins were staying with their parents, she decided that was it. This wasn't the day for her feeling that she never really got along with those two to be confirmed.

Arriving back at The Sylvan Barn she began to cheer up a little. Shortcomings there might be in this Parker household, but they were far exceeded by those prevalent in the other!

Getting out of her car, she glimpsed someone moving around beyond the side of the house. Her mother was busy with something in the vegetable garden. Calling to her, Amanda strolled across to investigate.

'Need any help?'

Caroline straightened her back and smiled. 'Up to you. I wanted some spring greens for this evening, but gathering them's a bit laborious. Afraid we've had the best of the crop.'

'Let me do that,' Amanda suggested. Out here she felt she could breathe more readily. And even a simple task was preferable to sitting around indoors while the fact that

Keith Clifton had gone off with Anne Newbold kept surfacing no matter how determined she was to suppress it.

'Just be careful,' Caroline warned. 'That knife's recently been sharpened.'

'Mum! Rebecca's the baby, remember. I *have* handled a knife before.'

'OK, OK. If you're sure, I'll take the hint and see if she's awake and in need of changing.'

Left to it, Amanda began to enjoy cutting the greens. Even though some of the vegetation was starting to rot and was quite noxious, recent rain had released the smell of the earth itself, and the neighbouring jasmine had several blooms that lingered on its stems.

Gazing towards the jasmine, she savoured its scent. She was no expert on gardens, but this seemed somehow to be uplifting her bruised spirits.

The gash was deep, so deep that Amanda didn't feel any pain until she felt the wetness, glanced down and saw blood surging from her wrist.

The knife couldn't have slipped that far, surely? Almost hypnotised by the quantity of blood, she froze. Soaking into the ground, it didn't appear quite so horrific, but it was running over her pale tights, her cream-coloured suede shoes.

Amanda ran for the kitchen door, arrived

there trailing blood which spattered her skirt and the immaculate floor tiles. At the sink, she turned the cold tap full on, forced herself to thrust her wrist beneath the flow.

'Is anybody around?' she shouted, feeling a fool, but suddenly rather ill.

The water had done no good – blood was streaming from her wrist. She couldn't leave this sink while the mess her stupidity had created threatened to ruin every part of the house.

Malcolm came running to investigate.

'God, what have you done?' he demanded, appalled.

Amanda's face was pale, waxen, and it was evident that the reason was this seemingly unstaunchable flow of blood.

He swiftly located clean towels in a drawer, wrapped one around her wrist and hand, then found her a stool.

'Sit there for a moment – I'll phone the doctor. Could be quicker than getting an ambulance to come all the way out here.'

'I'm afraid you'll have to explain just where that is,' said Tom Hannah when Malcolm gave the address after explaining Amanda's injury.

'Would it be quicker if we came to the surgery? My car's outside. I can have her there in minutes. If that *is* where you are?'

'Yes. Thought I ought to spend today getting my bearings. Not quite swiftly enough, by the sound of this.'

Amanda was feeling faint by the time Malcolm parked outside Birch Tree House. Although Caroline had bound the wound tightly with towels, she hadn't managed to stop the bleeding. Amanda was shocked, badly scared, and wishing fruitlessly that her own father was there, instead of Malcolm Parker.

'Tom Hannah,' the locum introduced himself, concern erasing his smile when he saw the extent to which Amanda was injured. Without wasting a second, he led her to the examination room and sat her in a chair beside the surface where he'd set out dressings and sutures in readiness.

'That's quite spectacular,' he exclaimed, unwrapping the saturated towels. 'Luckily, my experience of A&E is relatively recent. Should be able to stop the bleeding and stitch you up. How on earth did you do this to yourself?'

'Cutting spring greens for our meal.'

'Don't tell me – in the garden? I trust your anti-tetanus jabs are up to date?'

'When should I have had those?' Amanda asked him.

'Before tackling any gardening. Do I take it you've never had the jabs?'

'Don't believe I have.' It sounded better than admitting that she hadn't.

Tom was prepared with a syringe of anaesthetic to use before stitching the wound. His blue eyes glinted wickedly, reminding her of Chris. 'This is only to numb your wrist. Just wait till I give you the anti-tet jab!'

'Do I have to have it?'

Malcolm grasped her shoulder. 'It's wisest, Amanda love. You don't want to risk lockjaw.'

'Too right,' Tom agreed. 'Quite aside from its unfortunate way of curbing the ability to talk, the complaint is decidedly disagreeable.'

While he talked, he examined her cut, staunching the blood repeatedly, and wondering how much she had lost already. He had to wait for the anaesthetic to take effect, but even applying pressure he was having difficulty controlling the flow. Tom was relieved when he could select a suture and commence stitching.

Initially, he must concentrate on closing the wound as swiftly as the pauses to wipe away fresh blood permitted. He also must be thinking ahead. The girl wasn't his patient, of course; he couldn't readily assess how she would be affected by the shock coupled with all this blood loss. No doctor liked taking risks. In unfamiliar circumstances nothing could be left to chance. But until he had finished the immediate task, the girl shouldn't have to endure further anxiety.

When Amanda closed her eyes and swayed to one side on her seat, Tom decided. She'd have to go to the local hospital, where facilities existed for any further treatment, possibly a blood transfusion.

Amanda took the news well. She hadn't felt the stitches going in, and when the doctor began applying the necessary massive dressing she felt her relief growing. She needn't look at that wretched cut for a moment longer, might even begin to hope that she could think about something else. Until the numbness wore off. She wasn't enough of a fool to imagine there wouldn't be any more pain.

'I'll give you painkillers for tonight,' Tom told her. 'I want you to have something in case the hospital sends you home. And a prescription for a supply to keep you going into the week.'

'Thank you for that, and for being so brilliant.'

The doctor smiled, turned to Malcolm. 'Can you get her to the local A&E, or shall I arrange an ambulance?'

'I'll see to all that – don't worry.'

'I'm going to ring through to them, see if I can speed things up for you.'

Amanda hadn't reckoned on having a stay at the hospital while the drip replenished the blood that she had lost. But she still felt so weak that she appreciated having care to hand. Assuring Malcolm that she would be fine there, she encouraged him to go home, where he would await her call to say when she would be released.

'Tell Mother not to worry. I know how she'll be feeling. But she did warn me how sharp that knife was. The accident's all down to me.'

Her stay in hospital was short, and following the transfusion Amanda felt so much stronger that she was convinced the visit there had been warranted.

'I want to thank that nice locum doctor of yours,' she told Caroline on the Monday morning. 'Do you think it'd be all right if I called round there?'

'Why not? We all appreciate it when people don't take us for granted. Why not give him a bottle of something – Malcolm will find you one from his cellar.'

At her mother's suggestion, Amanda arrived at Birch Tree House just as Tom Hannah finished morning surgery. Smiling, he greeted her warmly when he emerged from the consulting room to show out his last patient.

'You survived my torture then!' he exclaimed, a grin warming his blue eyes.

'And they evidently didn't keep you too long in hospital.'

'Just to replenish all that blood. I must

have looked a sight when Malcolm got me to you! But you did a brilliant job – the hospital doctor was surprised that the bleeding had been checked. He could tell by my clothes how much I'd lost.'

'To say nothing of the amount drenching the consulting room here.'

'Did it make a dreadful mess for you?'

Tom laughed. 'That was a joke. Don't you remember how well covered in towels you were?'

'That's good. Everyone at The Sylvan Barn has been teasing that I ought to have been discharged earlier, to clean up all the blood.'

'No doubt they're really just very glad to have you home.'

'Oh, actually, that's not my home. I was staying for the weekend.'

'I suppose you have your own place,' said Tom.

'Not yet. I live with my stepmother, my father's second wife. He died the other week.'

'Oh – sorry to hear that. Not the best of times you've been having then.'

'Not at all. Although this cut could have turned out much worse than it did. Thanks to you. That's what I've come for really, to say thank you properly. Just a token,' she added, handing Tom the bottle.

He unwrapped the tissue, inspected the

label. 'A good French red – that'll be greatly appreciated. Help me unwind after surgery tonight. Was there something I could do for you now? Want me to take another look at that cut?'

'Not at the moment, thanks. They OK'd it before I left hospital.'

'Perhaps you need a note from me for your own GP? Where exactly do you live?'

'A few miles over the Sussex border, quite near to Northiam.'

'Pleasant countryside, I believe – wouldn't be surprised if I settled somewhere in that area. However, do you want me to jot something down for your doctor?'

'Would it be possible to come back to you? I'm in the village every day – I work with my mother, Caroline Parker.'

'I'd certainly like to take another look at my handiwork. We'll fill out the form to cover for yesterday – when you were resident in the village – and see how it goes. Of course, when Dr Newbold takes over again, it'll be up to her to say.'

'No problem. With working for my mother our hours are quite flexible – she won't mind if I have to arrive late or leave early to see my own GP.'

'What sort of business is it?'

'Public relations – it's interesting because every day is different. Though we tend to specialise – lots of our clients are writers needing promotion for their books. Then there's various award ceremonies, and stuff.'

'Sounds fun.'

'Can be. Most of the time it is.'

'Which is as much as one should expect from any work, eh?'

'Except something like yours, where there's always the satisfaction of being really useful.'

'Can it be wrong, just for a while, to be thankful you're not obliged to be of use all the time?'

Keith looked up at Anne's words, and grinned. 'Let's say we're prepared to make the most of not being in demand, shall we?'

'You scared of having even a few days when you're not needed?' she teased.

His brown eyes lit up with mischievous good humour. 'But I thought I was – last night you almost convinced me!'

Anne felt ridiculous high colour rushing to her cheeks, glanced down at her plate, avoiding his gaze. Keith had surprised her, and she'd surprised herself rather more. They had eaten out quite late at a country inn somewhere between Ilkley and Bradford. It had been dark long before they came out to her car, seemed darker still when Keith drew off the road, and she felt his arm come around her.

His kisses were tentative at first, but soon

grew demanding, so passionate that the answering response began to alarm her with its intensity. Not for years had she wanted a man so fiercely; never since Malcolm had anyone attracted her so insistently.

Drawing apart at last, they had been quiet during the drive to their hotel, had seemed a little awkward with each other as they headed upstairs to their separate rooms.

'I must say a hasty goodnight,' Keith admitted ruefully at her door. 'Or there'll be no keeping to those promises I made so easily.'

There had been little awkwardness between them today. They had walked and talked, relishing dry weather and enough exercise to warrant an agreeable lunch at a good cafe in York. And now they were eating again, this time in their hotel.

They had both needed to talk. Arriving in Yorkshire had brought confrontation with realities that scarcely disturbed the majority of farmers back home in Kent. The foot-and-mouth crisis in the news over the four months since February was very much in evidence here among the Yorkshire Dales.

With whole areas closed to the public, few visitors around, and the ominous purpose of animal transporters all too plain, they had felt guilty about coming north for enjoyment. Together they had concluded that they might have needed this reminder of the true situation.

Anne wondered how this day would end. And tomorrow Keith was going off on his own, to discover details of the parish that was becoming vacant. Anne felt strangely uneasy, as though sensing already that he was making this move and it could take him away from her, permanently.

'You've gone quiet,' he remarked, his eyes willing her to confide the reason. Because it mattered to him – she mattered.

'I'm fine, really. Just being stupid.'

'You're never that.'

She tried to laugh it away. 'How can you be sure? You haven't known me long enough.'

'I need to know you better.' He was serious now, gravity intensifying his steady gaze. He took her hand as it lay on the table.

Her hand still in his, they strolled across the foyer and up the stairs. Anne unlocked the door of her room, drew him inside with her.

Keith's arms enfolded her, pulled her sharply against him. 'What's worrying you?'

She shook her head. His kiss was light, and then he persisted.

'You ought to tell me...'

'I've no right to interfere – it's your life.'

'Is this about that vacancy I'm pursuing tomorrow?'

When she couldn't reply Keith kissed her,

as fiercely as ever before. 'I wouldn't readily settle up here without you.'

'But—'

His mouth returned to hers, taking her breath, preventing her from adding another word.

'I love you, Anne. I know I've sprung this on you. We need to talk. Only first there's another urgency. And I'm not certain I can contain every element.'

One hand went to her spine, anchoring her against his need; she felt his fingers at the buttons of the soft-textured jacket she'd worn for dinner. His caress was gentle on her breast, exploring, seeking her approval.

Keith sank into the huge armchair, drew her down with him, kissing her, his tongue searching her mouth, exciting wild pulses of desire deep within her. Anne stirred and so did he; his hand traced her hip, sank lower over the cloth of her trouser suit. And then his fingers were sliding within its cloth. She heard him groan.

'I need you so much, darling Anne. But I can't feel it's right, simply to ... to take you.'

'We're both adults, both free,' she reminded him, yearning for satisfaction. And then she thought of the work he did, the person he was. She smiled against his mouth. 'I'm sure we'll find a means of keeping within certain boundaries.'

'I only hope this unnatural restraint isn't

destined to last for ever,' said Keith.

Anne's inward smile was rueful. She couldn't agree more fervently. But he had said so much, had used these other means as well to emphasise his feelings. She must not let imperative desire compel her to abandon reason.

'You have changes in mind,' she said quietly. 'And I've become a creature of habit, entrenched in a way of life which seemed ... more than acceptable. How patient are you, Keith?'

'Wish I could say "very" – that I'd wait for you for ever. That would do neither of us any good. I can only ask that you consider my longing to have you share whatever my life brings. You have my word I'd always do my utmost to accommodate all your thoughts, your plans for the future.'

It was a surprisingly considered suggestion – she couldn't have wished for a more straightforward expression of Keith's hopes. But was she ready for such a commitment? Was he the man she wished to be committed to?

Ten

Feeling quite apprehensive, Amanda drove home on the day that Emma was arriving back from the short stay with her cousin. Even disregarding any potential difficulties between them, she felt less than ready to cope with the evening.

The wretched cut had hurt her every bit of the day; she'd been obliged to grit her teeth whenever she had to use the computer keyboard. Driving felt even worse – she wasn't at all sure she should have tackled this journey.

The one bright portion of the day had been dropping in at Birch Tree House, where Tom Hannah had welcomed her with such a genuine smile that Amanda had wondered if he always looked so pleased to see every patient.

'Glad you're looking so much better,' he said. 'You're evidently over losing all that blood.'

The wound, however, had looked worse. He had frowned over one spot where some degree of infection seemed likely to prevent clean healing.

'We'll not take any chances with that,' he told her as he began cleansing and re-dressing the area. 'I'm prescribing a mild antibiotic – just to make certain you heal thoroughly. The last thing you want is trouble now, or more scarring than we can avoid.'

She had been rather disappointed when Tom had explained that Anne Newbold would be back by the end of her week's supply of antibiotics.

'You may as well see your own GP, if you need to. Although I trust that this will do the trick now.'

When Amanda began thanking him again for all he'd done, Tom laughed. 'Even if it hasn't totally succeeded yet?'

'It's still heaps better than when I was smothering everything in blood.'

'Glad to be on hand. In fact, I'm glad to have met you – made a pleasant change from some of the old miseries stomping into the surgery.'

'Don't let Anne hear you say that – she's devoted to her patients. Or so Malcolm and my mother always claim.'

'Take no notice of me – I'm really not whingeing about the time here. Just can't wait to have my own practice.'

'You really haven't got your eye on somewhere then?' She knew very little about doctors in general and locums in particular, had no idea how or why some didn't have a place of their own.

'Didn't I tell you earlier? I'm looking around. Love Sussex, for instance. Didn't you say that's where you're from?'

'Right. Just over the border from Kent.'

'Want to keep in touch? I'd like that. If you gave me your number, I'd contact you if I was able to settle on a practice somewhere near you.'

At the time, Amanda had been delighted. She had liked Tom Hannah from the start, and was flattered that he appeared interested in her. As the afternoon passed, though, she'd begun to realise how insubstantial was the prospect of meeting him again. With her luck, she would wait in anticipation only to discover eventually that the idea had come to nothing.

And it was *now* that she needed someone around. Especially to counteract the effect that her stepmother would have upon her.

Despite all misgivings, Amanda was pleasantly surprised by Emma's greeting at the bungalow. She had only just parked the car and was walking up the path when the door was opened to her.

'Good to see you again, Amanda. Come along in. I've got dinner on the go – you've just time to wash your hands and so on.'

'That's nice. How was the weekend?'

'Pretty good,' Emma replied. 'Dick has advised...' She got no further. Amanda was removing her jacket, revealing the heavy bandaging. 'Oh, my dear, you're hurt. Whatever have you done?'

'Cut myself. Over at Mother's.'

'Doing what? That looks pretty serious.'

'It bled a lot, at first. Had it stitched, though.'

'You still haven't told me how it happened.'

'Would you credit that I was gathering spring greens? The knife was sharper than I believed, I guess.'

'Or you were thinking about something else?'

'You know me too well!'

Emma laughed. 'Takes one to know one, as the saying goes. Yes, Amanda, I enhance boring tasks by planning something more interesting. Or at least I did.'

These days, forming clear ideas felt to be impossible. Much as she'd welcomed staying with her cousin, Emma had come away rather more confused than she had been earlier.

'And your plans for this place – the vineyard, I mean – are you going to tell me?'

Her stepmother gave her a look. 'Has Christopher Parker put you up to quizzing me?'

'Not at all. And I know it's not my business. In any sense of the word! But I do care. Because of Daddy. Chris, too, I suppose, when he's not coming all high handed.'

'You admit that he can seem that way then?'

'He's male, isn't he? Seriously, Emma, do you want to talk, or would you rather I kept right out of all this?'

'My cousin Dick started to clarify my thinking, to a degree. Must confess, he then made me see both sides, which renders decision-making no easier. If I let Chris have his head, I'll be obliged afterwards to go along with any consequences. Might also leave myself open to concurring with his schemes again.'

'Not necessarily. If circumstances change, there'll be nothing to warrant your automatically falling in with his thinking. If it was up to me, I'd be inclined to go into his reasoning behind projected developments, make an informed decision, and worry about future alterations at a later date. Much later. When you're not still so hurt by losing Daddy.'

'I'll always be hurt by that, dear.'

'I do know that. But you've survived bereavement before, and reached a point where you were coping.'

'But not with half-shares of a vineyard where I feel out of my depth.'

'You could try being honest with Chris

about that feeling. Get him to explain his ideas more fully, until you're sure of all the pros and cons of developments. You might learn he's really only concerned with working the vineyard to capacity, by trying different varieties. Would that prove too drastic for you?'

Emma sighed. Another rational argument, and she had heard so many! Dick – ever reasonable – had made the point that unless, or until, she learned viticulture thoroughly she wouldn't be able to disprove the viability of even one of Christopher's schemes.

Emma seemed to go along with Amanda's thinking, and that made their first evening back together quite congenial. After a delicious meal, they cleared away dishes while a classical CD filled the bungalow with music.

'I used to play, you know, the violin,' said Amanda. 'Did my father tell you?'

'Not that I recall. And you never play now.'

'I wasn't terribly good. I've realised since that leaving me unaware of that *wasn't* a kindness.'

'Julian could be very indulgent.'

'Quite.'

'And *now*, Amanda – what do you yearn to do with your life? Is working with your mother the be-all and end-all of your existence?'

'It's fabulous work – I love it a lot. And she's a good boss, has taught me an enormous amount. But it is only a job.'

'And you need a life away from it.' There wasn't a question in Emma's voice.

'Family, children, somewhere of my own. These days, I don't mind admitting there are too many babies around for comfort, Emma.'

'So you're settling for living here, with me. To avoid the emotions aroused by those infants?'

'Could work,' Amanda suggested.

'Only until you have a place of your own, somewhere to fill with everything you want from life.'

'Reckon I ever will?'

Emma was being so understanding that Amanda was feeling unable to be other than honest. About her hopes, about those eternal fears.

'Still looking for someone like Chris Parker?' Emma's question sounded sharp. Amanda guessed her stepmother still couldn't really understand the situation with Chris.

'Chris and I will always have a sort of ... bond. But it's not romantic – or not any longer. And I suspect that was all on my part. He's not the one for me – I do know that. I just worry that no one else will be either.'

Since Julian had died, so much was altering – in the bond with Chris, her attitude towards Emma. Each day seemed to demand some degree of rethinking.

'I'm having second thoughts about that parish over in Halifax,' Keith began telling Anne as soon as he joined her at their table for dinner. He couldn't pretend he was other than disappointed.

'Too drab a place?' she enquired, her impression of so many northern towns well remembered.

His laugh was rueful. 'Quite the opposite – much further from the town centre than I anticipated, with a modern church which appeared to draw its congregation from affluent-looking houses. I didn't even bother to see their church council representative. I'll have to ring him tonight – don't know how I'll explain.'

'That you suspect it's all too upmarket?'

'Sounds more as though it ought to be ideal, doesn't it?'

'You haven't really explained to me why it isn't.'

'Like our village, I guess – it's not gritty enough. For me.'

'We are talking twenty-first century, love. Most of the back-to-back houses surrounded by ginnels and outside lavatories have been superseded.'

'I'm trying to be serious.'

'Sorry, sorry. Go on.'

'I'm not looking for somewhere soft. I need to feel I'm making a difference.'

'Beyond disturbing their favourite form of service.'

'Quite. Don't you relish the tough problems that you face?'

'When I can do something to help put them right. But you see, Keith, that's how our work differs. Whether you live in a village like ours or an overcrowded city, folk still have their cancers, heart attacks, debilitating illnesses. And GPs everywhere seem to be overstretched.'

'So *your* complaint never is of being underused!'

'Hardly. I do see what you mean, though, love. And am beginning to understand why our parish mightn't have been your ideal choice.'

'Am I being a pain?' he asked, starting at last to study the menu. 'A part of me does believe in being able to serve, *wherever*. Only then I think of how swiftly life runs by. This is already my second career – I shouldn't be merely marking time.'

'Especially when you might do so much more.'

'We'd better leave it for today – I'll bore your socks off. We are supposed to be making this a break.'

He needed to overcome this disappointment. There had been another vacancy also, in Bradford, but he felt too dispirited to investigate its possibilities. No longer trusted his judgement of what he wanted.

Anne was concerned about Keith's evident dissatisfaction, but couldn't think how she might help. She wasn't surprised, though, when he made no attempt to hold her close that evening. Declaring that he loved her hadn't automatically removed the obstacles created by career uncertainties.

Their closeness of a different kind returned with the morning. It was a bright day, and they decided to take the car further up into the Dales. It didn't really matter where – she recognised that Keith was in as much need of a refreshing outing as she herself.

They headed north along quiet lanes in the general direction of Skipton, where they decided to pause for lunch. They strolled as far as the castle, exchanging memories of their previous, independent visits, discovering similar tastes regarding historic places and the joy of having their stories unfold.

Anne was at the wheel as they started along the road towards Settle. There was greater evidence here of precautions against foot-and-mouth disease. Farm gates were firmly locked, with warning notices and very conspicuous provisions for disinfecting vehicles and people.

'Do you think we should turn back?' she asked Keith. 'We mustn't risk spreading that wretched disease.'

'Just go a bit further, eh? They'd have closed the roads if cars were such a threat.'

Five hundred metres along, Keith caught sight of a woman running agitatedly down the track from a farm. Waving her arms to attract attention, she was yelling.

'Oh, please, please stop! I've got to get help.'

Anne parked beside the gate, wound down her window. 'Whatever's wrong?'

'It's Jack – my husband. Strung himself up in the barn. I cut him down, but I don't know if it's too late. I can't get help, not now the phone's gone.'

'I'm a doctor. Where do you say he is?' Anne tossed her car keys to Keith. 'My bag's in the boot – bring it, will you?'

The five-bar gate was padlocked, but Anne scrambled up and over it while the distraught woman was worrying about having no key on her. Together they ran up the rough track to a ramshackle barn where the farmer lay, still unconscious, on the dusty earth floor.

'How long's he been like this?' Anne demanded, running to kneel beside the man, who looked quite old but was more likely to be fifty or so.

'Nay, lass, I don't know. It were nobbut by

chance that I found him.'

'But when – was it long since?' The man's face looked congested, cheeks and lips were blue-tinged. If he was breathing at all, she couldn't detect any signs.

'Just a minute or two. I ran straight to see if I could spot somebody. The phone were cut off, you see.'

'Right.' Anne found a pulse in his neck, but it was slow, extremely irregular.

She turned the man on to his back, and tilted his head to check that the airways were clear. As she began mouth to-mouth resuscitation Keith arrived at her side. He offered protective gauze from her bag, but she shook her head. This was no time for refinements.

The man started to breathe within moments. Anne smiled up at his wife, felt Keith's hand reassuringly grasp her shoulder.

'He ought to make it now, but we must get him to hospital,' she said. 'I've a mobile in the car.'

'I've called the ambulance already,' said Keith, and turned to the man's wife.

'Do you want to get your coat, lock the house and so on? Make sure you pick up your key.'

'Eh, I've locked myself out already. I were that worried about Jack. He hadn't been in at dinner time, and I couldn't see him out in yon field. Been there most of t'time for days, he has. Since his cows was took. Culled, they call it. Destroyed, more like – and us along with our stock.'

'Let's see if we can find you a way into the house,' Keith suggested gently, then checked that Anne didn't require any help.

'We'll be OK till the paramedics arrive,' she assured them.

Although barely conscious, the man was breathing more strongly now, and his heart rate becoming steadier.

'I haven't done it, have I?' he croaked eventually. 'Can't bloody get owt right.'

The ambulance arrived to prevent further words, and Anne wasn't sorry. No suicide attempt could be treated lightly, and she never felt she'd mastered providing the words they really needed.

'Tried to top himself, did he?' one of the paramedics said when she went out of the barn to meet them. 'Poor bugger, like a lot more round here. Lost everything he lived for.'

Anne nodded. 'Except his wife. And they'll both need convincing that surviving matters. She sounded as low as he is, if not shouldering as much of the responsibility.'

'That's the worst of it,' Anne remarked to Keith while they hurried back to her car to follow the ambulance. 'Men like him take being the provider very seriously. Even when it's through no fault of theirs, they'll not accept they haven't caused all this trouble.'

'Maybe that should become my job – convincing them that it isn't all down to them. It's just shitty bad luck that's deprived them of all their stock.'

Glancing sideways at him, Anne smiled. She noted the black smudges across his face, dark dust in his brown hair, and the now grimy clothes.

'How did you get back into the house for that poor woman?'

He grinned. 'They have coal cellars round here still, with an iron grate – a *small* iron grate – providing access.'

Anne laughed. 'There's your reality you were seeking.'

'Or waiting for us when we reach that hospital?'

In fact, when they finally saw the doctor who'd examined the farmer on admission, they were happy to hear his reassurance.

'Thanks to your fortuitous arrival and prompt action, he should suffer no brain damage. He's fully conscious now, seems to have all faculties intact. Not that he'll appreciate that for some long while.'

'Is his wife with him now?' Keith enquired. 'I ought to have a word with her – it's a little early yet for talking to him.'

The doctor nodded. 'Poor woman daren't

leave his side. And I suspect that's the way she'll feel for some time to come.'

Anne agreed. 'Ultimately, that may be no bad thing. There's nothing worse for either partner than feeling that they're alone while facing insuperable problems.'

'Yet these Yorkshire farming folk are tough – women as much as their menfolk,' Keith remarked. 'Could be she's the one who'll pull them through this crisis. And gain strength herself in the process.'

Anne turned to the other doctor. 'Is it too soon to see them now?'

'His wife needs to thank you – she was adamant about that. As for speaking to him, I'd suggest tomorrow.'

'We could manage that, although we're only up here on holiday,' said Keith.

He sounded regretful, Anne noticed, and recognised how greatly he needed to do some good, somewhere.

The farmer's wife, who introduced herself as Angela Wood, thanked them both effusively, clutching at Anne's hand while tears streamed down her lined face.

'I'll never forget you to the end of my days. I were that certain my Jack were a goner. I just wish there was summat I could do to show how thankful I am.'

'There's no need. I'm simply relieved that it did the trick.'

'And you an' all,' the woman said to Keith.

'It was you as thought to get the ambulance to him.'

Anne noticed that the farmer himself was watching them through half-closed eyes, unwilling to acknowledge the rescue which he still obviously regretted.

'He'll be a long time accepting that his survival is for the best,' Keith admitted at the end of their next visit to the hospital.

He had tried to encourage the poor man to believe that his being alive still might be viewed as an omen for the future.

'Easy to say that, isn't it, lad. You're not the one who's had your reason for existing taken from you,' came the sharp retort.

Even when Angela tried to smoothe over her husband's curt manner, Anne could see that no one would make the farmer view their prospects more optimistically. Nevertheless, Keith had made one last attempt.

'You've been granted fresh life, whether you wish it or not. You love your wife, don't you?'

'I suppose so, aye. We've never fratched a lot. Now what're you saying?'

Keith smiled. 'Nothing very alarming – just that you shouldn't be planning to leave her to cope with this lot. Everybody has their breaking point, you know. Even wives. But if you continue to prop each other up, you'll survive until better times come along.'

'And where will they come from? You can't know that. How can anybody be sure that things won't get worse?'

'There are no guarantees, I know. But I do believe that we're never given something to endure without being provided with the means of surviving the trouble.'

'Eh, well, you've a right to your opinion, same as me.'

Angela gave her husband a look, then rose from the bedside chair and crossed to grasp Keith by the hand.

'I appreciate that you've come back like this today. Take no notice of Jack – he's had a bad time of it. Happen one day he'll come round to your way of looking at it.'

'And happen I won't,' came the growl from the bed.

'Time we were on our way, don't you think?' Anne suggested. She empathised with Keith's disappointment, but had seen that rigid refusal to concur already, far too many times. Patients at their lowest ebb couldn't be expected to foresee a more favourable future.

'That's what I mean,' Keith announced much later when they were driving to their hotel to pack for returning to Kent. 'I know I got nowhere near convincing that poor chap to be more optimistic, but it felt *right* to be there, in the heart of their difficulties. And if my best wasn't enough, spending time there might have provided opportunity for getting through to him.'

'There are people in Kent who are reaching the proverbial end of their tether,' Anne reminded him.

She was beginning to feel torn apart. Keith was slipping away, drawn by his feeling for this northern county and its folk. And she felt afraid. These past weeks of getting to know Keith Clifton had been good; during their holiday she had grown fond of him. She didn't want to picture a life where he no longer existed. And yet his suggestion that she should give up her practice to come here with him had been a shock. The only thing she was sure of was that the commitment such a move would entail mustn't be considered lightly.

'You could practice anywhere.' It was his turn to issue reminders. 'Effective doctors are needed throughout the country.'

Her smile was rueful. 'I know you've suggested that we should both change our location, but isn't that a touch excessive? We've known each other how long?'

'Depends how much a solution matters to you.'

Although feeling very fit after taking the holiday with Keith, Anne remained quite disturbed. Keith had made his affection for her evident enough, and with that his hopes for the future they might have. She could understand that his unease since coming to their village might make the prospect of any change welcome.

She herself had never been particularly impulsive, and could hardly believe now that she was feeling compelled to consider his suggestion that they move to Yorkshire, *together*. She had a good rapport with Keith, but she wasn't in love, or didn't think that the emotions surging through her qualified as love. Excitement, yes. But excitement was a very different matter.

Anne had experienced passion several times in the past, and the previous occasion had left her emotions raw. The fault had been her own. Unfortunately, life did not always provide the freedom for both parties to indulge their undeniable affinity. She still remained troubled that she'd once come closer than anyone had suspected to surrendering to impulse. How could she trust her own judgement?

Keith certainly was a very different man from any who had attracted her in the past – and she herself seemed to be at a very different stage in her life. Where she might once have welcomed upheaval, taking a chance, today she felt she had to spend time weighing all the prospects.

She had made her own niche here in Kent, serving her village on the parish council as conscientiously as she ran her surgery. And if the struggle to prevent the rail link savaging their quality of life had proved less than a success, she had battled for the good of her people. They knew whose side she was on, counted on her.

The same might apply equally elsewhere, Anne reminded herself, and sighed.

Was the near completion of that rail link the sign that she might pursue some other worthwhile cause in a different part of the country? With experience gained these past several years, mightn't she work more effectively among people who weren't already testing the breadth of her abilities?

She had felt good, she could not deny, when her efforts to save that farmer had resulted in his physical recovery. But what of his mental anguish? And that of folk like him who were devastated by life's blows? Like Keith, she might strive to help such people through the months and years to come. *With Keith...?*

Working as a team, however briefly, felt great. Anne wasn't entirely sure that he was right to limit his future ambitions by qualifying that he should be helping people whose situations were especially daunting. She certainly respected his concern for folk, his quiet way of providing assistance, that earnest desire to make a difference. She loved him for that. But was that the limit of her love?

She was too old to be carried away by desire, too old to marry for anything less than love, too old to risk what might be a catastrophic mistake.

For Keith also there must be no such misjudgements. Was he being too incautious? No priest should risk entering an unstable marriage; his career more than her own would suffer if the life they tried to make together should fail.

Anne was relieved that Tom Hannah had a free day before taking up another post as locum several miles away in Surrey. She needed something else to think about while they discussed the cases he had handled in her absence.

'I think most of your patients have taken to me more readily than I expected,' he said cheerfully. 'I've enjoyed my time here. In fact, if you ever think of moving on, let me know. I'd be happy to discuss the possibility of taking over from you!'

It was said lightly enough, but Anne could have done without anything that suggested her time in the village might be limited.

Although he did wonder if rural Yorkshire was quite the best place for him, Keith had few misgivings about deciding to move on.

He had reminded Anne that he hoped she would choose to go with him, but he'd stressed that he didn't expect a swift answer. But nor did he expect to remain inactive awaiting her decision.

Seeing his bishop – as he felt that he must, because he was staying in Kent for so short a period – became an uncomfortable prospect. Keith anticipated a degree of disbelief, to say nothing of the suggestion that leaving the parish was a hasty conclusion.

What he received on that overcast day was the implication that he was being unfair to his parishioners.

'I hoped for more from you, I must confess. A younger man who'd taken orders while relatively inexperienced might have been excused wishing to cut and run at the first difference of opinion. I expected tolerance in a man of your years, a refusal to seek the easy option.'

'Easy?' Keith exclaimed, infuriated by the senior priest's misjudgement. 'But you've got me all wrong. The very reason I need to move on is because life's *too* easy in a parish like that.'

He wanted to explain how he had felt that day in Yorkshire, but couldn't find words which wouldn't sound self-important. His bishop had plenty to say.

'Nonsense. Every church has its share of needy folk. I suspect you've not been seeking them out. I suggest you give this more thought – prayer as well. I didn't have you down as a quitter.'

The bishop's words made Keith more positive about going. If more regretful too, because of feeling misunderstood. He hated anyone to believe him capable of just giving up, and he'd been reminded that he hadn't persisted with real efforts to tackle the first difficulty he'd encountered concerning the style of services.

Even so, he reflected, everything that goes on in that church is only a small part of what my work should be. It ought not to assume so large a proportion.

Keith might have delayed advising the church council of his intention; he could believe they would criticise his reluctance to allow more time for things to work out. And he longed to accommodate Anne's need for time in which to think through her own future.

Everything changed within fifteen minutes, when he saw on television the rioting in the streets of Bradford.

Had it been in any other city he might have done little more than sigh over the local problems. But he had learned of that vacancy in the area, couldn't just do nothing. This, surely, would be the place where he might strive to have some effect upon the situation.

As for Anne...? Sad though he would be if she could not agree, he wouldn't now be able to let her influence him against taking on this challenge.

Eleven

Anne was surprised to find Christopher Parker among the patients in her waiting room during her first week back at work. Chris was normally fit, so very fit that she couldn't recall when he'd last called in at her surgery.

Today, he seemed rather awkward as he took the seat across the desk from her. She smiled encouragingly.

'What's troubling you, Chris? Must be quite bad – you're not one of the regulars who pop in as part of their routine.'

He grinned. 'Actually, I was wondering if you might even turn me away. I'm not living in the village now, you know. But I haven't done a thing about registering elsewhere.'

Anne found his records while Chris was speaking. 'I've got everything here, but you will have to register local to you. Meanwhile, is there something urgent?'

'I've got a blinding headache – a problem

I keep getting. Nothing seems to shift it for more than a couple of hours.'

'I see. Let's start the elimination process – is your eyesight all right?'

'A hundred per cent – or whatever the grading they use. Had it checked out last week.'

'Right. Well, you're rather on the young side for high blood pressure, but we'll make sure while you're here. Could it be stress-related?'

'Ah.'

'You'd better tell me, hadn't you? One of the most useful assets of a GP is their clause of confidentiality.'

Chris nodded. 'One reason I'm here. Got to talk, you see. Can't at home – they'll think I'm nuts.'

Anne smiled again. 'Whereas if I do, no one's to know.'

'I've got myself into such a mess,' he began, then halted while he sought the words to express all the confusion and its source.

Anne frowned. She hadn't expected this. Chris Parker had done so well, become such a fine manager of that Sussex vineyard. But perhaps with Julian's death he'd become overwhelmed with responsibility. Even relatively young men like this could feel a job was too taxing.

'Is it your work?'

He laughed, grimly. 'I wish. There's always some solution regarding work. No, this is private. Intensely so, which makes it worse. There's this woman – somehow I've become more involved than I ever intended. You might say obsessed. And she's married. I didn't know at first, didn't care enough then to notice if one of her rings was on that finger. I can't extract myself. And I've got to. Soon. He's ... he's been away, but he'll be home. Very shortly. Call me an idiot – you're entitled – but I cannot end it. Nor must I continue seeing her.'

'I'm very sorry, Chris.'

He sighed. 'Don't know why I'm here really – nothing you can do.'

'I can *listen*. Like this. Mild medication to see you through could help, but...'

'Drugs aren't a solution?'

'As you say. I'll prescribe something for the physical side, the headaches. For the root cause...'

'Get myself a life? A different one?'

'Easier said than done?' Anne suggested. She yearned to be of more use. Could scarcely restrain the very personal compulsion to help this young man. Chris was so like his father now. Despite the eyes being blue rather than that beautiful grey, he seemed to possess that same endearing look – a mix of self-assurance and vulnerability. She felt she might have hugged him.

After she had checked his blood pressure, Christopher stood up, shrugged.

'Men get hurt more than some people think, you know. By ... by emotional loss, separation.'

Anne felt a shiver reach the hair at the nape of her neck.

Much later as she was locking the surgery doors Christopher's words recurred, and again she experienced that shiver. She had seen Keith hardly at all since their return to Kent – had kept it that way, reluctant to have him influence her ultimate decision.

She hadn't meant to be unkind, was only now really beginning to believe how deeply her future life might affect his. He was determined to leave – that much had filtered through to her; villages were not famous for containing information concerning people in responsible positions. This past day or so, her liking for Keith had grown as she realised that he was not about to pester her with either details of his plans or suggestions for her own.

On the other hand, Anne thought ruefully, she might have responded if he'd rushed over to repeat the plea that he didn't wish to move without her!

He has left me in no doubt already, she reminded herself. And she and Keith were both free.

Strangely, seeing Malcolm's son that day

was all it took to accelerate her decision about marrying Keith. The old life was closing fast, with the more mature generations in the village settling into a routine of quiet, peace. And while the younger folk relived the uncertainties, passions and ambitions of their predecessors, human failings remained.

She herself must prevent what she'd always believed was a great failing – she must not, *could not*, refuse to tackle the challenge of a fresh existence.

As soon as she saw Keith, Anne recognised that he was happier. He began explaining that his plans were reaching a conclusion.

'Swifter than I ever would have believed, once I saw that any rural community might seem too reminiscent of our village. I've applied to a parish in Bradford.'

One of the places where there's been such dreadful rioting, thought Anne immediately, her heart thudding agitatedly. And she knew Keith – he would be out in the thick of it, struggling to make the folk there see each other's disparate views. She certainly couldn't let him go there without her. She'd never know that he was all right from one day to the next.

'So, I'll have to find work in the area,' she said swiftly. 'If only as a locum or something initially.'

'You'll come with me?' His eyes widened

and he began to smile.

'I'd all but decided before you told me where you're going. I couldn't bear it if you tackled working among any trouble while I was so far away.'

Keith was ecstatic – not normally a mood Anne associated with him, and surely sufficient assurance that her decision pleased him. She was thankful now that she'd gone to him without further hesitation, even before giving a second's thought to contacting Tom Hannah about her practice.

'You'll have things to sort, just as I have,' Keith exclaimed as he allowed himself to begin taking a fresh look ahead. 'But if you wish, we could marry before we leave.'

Anne laughed. 'Wow! You don't mean to allow me time for much thought.' Smiling, she continued: 'I suppose we've done thinking enough – we're hardly teenagers any more, ought to know our minds. And yes – I might come to believe marrying here could be very good.'

Keith clearly was equally eager to be planning. 'We must start compiling lists – people we'll invite. Do you realise I don't even know what family you have?'

'Few close relations – a couple of aunts, a cousin or three. One who might give me away. Or I'd prefer my nephew, my sister's son. She's been dead for years.'

'I've a brother in South Africa – I'd like

him for my best man but I doubt if he would make it. Or I could contact one of my army pals.'

'Actually, I may find I've someone lined up for taking over the practice – Tom Hannah, the young doctor who did locum for me. He said he'd be interested – I'll have to discover if he was serious.'

'The church council accepted the news of my departure with unflattering alacrity. So, no problem there, except for covering a potentially long interregnum. And I've spoken to the bishop – he's accepted that I'm going. Assuming we want him to conduct the wedding, I'll have to have another word...'

Anne felt quite breathless, swept along by Keith's enthusiasm and the mass of practicalities needing to be sorted. By the time she left him that evening, the list had grown to include her imminent resignation from her various local committees. She would be sorry to surrender her role with some of those, was already resolving to do similar work around her new home.

Their time together had been brief; Keith was committed to visiting an elderly man, a former churchwarden who had recently lost his wife. Before parting, though, he held Anne close, assuring her of his love, promising a future devoted to creating happiness for her.

* * *

The visit to Anne's surgery had helped, Christopher decided. The pills seemed to deaden the pains in his head, and their talk was clarifying his thinking.

He would give Diana up. Their investigation of that silver appeared to have reached the point where they would learn no more. The pieces which they assumed belonged to the Parker family had been dated and valued accurately enough for insurance. The Communion cup and flagon would eventually be donated to some church, if not, as he'd hoped, to the one where they originated. He had no reason to continue seeing Diana, would steel himself against creating one.

Filling his life without her shouldn't be too difficult. Since Julian's sudden death the vineyard was more time consuming than ever. The differences of opinion with Emma seemed predictably constant. Chris couldn't swear that she automatically opposed his every suggestion, but it often felt that way.

Only recently he had experienced massive guilt on account of the distress his latest idea caused Julian's widow. Until the day of her outburst he'd merely sensed that Emma was resenting any kind of change. During the early days following her bereavement, she had remained reluctant even to hear him out, but she'd finally promised consent to a couple of experiments involving fresh types of vine.

Confident that his judgement was right, Chris had gone ahead with ordering new stock, and soon was beginning to clear out suitable areas for their introduction. The ground was poor, but that stony, impoverished soil was ideal for the long-rooted vines which plunged down somehow even when they encountered rock. He must, nevertheless, be rid of any neighbouring old stock in order that performance in these new trials should show some accuracy.

His misfortune was choosing to begin clearing the ground on one of the rare days when Emma decided to take a look at the vineyard.

Relishing the exercise, spade and fork alternating as he dug out the old stock, Christopher didn't see or hear anything until Emma screeched at him.

'How could you! Who the hell do you think you are to ruin everything my husband cherished here!'

Startled, Chris straightened his back and faced her. 'You did agree,' he began, and was interrupted.

'Not to such total devastation. You couldn't have explained fully. I'd never have consented to this scale of destruction. I won't stand by and let this happen, do you hear? You've got to put this right. I don't care how long it takes.' Emma drew in a sharp breath, swung out an arm to indicate the heap of uprooted plants. 'You can start now by putting every one of these back where it came from.'

'Emma, no – it wouldn't work. And even if it could, they'd never be viable. I told you we need to try something fresh.'

'Julian cherished those vines,' she repeated, 'devoted his life's work to making them the best. I can't bear to watch you destroying him.'

She was weeping copiously, close to hysteria. Chris didn't know what to do.

'Please don't,' he said. 'It will be all right, you'll see. When these are replaced and you see fresh growth beginning.'

'Stuff *you've* planted? Don't ask me to accept that!'

He hated himself for being unable to calm her, for letting her turn and trudge away towards the house so forlornly. Never believing he was good with women's emotions, Chris was totally at a loss when it came to Emma's.

The only good thing that day was hearing Amanda's car in the drive, and knowing that Julian's widow need not be quite alone.

Chris did not know that Amanda was home early from the office simply because she was too upset to concentrate. Her mother had taken the morning off to drive Rebecca over to the surgery for some routine inoculation or other. Initially, Amanda was delighted.

Although the promotion Caroline had given her acted as a boost, the trouble was that Caroline herself was always around so constantly. With her mother in the room, it was instinctive to consult her over any tricky point that arose or for advice on strategy. Only when left to cope alone did Amanda ever feel that she was any more capable than she'd been years ago.

On this occasion, however, any brief satisfaction about having her head was banished the minute that Caroline returned and placed the carrycot in its usual corner of the office.

Looking particularly happy, she glanced towards Amanda. 'Guess what – but I don't suppose you will. You'll be as surprised as I am. Our dear doctor is about to be married. By special licence, no less – to Keith Clifton.'

Amanda *was* surprised, and quite severely shaken. Hadn't she been reassured recently by local gossip that Anne and Keith appeared quite cool towards each other following their trip to Yorkshire? When he'd looked rather preoccupied if not exactly dejected in church, hadn't she begun to visualise herself as the person who one day would make up to him for anything that had gone wrong?

'What is it they say about still waters?' she'd said to Caroline. The news had rendered her incapable of stringing together more original words.

But that saying about still waters had intimate connotations, and Amanda could not bear to consider what might have occurred between Keith and the village doctor. It all seemed so *wrong*. And wasn't Anne Newbold rather old to be marrying? She'd thought of her as being of the same generation as her own parents.

Recognising her daughter's anguish and having more than an idea about its cause, Caroline had enquired if she had a headache, and should she call it a day?

'Could be that time of month,' Amanda had agreed readily, and rushed off to her car.

For once, finding her stepmother distressed was almost a relief. Setting aside her own massive disappointment, Amanda threw herself into being helpful, the one who'd rescue this older woman. Nothing mattered now, anyway – filling the hours with something that obliterated thinking would serve to give her purpose.

'Trouble out there?' she asked, escorting Emma into the house and out of sight of the vineyard. 'Let me pour you a drink while you tell me.'

'Only if you promise not to go telling

Chris Parker,' Emma said eventually while they each sipped from a large measure of gin. 'I've said my say to his face, and it's made no difference whatsoever. He's seen I'm upset rather than annoyed this time. I'm not looking for his pity.'

'But you'll let *me* understand?'

Emma was considering her, the eyes still wet with tears suddenly appearing hopeful.

'I'm glad you want to try, Amanda. It's all a bit of a mess, isn't it? Nothing's the same, never will be. And I keep trying to hang on to ... to what we had, I suppose. It was just those uprooted vines: seeing them got to me. I could picture Julian working there with them, and now they're going...'

'Chris is replanting, though.'

'Oh, yes. With *his* stock, according to *his* ideas, *his* decisions.'

Amanda smiled slightly. 'It reminds me of working at The Sylvan Barn – the way things are between me and my mother.'

Emma raised an eyebrow, gave her stepdaughter a curious look. She'd always believed things over there were so perfect.

Amanda's smile widened. 'It's partly the age thing, I know – generations and all that. And the ones with experience not wishing to let go.'

'Only I don't have experience, not of viticulture,' said Emma, more sagely than Amanda would have expected.

'As a devoted observer, you have,' her stepdaughter reminded her. 'You know how much Daddy put into his work. It's only natural to try to preserve it.'

'To preserve *him*. As we cannot. As we know that we cannot, eh?'

'Horrible, isn't it. Do you think another drink will help?'

Emma shook her head. Together, they went to prepare a meal – routine tasks that solved nothing yet eased the pain. Very slightly.

Was it partly because of losing my father that I turned to Keith? Amanda wondered much later. Had she tried to replace one person's caring concern with another's? Or was it really as she was beginning to fear – that she regularly became besotted with the nearest unattached male?

Just let him go, she thought, reflecting on Keith's imminent departure. And don't let anyone expect me to attend his wedding.

When that day came only one person connected with the Parker family attended the ceremony, a family crisis preventing the remaining members from being there.

The crisis, which happened overnight, was announced before breakfast in a telephone call from Malcolm's brother Graham.

'You'd better get over here, smartish. It's Mother – she collapsed in her own apartment, just managed to ring through for us before losing consciousness.'

The day was a Friday and Amanda was due to run the office unaided, freeing Caroline to attend the wedding with Malcolm. Chris and Nick along with Bianca were invited too, as was Amanda. Making manning the office an excuse for refusing had felt good. She couldn't like Anne Newbold for the invite, any more than she could for snatching up Keith Clifton. Of course, she knew he was too much his own man to have been coerced by anyone. But she needed to take comfort in some of her own instinctive feelings.

Arriving at Graham's home, Caroline and Malcolm were greeted by Kate, and shrank immediately from her very evident anger.

'You could have told us,' she snapped. 'You should have. How could you expect me – *us* – to care for her properly without knowing?'

Their own doctor had surrendered the old lady's wishes to his own judgement, and revealed the nature of the illness an hour ago.

'Never mind that – how is she?' Malcolm demanded, beginning to stride past Kate into the house.

'You'll not find her there. She's in her own place – refused to let us look after her properly.'

As she would, thought Caroline, following Malcolm around to the entrance of Isabel's apartment.

Kate pursued them, her voice relentless. 'You can't pretend you didn't know. As soon as she recovered slightly she admitted to confiding in you. God knows why. We're the ones on the spot, always have been.'

'I think that contributed to her reasons,' Caroline told her sister quietly. 'Isabel didn't want any fuss.'

Malcolm turned and faced them both. 'And nor did she intend to impose the misery of her cancer on anyone living around her.'

'Graham won't see it that way, no matter what you say,' Kate retorted.

Neither Caroline nor Malcolm said one word. Nothing would mend the situation, and Isabel must remain their chief concern.

Graham met his brother at the door of their mother's bedroom. 'I shan't forgive this ... this *silence* of yours. We ought to have known from the first. How otherwise could we be expected to provide the right care and understanding?'

'She didn't tell me.' The grimness of Malcolm's voice witnessed to lasting annoyance, disappointment.

Graham's eyebrows shot upwards. 'What's so special about Caroline?' he muttered.

His brother shrugged. 'Not being family,

not living here...? I believe Mother needed to retain her dignity.'

'She's lost that now.'

'But not months ago,' Malcolm suggested. 'To her, that mattered.'

Beyond them in the room, Isabel was resting. Barely asleep, yet not fully aware. They were here, though, she knew. Both of her sons. Arguing, but when had they not? She'd endowed them with her spirit. She had nothing else to give, little left now to provide purpose for continuing her own life.

Kate had fussed as Isabel had known that she would, tending pillows, bringing unwanted drinks, wearying her with suggestions. The doctor had been better, administering the drugs she craved to counteract the pain which had so suddenly overcome her determination to stay aware.

The doctor wouldn't say how long she'd got, or could not. For the moment, Isabel did not care. She remained intact – when conscious, in control. Neither the cancer nor her well-intentioned family were controlling her.

Dying seemed less of an evil when viewed from her current state. Who could like this disordered body of hers, wish to prolong its existence? It seemed years now, though it was but a matter of weeks, since she had sat upright as ever in her chair. Walking had grown into a trial, eating worse than that, and she despised every one of her necessary functions.

'How are you, Mother?'

Malcolm, as ever, kind. If fatuous in his questions, however well meant. She could be kind in return, ease his alarm perhaps.

'A little better, darling. I've a good doctor.'

'He serves you well.'

'Panders to me, you mean? Keeps confidences, eh? Caroline told you, though, didn't she?'

'Eventually, when she had to.'

Her laugh sounded strangled. 'I didn't mind your knowing. It was the others. Kate would have hauled me from one consultant to the next. Or found so-called remedies. If she'd been my own daughter, we'd say she'd inherited my organisational skills. As things stand, well, she's good for Graham, always was.'

'Shouldn't you be sleeping?'

'Time enough for that when this lot takes a firmer grip on me. Tiredness matters not a jot, you know, when you're near that final rest.'

'Even so...'

'Malcolm, you're as bad as your brother. You're going to need to let go – and that won't be achieved while you struggle to preserve me.' Isabel paused, reflecting. 'I dream a lot, you know, often scarcely distinguish between dreams and reality. The past intermingling with today, people hardly remembered, transposed, as though to draw me towards *their* reality. It's not unpleasant.'

Explaining to Caroline while the old lady slept, Malcolm began to feel comforted. He tried speaking in a similar way to Graham and Kate, was confronted by blank opposition.

'I'll never forgive you for keeping me in the dark,' Graham persisted.

Kate was nodding, fortifying her husband's displeasure. 'What right had the two of you to withhold this from us?'

Graham seemed unstoppable. 'For Mother's sake, you should have felt obliged to ensure we all co-operated to provide everything necessary. Furthermore—'

Caroline checked him. 'For your mother's sake, I was obliged to comply with her wishes. Given those circumstances again, I'd still respect her decision.'

While Kate and Graham continued their berating, Caroline sighed, turned away.

'I think I shall sit with Isabel.'

Frail though she was, her mother-in-law glanced up as Caroline went into the room. Unlikely though it seemed, Caro thought that the old lady winked at her.

The voice hardly resembled the assertive tones that once had been so forthright.

'You may blame me quite freely, my dear – no one's annoyance will follow me where I am going. I do trust, though, that my gratitude will remain with you, for respecting an old lady's request.'

Caroline smiled at her, covered one bony hand with her own. 'Even a sadness like this can breed affection, and it has. I shan't forget how you trusted me.'

'The others will get over their irritation. You will need to remind Malcolm of that fact until the ice begins to thaw.'

'Is there anything you need?' Caroline enquired.

'Peace – not something I've always relished, any more than I always created it. Oh, there is one thing – Lucy and I have had a good understanding. Is there a chance she might...?'

'Come to see you? I'm sure she'd be sorry if there was no opportunity. I'll give her a call.' Caroline wondered if Amanda would be free to drive over to Folkestone for Lucy, who would be distressed by news of this illness worsening.

Isabel was nodding. 'If ... if she doesn't make it here, er, in time, do tell her what I would have liked.'

Caroline swallowed, surprised by the strength of her emotions. Why had she never felt particularly fond of her mother-in-law? She hadn't completely understood how greatly she admired the old lady's spirit.

The hours trudged by. Isabel seemed to

rally a little, managed a few spoonfuls of Kate's home-made soup. Neither Caroline nor Malcolm gave much thought to the marriage due to take place in their village church, except to contact Chris before he left his flat to attend the ceremony.

In the PR office, Amanda was thankful to take her mother's call, which sent her driving off immediately to pick up Lucy.

Disturbed by the severity of his grandmother's illness, Chris rushed over to see her, and arrived just as Caroline emerged from Isabel's bedroom.

'How are things?' he asked, rather afraid he might learn that he was already too late.

'She's sleeping, I think. But she'll be glad you're here. Try not to disturb her if she doesn't waken, though – she needs peace now.'

'What happened? Is it her heart?'

'No, darling – cancer. We've known for a bit that it's terminal.'

'You never said—'

'Her decision.'

'That figures. I left a message for Nick, at the school. I'm sure he'll get here when he has a free period. Sooner than that, perhaps.'

'Bianca will have told him as well. She's looking after both babies.' When Nick hadn't arranged time off for the wedding,

Bianca had opted to care for Mark and Rebecca instead.

'Don't know what to do, about the wedding. Especially with Keith's insistence that he wanted me to be an usher.'

'See how you feel, Chris, when you've seen your grandmother. Did you have a word with your father on the way in?'

'Out there, in front of the house. With Uncle Graham. Thought Grandmother had died, they both looked so grim.'

Isabel roused sufficiently to respond with a smile to Christopher's hand on her arm, and then to whisper 'Hello' when Nick arrived to join them.

Later than intended, Chris finally set out for the church. He liked Keith too well to let him down on this special day, and no one seemed to believe that his Grandmother's condition would worsen before nightfall.

The church appeared full – the village doctor was popular there, if their rector had proved less so. Regretting that he wasn't early enough to fulfil his role as an usher to the full, Chris joined the other young men conducting the last few guests to their places.

The service began with the usual stir as the bride entered, drawing everyone's attention, for Anne Newbold looked far younger, suddenly quite beautiful. She had chosen her outfit well: a closely fitting suit of some pale creamy-coloured cloth, and a toning hat far more frivolous than Chris, for one, would have expected.

Smiling privately, Christopher thought of his father, was no longer surprised that this glamorous woman once had figured in his conversations so regularly.

There could be no doubting now that she had no thoughts beyond the man who was awaiting her beside the front pew. Chris envied Keith his committed future, but willed himself to push his own dissatisfaction to the back of his mind, if only for today. He needed to make up to Keith for his late arrival at the church, and to help the couple celebrate.

The ceremony was long, incorporating as it did the Communion service and an address by the bishop. Although trying hard to concentrate upon every word, Chris found that his mind would persist in straying to his grandmother. He wished with all his heart that he had understood her better while he was young; so many years had been wasted while he remained intimidated by her manner.

He hadn't known then that Isabel Parker possessed such a humane side, had perhaps only begun to see that facet during the time that she was showing particular kindness to Nick and Bianca. That had been during those awful years when it seemed that each time Bianca conceived it ended in disappointment.

Chris prayed his grandmother might have a quiet end; no one could say that she'd been an easy person in life, but she deserved the peace which her sick body so evidently was craving.

He wished he could believe he might have more time with the old lady. Today, he experienced a strange intuition that she could be the only one who'd give him some hint that would lead to finding a solution for the troubles in his personal life. And yet, even if she were to remain conscious for long enough, how could he justify bringing his difficulties to her?

Anne and Keith, their guests assembling behind them, were leaving the church. Both smiling light-heartedly, they looked entirely well matched, completely happy.

Without knowing details of any past traumas in either of their lives, Chris suddenly felt heartened. He could believe, for now, that there might be some pattern to the existence that each person lived out. Could it be that tuning in to its purpose was all that we needed?

Twelve

No matter how speedily arranged, the wedding of Anne and Keith Clifton became an enjoyable occasion, and for Christopher, at least, relieved personal traumas. The couple celebrated with their guests far into the night. They weren't going away; a honeymoon had been postponed to accommodate all that they both needed to organise before they finally would leave Kent.

Renewing acquaintance with an old friend who was Anne's nephew, Chris was drawn into the heart of the gathering, permitted no regrets that he was attending alone. By the time somebody dropped him off to sleep in his old room at The Sylvan Barn, the wine and the company had ensured that he was feeling euphoric.

He awakened next morning to sounds of Caroline playing with Rebecca, and soon identified another woman's voice as belonging to Lucy Forbes.

The two women exchanged an amused glance when he roused himself sufficiently to wander downstairs and join them.

'I see you had a good time at the wedding!' Caroline exclaimed. 'I take it that everything went off all right?'

'It was fine, yes.' Chris crossed to give Lucy a kiss. 'Good journey?' he enquired.

'Oh, yes. Amanda came over for me, you know. She's very capable.'

'And how's Gran Parker?' he asked Caroline.

'Still holding on. Your father stayed over there and rang through first thing this morning to let me know the situation. Mother and I are setting out shortly, if you want to come with us.'

'Think I'd better. Not certain the drinks I had yesterday won't still be in my system. Didn't dare drive here afterwards.' And he certainly couldn't have faced the journey back to his own flat in Sussex.

There seemed no change in Isabel Parker's condition. They all felt appalled to be seeing her like that, drained of everything but the fragile strands of life still keeping her with them.

Caroline noticed how shocked Lucy was to see her old friend slipping in and out of consciousness. Gone were the indomitable spirit, the forthright nature, and that straight back which symbolised her refusal to compromise. Worst perhaps of all, her ability to reason was fast diminishing.

During that day the rare moments when

she managed to speak revealed only a mind sadly clouded, where present and distant past were fused, inextricably mingled in a manner that the Isabel they knew never would have permitted.

Late the previous night had been worse: she was distressed, her soul anguished by the belief that the weight anchoring her to the bed was her husband's death, and she herself too incapacitated to attend his funeral. Witnessing his mother's sobs, Malcolm had been immobilised by emotion.

Caroline had held the old lady to her, soothing and talking until her mother-in-law's weakening brain surrendered to their reminders that she had been a widow for over thirty years.

'You mustn't feel like that. It's all right,' Caroline had assured her. 'You participated fully in your husband's funeral.'

Malcolm had grasped Caroline's shoulder, his thanks sincere for coping with a situation that seemed beyond him.

'It's hard, I know, when it's your own parent,' she had said, and wondered what Isabel's troubled brain might next unearth.

Unearth appeared to be apt, so apt that they began to suspect that Isabel's subconscious was aware of the prospect of her own imminent interment. Graham had taken over early that morning, and emerged eventually, no less distressed by Isabel's meanderings about the burial of her own mother.

'She knows she's going, doesn't she?' he said after recounting the gist of the old lady's ramblings.

'Perhaps it's better that she does know,' suggested Chris as he and Nick went through into the darkened room to sit with their grandmother. 'I think I'd prefer to have some inkling rather than just be snatched away.'

Nick nodded agreement. 'All a bit of a mystery, eh, Chris? Times like this, we feel better for believing it isn't quite the end, though.'

'Of course it isn't.'

Startling them both, the words came firmly from the bed. Isabel's eyes jerked open. For the first time in many hours, they could be positive that she saw and recognised them.

'That boy you lost, Nick – he is *there*, wherever ... And I don't mean in the ground where we placed him.'

Chris glanced anxiously towards his brother, saw his eyes fill with tears. Maybe that was no bad thing. When in this life was a grown man to express the deepest of emotions?

'They were digging a hole on that other day,' Isabel continued, eyes closed once more, her voice so weary that they felt with her the effort of dredging up events from her past.

'It's all right, Grandmother – rest now,' Chris suggested gently.

Isabel persisted, trying to clarify some old memory. 'Not ... not a hole to take a long wooden box. But it was sad ... I was sad. Father had to go off to fight. He ... I didn't understand, because he wasn't hiding it near our house.'

Nick sighed. 'Rambling again, I'm afraid,' he murmured to Chris. He touched their grandmother's hand, smiled at her. 'It's all right now. It doesn't matter.'

The frail voice continued. 'Was it a grave, though? I saw a vicar, all in black. Can't remember what he was saying. And he laughed. It wouldn't be a person, would it, going into the ground?' she asked agitatedly. 'They put a big stone there, with the dirt...'

Her eyes were open again, but scarcely seeing them.

'A flat stone,' Chris confirmed, and smiled.

Nick gave him a look. 'Where you found the silver?'

His brother nodded. 'Never thought it could be her side of the family, rather than the Parkers'. And I'm afraid it's too much to expect her to tell us any more.'

Nick gently squeezed the old lady's hand. 'It was some silver they buried, Grandmother. And it's still safe – Dad and Chris found it.'

Did her thin lips smile?

'She looks quite peaceful now – might be asleep.'

Chris could see she was still breathing. Isabel Parker was not one who would surrender life readily. And she may well have told him sufficient, certainly more than he had learned already.

'Think we ought to fetch Dad and Uncle Graham?' he whispered.

'Probably. Can't be much longer.'

But before they could call them in Isabel roused sufficiently to assert her own wishes. 'Did I hear Lucy's voice? If she has arrived, I must see her.'

Lucy struggled to hold on to her emotions. Isabel appeared too exhausted to speak, but clung to her hand, and nodded as though to confirm that she knew who was with her. Lucy felt glad that Isabel wanted her, was pleased for her that she had such a dependable family.

Caroline had been so staunch, but was showing the strain. Lucy resolved to protect her daughter from any other disturbing thoughts. Caroline didn't need to learn that Paul Saunders had married. And certainly not at a time when everything seemed out of perspective, destabilised by the nearness of death.

'Wish I'd had the wit to ask Grandmother about her parents ages ago – it never occurred to me,' Chris said to his brother outside the room. 'I could use more clues to whose that church silver was – and why was *her* father concealing it? Was Dad wrong to think those monograms on the family stuff are Parkers'?'

'Looks like he was. Quite simple – didn't you know, Grandmother's maiden name was Prescott,' Nick told him as they went to find their father.

'You sure about the name? How do you know?' Chris asked Nick after making certain that Malcolm and Graham would go to their mother.

'The diaries, of course. Remember she gave Bianca and me a lot of old books? Three of them turned out to be diaries. We offered them back to the old gir—... to Grandmother, but she said to keep them.'

'And you have?'

'Of course. Who would dare not to? Bianca took a look at them, but wasn't keen, not while she was pregnant. Mostly war experiences – harrowing, I think.'

'World War Two, you mean?'

'Hardly. The first lot – 1914, and that. Trenches, and stuff.'

'We need to have a look. Let's hope they begin before Great-grandfather set out.'

* * *

Bianca found George Prescott's diaries for them the next day, while they were there to tell her more about the way that Isabel had died quite gently surrounded by her sons and grandchildren.

Both Chris and his brother were thankful to have some distraction from their loss, and glad that seeking the relevant passages seemed appropriate. Almost a task they might complete for their grandmother.

Following a lot of quite mundane entries they came across the first mention of any silverware.

> 25th January 1915. This time the Germans lost the battle of Dogger Bank, but they'll be back. Cannot remain here, just letting this diabolical thing happen. Gwendoline will be all right – Isabel is three, company for her. Charles Hewitt called en route to enlist; he'll make a good padre. Wanted to leave with me some church plate he was given (very old – too good to take into battle with him as intended by his parishioners).
>
> Thinking to preserve his silver against possible invasion, I buried it. And also our best pieces. Well away from the farmhouse, that way less likely to be discovered. Dare not assume that the Germans won't invade; if they should do so, no home may be safe.

This fresh information gave him good reason to contact Diana, who was, as ever, eager to do more research. He had rationalised getting in touch – she deserved to know what he had learned. She received the news enthusiastically, and swiftly provided the first lead to discovering more about the Reverend Charles Hewitt.

'Crockford's,' she said over the phone as soon as Chris put her in the picture. 'The clerical directory. We only need to go through back issues until we find details.'

Her discovery of the entry concerning Charles Hewitt was the only good news during those early days after losing Isabel Parker. Despite her considerable age and the inevitability of her death, the whole family felt her loss very keenly.

For reasons that he could not really explain, Christopher suddenly felt that he ought not to allow himself the luxury of pursuing the history of that silver until after his grandmother was buried. Perhaps he needed to know that she was at rest before he would feel free to continue the investigation into this inheritance.

'She is not really absent, or no more so than someone who has slipped out of the house,' Keith Clifton began, addressing Isabel's family and friends during her funeral service. 'She remains a part of your lives, so real to you that time alone will convince you that she won't ever walk in through your door again. Saddening though it will become, the realisation that Isabel is no longer around here is a gradual process. There will be pain in recognising this situation; there may be times when feeling that this is just some dreadful dream creates particular hurt. But the gradual nature of our acceptance of a dear one's loss does serve a purpose, and is geared to accommodate our human spirit – which can't always manage swift adoption of unpalatable facts.

'And so, as days turn to weeks and months, and you learn to live lives rendered different by this passing, emotions will adjust. We pray today that as you continue to support each other, Isabel Parker leaves as your heritage a portion of her strength. And as you grieve for the loss of the family mother, you may find consolation in the understanding of our one, true Father.'

'Grandmother left us more than you think,' Christopher told Keith after the interment as they were driving towards Isabel's old home. 'Today's not the time, and this isn't the place, but I do need your help. And I'm not sure how much longer you'll be around here.'

'Sounds interesting. What's this about?'

'We're on the track of the true source of that church plate.'

Diana had telephoned only the previous day to say that according to the relevant Crockford's Clerical Directory, the Reverend Charles Hewitt had indeed served as rector of their village church.

He explained this to Keith, and suggested that they should meet him at the rectory one evening in order to go through any records of the relevant period.

'We haven't talked about it a great deal at home, as you'll imagine – there's been too much on because of Grandmother's death. But I'm sure all the family will think, like me, that the church stuff's got to be returned.'

Ascertaining full details of the silver's history continued to be just as complex as it had been all along.

'Disappointment again. I'm sorry,' said Keith, glancing across the books which he had spread before them on the vestry table. 'Even given the information you've come up with, I still can find no record of such items.'

'But he was the incumbent here during that period,' Diana insisted.

Keith smiled. 'Yes, indeed. Here's where he is mentioned, although not for long. Just up to his departure for World War One, from which he certainly didn't return to this parish.'

'That's what you found too, isn't it?' Chris said, turning to Diana.

They were meeting for the first time in ages, and their phone calls about this clergyman hadn't always seemed satisfactorily conclusive.

She nodded. 'Crockford's had no further word of him after the war ended.'

'So presumably he died, which explains why the incumbent here was the same chappie who took over in 1915.'

'And the silver Communion cup and flagon?' Chris persisted. 'Are we never to learn more than that bit I told you from his diary? That they were given to him by the parishioners of the time.'

'I've been thinking about that,' Keith said, closing the volumes in front of him. 'We could try asking some of the really old stalwarts of the parish. There are one or two still around who could have memories going back that far.'

'And often fresher than recollections of more recent years,' Diana suggested.

Christopher was happy to make arrangements to visit anyone whom Keith suggested, and pleased when Diana was to accompany him.

The third person they saw was William Warner, who, at ninety-eight, was remarkably articulate, and soon proved to be just the man they were seeking.

'Are you telling me that'd be the stuff that was presented to the Reverend Hewitt when he was going off to the Great War? But that was lost along with him, wasn't it, near Ypres.'

'That's where he died, is it?' asked Diana.

'So we heard afterwards. When he didn't come back.'

Christopher began explaining how those silver items had been judged too valuable to risk near any battleground. 'We've learned recently that my great-grandfather buried them at the Reverend Hewitt's request, for safe keeping.'

The old man beamed at them. 'Well, there's a surprise. And how do you say it came to light?'

'Father and I were preparing ground, following all the upheaval of the rail link construction. My spade turned on this stone slab, and there beneath it was—'

'Charles Hewitt's silver,' Diana finished.

William Warner chuckled. 'Eh, if only my old dad could have known that. He was mortified, you see, to think that stuff was lost.'

'Had it been purchased locally?' Chris enquired.

'Only in a manner of speaking. There'd been a collection, from the parish, to send him off with something to remember us by. Only it hadn't amounted to very much – nobody could afford it in those days. That was when my father had the idea. He donated the cup and the wine flagon. I reckon that was at a substantial loss to himself, but that's the way he was. If somebody impressed him, nothing was too good for them.'

'I don't suppose you also know where your father had acquired that silver? We believe it's very old, you see,' said Diana.

'He kept a record of that. Might take a bit of finding now, but I have it somewhere. Interesting, I remember him telling – came into the family when there was some sort of split. Generations ago, the story goes, one brother and his lot turned back to being Catholic. Had their own tiny chapel in the house here.'

'As a result perhaps of Kent's proximity to French influence,' Diana suggested.

'They wouldn't have anything to do with the Protestant religion – made out that only the Roman Church had vessels fit to hold their wine, if you get my meaning. Anyway, the other brother died young, but his daughter was against the Catholic faith, seemed to think that the cup belonging to her father mustn't be contaminated with all that popery, and such. That's how it came to be preserved here, in the house.'

'And how it was donated to a twentieth-century rector,' Chris finished.

'I'm eager to see it, naturally,' the old man told them. 'But it'll go to its rightful place then, and that's the church in our own village.'

Although Keith was delighted to receive the two items of church plate on behalf of his parish, and showed Christopher and Malcolm where he recorded their return, Chris remained almost haunted by its history. It seemed as much a part of his own background as the Prescott pieces. He caught himself longing for some form of contact with his predecessors, an emotion all the stronger while he felt the loss of Isabel Parker more keenly than ever he'd expected.

Nick had left with him George Prescott's diaries, and Chris was studying them most weekends at The Sylvan Barn. He was reluctant to leave such important documents in his flat, which was unoccupied during each workday.

His father had looked at a few pages with him, but was mainly occupied along with Graham in beginning to sort Isabel's affairs. Chris was pleased when Amanda became interested on the Sunday that they'd both had lunch in the family home.

'I'll show you how far I've got, if you like,' he offered. 'Though I have to warn you – it's not a pleasant read.'

Chris explained that he'd passed the descriptions of Prescott's enlisting, and the early days of training. Such as that training was – the men appeared to be ill-prepared for battle when they went overseas.

> October 1915. We fight as best we can. Near Loos we persist, but fear the Germans have the advantage – in arms as well as skill. Spirits are low; news reached us from Brussels today of Edith Cavell's execution. And we are so filthy, facilities are dreadful, lice resist all our attacks with powder.
>
> Thoughts turn to home, with prayers for the safety of loved ones. Little Isabel was four last week. Cannot bear to think that she and my dear Gwendoline might not survive the bombs dropped during Zeppelin raids.

Amanda's sigh was heavy. 'I never realised what the First World War was like – didn't know there'd been bombing raids before the one that began in 1939.'

She looked so sad that Chris leaned sideways, hugged her shoulders. 'If this is upsetting you, you don't have to go on.'

She smiled. 'No, I'm all right. It's something we ought to understand, isn't it. And besides, it is a part of your family.'

Chris smiled back at her. He was pleased to discover that Amanda still felt this interest in him, in his people. Over the years their friendship had kindled and then waned, deepened and seemed to evaporate. No matter that they'd never have a romantic relationship – strong ties would always bind them.

'Let's see some more,' she suggested.

George Prescott evidently spent much of the war in Belgium. He was still in the region near Passchendaele in the wet summer of 1917.

> The mud beggars description. And there's nothing else – the town that was Ypres is ruined, its Cloth Hall tower all you can see still standing. Lost our fine sergeant today in heavy shelling, and were denied the right to remove him with dignity. I was the one who found him, didn't believe much was wrong. Till I tilted his helmet to find out if he was conscious. His face was blasted clean away. Couple of lads and I made a sort of stretcher, tried to get him out of it.
>
> Wouldn't believe so much mud existed. Up to our waists we were, stumbling and staggering, in and out of shell-holes that were deeper than the trenches. Even between them we could make no progress. The third time we fell,

the poor chap slithered into a waterlogged crater. Enemy fire started up again, was coming closer.

'Have to leave him, chaps,' one mate said. 'Or we'll be in there with him.'

May God forgive us, we had to abandon him.

'I wonder what the area is like now?' Amanda said. 'Where exactly in Belgium is it?'

'Not all that far inland from Ostend. I'm going to go there – got to. If you want to come, we'll see the region together. There's more of this I want to read first, and then I need to swot up on Ypres itself.'

The Prescott diaries were full of similar grim accounts, of trudging through mud to their thighs, comrades lost and others breaking down under the constant shelling. There were gas attacks too, though Prescott gave those little attention. Until he saw a compatriot suffer.

I was lucky to miss it. Neil caught it full in the face, was sickened. He scrabbled at his mask, desperate to throw up. Then they fired the next lot of gas, when he was most vulnerable.

We were obliged to leave him incapacitated like that. Or wait behind and be shot.

I hate this bloody war.

Chris couldn't read much more that day, and felt sure that Amanda must have had her fill of such dismal reading. He increasingly felt glad to know she cared. He was very conscious that this great-grandfather of his was no relative of hers.

'Can I really go there with you?' she asked before going home to Emma.

'Of course – that'll be fine. I'm going to ask Nick as well, but I'm not sure he'll wish to. And it'll depend on fitting in around school term-time.'

'And Bianca?' Amanda enquired. 'We've been such friends.'

'I suppose she might be willing to leave the baby with her mother. It won't be a long trip, but it's hardly an occasion for an infant.'

Amanda was thankful that the journey seemed certain to go ahead. She would welcome anything to provide a change of scene, and in such good company. *Reliable* company, she reflected wryly. Chris was just the person to make her lighten up. With anyone else she'd still feel wary, unable to trust her own assessment of people.

She must have misread all the signals from Keith, who, despite his dog collar, appeared to be a bit of a ladies' man. He surely had made a fuss of her, while all along he fancied Anne Newbold.

Amanda was embarrassed that she'd

succumbed to being flattered by having his attention. That she'd needed that. Looking back through the whole episode, she herself seemed so *sad*. It was high time that she got about more. Around home it mattered less that she was something of a loner. But if she had made more friends, she would be travelling quite widely now that she had a bit of spare money. She'd been a fool to neglect creating a social life. Even seeing how that had happened while she worked alongside her mother was no real excuse. If she stuck around Chris for a while she was likely to get to know more people of their generation.

This trip to Belgium should be great; she must ensure that she made it the start of a whole new way of life. As soon as they returned she must tackle the question of where she would live – she need not remain with her stepmother for ever.

'I suppose you're not interested in going across to Ypres?' Chris asked his brother the next time he saw him.

Nick was surprised. 'You mean, something to do with that silver, because of the people who buried it?'

'That sort of thing, yes. And as a, well, a tribute, I guess, to Grandmother, and her father. Even if we didn't know him. We always considered her the head of the

Parker clan, didn't we? Never even gave much thought to her having come from a family of her own.'

'I'll go along, if that's what you want. Provided you're not intent on touring all the World War One battlefields.'

'I only want to visit the area where he and that padre died. I have this feeling that they might have been lost together. Or is that fanciful? I suppose I need to make this effort to see that our great-grandfather is commemorated somewhere. And that parson. *If* we can find him.'

Chris wasn't sure that Amanda would, in the end, go with him, but he would be pleased to have Nick along. They hadn't travelled abroad together since he'd gone off to agricultural college.

They settled on a date during August for the trip. Nick wouldn't be at school, and nor would they be reaching the end of the holidays, when he might be involved in frenetic preparation for a fresh term.

His father's new vines were keeping Chris busy when he wasn't up to his eyes in work at his own vineyard. There had been a further disagreement with Emma, this time on the number of days they should provide escorted tours and wine tastings.

Chris had always viewed these as necessary rather than enjoyable, but Emma evidently considered that having visitors constantly passing close to her bungalow was an intrusion.

'We should limit the tours to weekends. In that way, I could arrange to go elsewhere when an invasion was expected.'

Chris couldn't agree, and saw no reason to pretend that he might do so.

'They're a vital part of familiarising the public with the range of our wines. In the tourist season especially, we need to get all the people we can interested. Let's face it, there's little enough enthusiasm for what's produced over here – we've got to ensure that ours is a name that's recognised.'

Emma said no more, but she strode off in a huff, slammed the door of the bungalow after her.

Smarting from yet another difference of opinion with her, Chris shook his head wearily, sighed. Didn't the woman realise that her home and her standard of living owed everything to the business he was running?

Despite his tiredness, he could not sleep that night. At one in the morning, he reached for the Prescott diaries as an antidote for the sour taste Emma had left him. Instead of continuing to read where he had set them aside previously, Chris did something which he had been resisting while studying in chronological order. He turned to the last page of all, was surprised to find it completed in a child's handwriting, and on paper that was gummed into the cover.

> These books belonged to my father, George Prescott, and were sent home to us by his captain.

Anxious to learn more, Christopher turned back one page to what should have been the final entry made by his great-grandfather. Only again the writing was a stranger's, addressed to Gwendoline Prescott.

> It is with great personal sadness that I have to inform you of the death of Rifleman George Prescott, a loyal member of my brigade. He died, as he had served, with unhesitating courage.
>
> Going to the aid of a wounded fellow soldier, Rifleman Prescott was shot in the head at close range by an enemy sniper. In the face of a renewed German onslaught, we regret we were only able to bury him in the trench where he fell. I can tell you no more than that he died amid the battle of the Menin Road.
>
> It is my intention to provide him one day with the grave he deserves. I hope at some future time, when hostilities cease, that I may be able to pass on to you some further information.

Christopher's sigh was rueful. In the absence of any more details, he could only assume that if his great-grandfather's commanding officer had survived the war, he had been unable to do anything about transferring George Prescott to a final grave.

At least the Menin Road seemed apt, he thought, liking the idea that his ancestor might have this link to the great arched gate that had been created as a memorial.

Amanda planned meticulously for making the trip with Chris, his brother and Bianca. Her only journey abroad since school had been that dreadful visit to Spain to collect her father's body.

She meant this to be so different, and hoped to prove her ability to cope in a foreign country, and perhaps even impress Chris with her self-confidence. As a foursome, they could be great fun; she for one would make the most of the experience. And if Chris and his brother should find the purpose of the visit a little gloomy, she would be there to ensure that they all discovered some enjoyment.

A change of plan came when Nick announced that he might not, after all, be joining them. And Bianca certainly was remaining at home.

'It's all rather exciting,' he told them, his

grey eyes glowing. 'We're expecting another baby, and although everything's supposed to be fine, we're taking no chances. Well, you know our past history...'

The prospect of going alone with Chris to Belgium was no problem for Amanda. Her intentions remained the same: she would cheer him up whenever the purpose of going to Ypres got him down. And they were to stay in Ostend, which sounded like a lively port.

A further threat to her plans came after a phone call from Tom Hannah. Hearing his voice was exhilarating enough; learning his reason for calling made her even more delighted.

'Remember me?' he began. 'You'll never guess what's happening! You'll have heard that Anne Newbold's leaving the village now she's married. Can't quite believe it – she's approached me about taking on her practice.'

'That's great.' Amanda was thrilled that she was the one he was telling about his plans.

'Thing is, I need someone to help me familiarise myself with the area. Acting locum didn't allow much opportunity for exploring...'

'I'd love that,' she said. 'When do you suggest?'

The blow came when Tom gave her the

dates of his visit to Kent. As he arrived there, she would be landing in Ostend.

Amanda couldn't turn him down, but nor could she renege on her promise to accompany Chris to Belgium. Frantically trying to calm her agitation and find a solution, she stammered into the phone.

'I really would love to see you like that, but I'm not certain about the date. Er, can you give me your number? I'll ring you back.'

She could have wept – this was just her luck. After going nowhere special for ages, she had this opportunity to meet up with a man she liked a lot, and just when she was committed to going somewhere else.

Should she talk to Chris, explain? He might not mind too much if she cancelled. The only trouble was the nature of the visit to Ypres. She'd expected all along that he would find the circumstances gloomy. It did seem unfair to let him down, especially now that Nick and Bianca were staying at home.

Christopher had booked his car on board the ferry, and had acquired all the necessary documents for driving in Belgium. His feelings about the trip were mixed; he didn't expect to enjoy much of the experience. He would be glad of Amanda's presence, perhaps the only company that would serve – going there with anyone else might create unease when he needed to hide his emotions. He was afraid of turning soft, couldn't guarantee that his feelings would remain contained.

Chris was sitting one evening, wondering how he would react if he finally found George Prescott's name on the Menin Gate, when he took a call from someone whose own emotions all too evidently were shattered.

'Diana! Whatever's wrong?'

She was almost incoherent, crying so much that he could make little sense of what she was trying to tell him.

'I can't credit he's doing this, Christopher. Such a shock – the very last thing I expected.'

'Hang on,' he said urgently. 'You're in such a state, I'm coming over.'

Snatching up his keys, Chris ran out to the car and sped across country to Diana's cottage.

'I had to come,' he told her. 'This doesn't sound like something to be sorted over the phone.'

Diana nodded. Her beautiful eyes were red-rimmed, but moist no longer. And why did Christopher sense that she was angry as much as distressed?

'Could you even tell what I was saying?' she asked, aware that she had been scarcely intelligible.

'About your husband, wasn't it?' He

noticed there was no ring on her wedding finger, wondered how much that mattered.

'Vernon, yes. As you must have known, I was expecting his release. I won't pretend I was counting the days, but I was preparing to try to make a go of things with him. Getting ready for his arrival even.'

Chris nodded. He hadn't wanted to accept that her husband was returning home, but he had visualised her preparations.

Diana swallowed. 'With his history, he was unlikely to work in the antiques trade again. He'd depend on me financially, if only until he found other employment.'

'Only now what's happened?'

'The very last thing I could have anticipated. At their prison, as in many, they've been provided with various projects. Their most recent was staging a play under guidance from a professional director. Evidently, Vernon was heavily involved. Has become involved with her! She runs a company in the West Country somewhere, and she's invited Vernon to join them. According to him, she can get him an Equity card.'

'So he'll be working away. Is the job seasonal?'

'I've no idea. That doesn't concern me any longer. I'm certainly not going to have him trot back to me when this scheme fades out on him. Or the season ends, or whatever! I've been such a fool, standing by him while he must have been laughing his socks off about his plans. I haven't waited around this long to have him go off with someone else.'

'You mean...?'

'I've told Vernon we're through. And now I'm cross with myself – much as freedom might ultimately be the one thing I want, ending our marriage *hurts*. Especially when I consider the years I've thrown away, simply hanging on.'

'How did he react to the ultimatum?' Chris enquired. He needed to be sure that Vernon really wouldn't walk back into Diana's life again.

'Coolly. He just said he was glad that we both would know where we stood. Have to admit I leapt in there to say that it would make quite a difference for me to know what was going on.'

'But you're still not happy?'

'Give me time. I've just written off ten years of a complex relationship. And no matter what he's done, I'm left to wonder what went wrong between us.'

'From what I know, none of the break-up is down to you.'

'Then why don't I feel better?'

Chris smiled. 'How long is it since you discovered what was going on?'

Diana glanced towards the clock. 'An hour maybe since he rang.'

'So, *time* is what you need. And a bit of

sympathy? I could stick around if that's–' He broke off mid-sentence, interrupted by his own mobile.

'Busy night for phones,' he remarked, before listening to the caller.

'Chris, I'm in an awful dilemma – can we talk?'

'It's not the best of times, Amanda.'

'Please. I'll never sleep if I don't sort this out.'

He sighed. 'Go on then. Make it snappy if you can.'

'Would you mind most dreadfully if I couldn't go to Belgium with you? Something's come up, you see, something very important. I don't mean that your trip over there isn't, but...'

Chris was smiling; suddenly everything was beginning to gel. 'It's fine with me, Amanda, don't worry. You go ahead with ... with whatever it is.'

He might persuade Diana to accompany him to Ypres; otherwise, he would postpone the trip, remain here with her. Either way, they would be together.

Thirteen

Tom Hannah called for Amanda when she finished work one evening. Briefly, he paused to chat with Caroline and knelt beside Rebecca to tease a smile from her.

'You could be seeing me around a lot,' he told Caroline as she walked with them to the office door. 'Have you heard that Anne's offered me her practice?'

Caroline smiled, shook her head. 'Even in this village, not quite every piece of news filters through that quickly.'

He laughed. 'And it's nowhere near official yet. I'm just testing the waters, as it were. Amanda here's got to convince me that I must settle in the area.'

Amanda swallowed, trying not to choke on her surge of satisfaction. She had been thrilled when Tom asked her to show him around, but so often in the past she'd been thrilled by a word of encouragement! She ought not to let this rush to her head.

She was surprised when he asked to leave his car outside The Sylvan Barn. 'I always think investigating on foot gives you a true picture of a place, don't you?'

Amanda agreed, but his suggestion generated some unease. This wasn't quite her territory, was it? Had he forgotten that her real home was south of here, in Sussex?

'If I do take this on,' Tom was continuing, 'one advantage will be your working so near to my base. Another will be your living just that short distance away. That way, you won't be my patient – and I'd hate anything to preclude our seeing each other regularly.'

Startled, Amanda gazed up at him. He was smiling, but his eyes looked serious. Until she nodded.

'Great,' Amanda murmured. 'Yes, great.'

'I'm too old to mess around,' Tom said. 'Don't believe doctors should. Might have had my fling, in a classic medical-student fashion, but that is over. Cards on the table time – I shall be busy, naturally, if I do set up here. But I like what I've seen so far of you, Amanda. Would love to know all about you.'

'Wow! You surely do believe in being straightforward. Makes a pleasant change.'

'Ah. Do I read that as "don't ask"?'

She felt her cheeks colouring, and wished that blush of hers didn't happen. 'Afraid so, or not for a while.'

'All a part of maturing, eh?'

They walked along a section of the Pilgrims' Way, talking intermittently of the men and women whose faith had compelled them to walk this route to Canterbury. Mostly, though, they talked about themselves, exchanging views and backgrounds, discovering differences and similarities that felt more than coincidental.

Tom had lost his father in an accident too; his mother now lived in Ireland. 'The part that's free, thank God – I'd die of anxiety if it were the north.'

'Did you grow up over there?'

He shook his head. 'In London. Dad was a consultant – they'd met when Mother was one of the many Irish nurses seeking work over here. Tell me about your father.'

'He owned a vineyard, quite a big one in Sussex. He and Mother divorced when I was quite young. She didn't...' Amanda paused, swallowed. 'I grew up with my father, still live there with his second wife. But it doesn't really work.'

They had reached a spot where the view extended below and beyond them. She was thankful to introduce a different topic.

'That's all Parker land down there – you met Malcolm, Mother's second husband. Just there, where the vines are starting to grow, is where Chris dug up some old silver. Most of it was family stuff, only...'

'Who's Chris – your brother?'

'No, we're not related at all. He's Malcolm's, from his first marriage. It's all very complicated. Especially as he worked with my father, and runs the vineyard now. We've always been ... pals, Chris and I.'

'Is he an only child?'

'No – you saw Rebecca, the baby that Mummy and Malcolm have together. Then there's Nick. He's married, teaches not far away.'

'I look forward to getting to know everyone.'

Amanda grinned. 'By the time you've sorted out the relationships among the Parkers, you'll be exhausted. And it gets worse – Mummy's sister Kate is married to Malcolm's brother.'

Tom laughed. 'No, no! No more, please – I can't take it in.'

'Do you have brothers or sisters?'

'Unfortunately, no. I can see I shall have to stick with you, and acquire a host of relations.'

'Or half-relations,' Amanda reminded him. 'There are times when I'm not too certain where the blood-ties are.'

'But the warmth between you all is sufficient.'

'I suppose it is. Dare I say the family bit can be a bind? Working with my mother. You won't breathe a word, will you? I'd hate her to know. But with someone unrelated, I could be far more assertive. Would get on much better.'

'Tell me about your job...'

They reached his car and could not part. Tom wanted to drive her home, she'd use a cab next day. And still they talked, revealing a great deal concerning their lives to date, their aspirations and more than a few dreams. Tom sympathised with the longing for her own place, said he understood delaying until she might create a real home.

Driving down into Sussex, Amanda mentioned that Chris had gone over to Belgium, but held back the fact that she was meant to have accompanied him.

'Have you had a good holiday this year?' she enquired. Their outing had exhilarated her, but also had tired her. She felt she was running out of subjects, and dreaded boring Tom.

'Not yet – too much hanging in the balance till I settle.'

'Any idea where you'll choose when you do want a break?'

'That rather depends on you.'

Amanda couldn't believe she'd heard correctly. Tom might be very direct, but he surely wouldn't be this certain of anything this early, be this certain of *her*?

He said no more about holidays, and nor did she. In fact, they had almost reached the bungalow, and, much as she had loved Tom's company – every minute of it – she couldn't feel sorry. The sudden arrival of all this happiness really was exhausting.

'Thanks for a lovely time,' she said, getting out of his car.

Tom smiled. 'Thank *you*. I'll be in touch.'

Amanda believed him, could believe also that what he had said about future holidays would prove to be true. There had been no kiss between them, he hadn't made any move to hold her hand, yet she sensed that, for certain, she could rely upon every word that Tom Hannah had spoken.

Unlocking the door and walking slowly through to greet her stepmother, Amanda began to understand. Although it really was ironical. For what seemed like the first time in her life, the thing that she liked least about herself – that she considered old-fashioned – had drawn towards her this really lovely man.

Even the drive to Dover felt good with Diana at his side. The weather was dry, and the breeze through the open MG felt invigorating. Chris had expected to rearrange the scheduling for the trip but, once invited, Diana could not contemplate any delay.

He had spent several nights in her cottage, unable to leave her there alone, but he'd been surprisingly circumspect, and slept in the spare room. Even that had seemed not to matter; he could believe that the new circumstances between them would rectify any problems. For the present, he felt content that Diana appreciated his being around for her.

There had been further calls from her husband, one to announce that he was out of jail, and a second to say he'd arrived in the West Country. Chris had heard Diana telling Vernon to clear out his possessions from the cottage.

'Come while I'm away,' she'd insisted. 'I don't want to see you.'

Her ease as she sat beside him in the car was showing Chris that the worst was over. She was free, and he was the one she wished to be with. He hoped that would remain so. He'd lived long enough to know that people reacted in one way while feeling grateful, but with no guarantees that the response would last.

After driving aboard the ferry and leaving the car, they went in search of coffee. The boat was crowded, and the throng of people beginning holidays created an atmosphere of anticipation.

I guess that's how I feel too, Christopher thought, even though this isn't intended to include much recreation.

They sipped their coffee and talked, mainly about the purpose of this visit. Re-establishing their relationship had mattered more than putting Diana fully in the picture about his forebears.

'I did tell you, I suppose, that my great-grandfather died on the Menin Road?'

'And that padre too, the one from your village?'

'Can't be at all certain about him. I suspect we may never find out. The War Graves people haven't found either of them buried so far. And, interested though I've been, I shan't be too perturbed so long as I find some record of my long-lost relative.'

'That makes sense, I guess. And it's rare to have all the loose ends tie in neatly. But it'd be good to discover at least one decent burial. From what you've said, those diaries were full of accounts of having to leave men where they died.'

'All quite distressing – brought home to me how frequently that happened. Anyway, Nick believes he might be able to pursue it through the MOD or some such. I think he considers that his bit, for opting out of this trip.' Chris paused, smiled across the table at her. 'Not that I mind – not in the least.'

'Are you going to show me those diaries one day? You know I'm interested in family histories.'

'Sure, whenever you wish. But choose a good day – they're not cheerful reading.'

'I didn't expect they were.'

They passed the voyage pleasantly, wandering through the shops then out on to the deck for a while. The sea was calm, and seemed to Chris attuned with the turn their lives were taking. Nothing had been said between them regarding their future, yet somehow he knew that separations were ending.

Driving off the ferry, Chris experienced an elation which was the direct opposite of the emotion he'd expected to feel when he arrived in Belgium. Ostend gleamed in the afternoon sunlight; they saw the harbour and its boats, church spires and towers, and an imposing building which they later identified as the railway station. And Diana looked good, the stress of her recent upheaval erased from her eyes, which were coming alive with interest.

They found their hotel – which overlooked the inner harbour – and went up to their rooms to unpack before emerging to explore the town on foot. They admired the masses of boats moored at the quay, their riggings chattering in the wind that was wafting scents of fish and the sea itself over them.

'I like it here,' Diana announced. 'A new place for me – I hope it is for you?'

There was so much to discover about each other, and they'd scarcely begun on that while sorting the priorities before making this trip together.

Chris grinned. 'The nearest I've been is Dunkirk, on a school trip that took in

Brussels, Antwerp, that kind of thing.'

He took her hand as they strolled, absorbing the scene while they walked around the quayside. A street beside their tall hotel took them through the town, past shops and cafes, until they reached the broad promenade.

They dined at one of the many seafront restaurants that specialised in fish, where Diana tested the local mussels, and Chris curled his lip in distaste.

'Never have liked shellfish, and certainly not those things!'

She laughed. 'I didn't have you down as so unadventurous.'

'You'd be sorry if you saw me ill. I'm much safer with a dish I can inspect properly.'

'You may inspect these,' she teased, proffering one of the shells from her plate.

Their choice of food was the only difference between them, and remained so that night in the hotel. Christopher was resolved to keep their relationship on even ground by subduing the urge to love her. He hadn't altered the booking for single rooms after Amanda backed down, and had sensed Diana needed space in which to reassess her life according to this single state.

During breakfast next morning he recognised in her light-heartedness that his surprising chastity had created greater ease between them. They ate well of the cold meats, cheeses and sundry kinds of bread, preparing for the journey away from the coast, and knowing that in this unfamiliar region locating somewhere to eat could prove prolonged.

Driving inland, concentrating on remembering to keep to the right of the road, Chris sensed that Diana was watching him.

'Do I pass?' he asked eventually. 'Is it obvious that I feel very foreign over here?'

'It isn't that at all. If you must know, my Chris, this is the first time I've allowed myself to really look at you – to learn each curve of your face, the laugh-lines, blue eyes that I could love.'

He swallowed; his own voice sounded strange when he responded. 'Don't do this to me now. I take my responsibility for this car – and its passenger – very seriously.'

He didn't need to see her face to know she smiled. 'I would never believe you'd do other than that. Just remember that I've waited a long time for the freedom to be this way.'

You might have said that last night, thought Chris, and I wouldn't have been at all chaste.

'We'll be different after today,' said Diana quietly. 'Sharing an experience that matters to you so much. I feel privileged to have come along with you.'

'Privileged? I hope you'll say that in Ypres.'

They drove on through flattish countryside that resembled England yet whose houses and farms often looked more colourful, indicating a different culture.

The distance between Ostend and Ypres proved shorter than anticipated, and they arrived without pausing to eat. Chris wasn't sorry that their route took them in to the west of the town, avoiding the Menin Road and its Gate, which mattered too much for him to want a chance encounter as they approached.

The Cloth Hall and cathedral were unmistakable from pictures that he'd studied. He found a place for the car, and they walked on through wide streets surrounded by impressive buildings.

'This is so beautiful,' Diana exclaimed, glancing all about them and up towards the gabled roofs that rose in steps, all so eloquently Belgian.

'It's hard to credit that this has all been rebuilt since 1918; they have taken such care to restore what must have been the original atmosphere of the place.'

'Was such a lot of Ypres destroyed?'

'I've read accounts and seen photographs of there being little but the Cloth Hall tower remaining.'

'Then the local people are to be commended for caring so much.'

I could love this land, thought Chris,

thrilled by the restoration achieved there. And then he smiled to himself, suspecting his benign mood was influenced by the woman beside him.

After a hasty meal at a pavement cafe, he got out his camera and took pictures of every aspect all about them, with Diana in the foreground of many.

She laughed, shaking her head at him. 'You might save some shots until I'm wearing a different outfit. Everybody'll think I've only the one dress.'

'There's always tomorrow – who's to say how many shots I mean to take of you?'

He only knew that after all the months and months of concealing his feelings, he needed to record every moment of this fresh relationship.

'I am surprised you're not reserving more of your film,' said Diana, serious again.

'I have more than one.'

And now he was delaying, considering a visit to the cathedral, and wasn't there a museum?

From time to time, quite unintentionally, he had glimpsed the Menin Gate, in the distance beyond the section where the street leading through the square had narrowed. It challenged him to approach, and scared him with misgivings about his purpose. How would he feel if he found no family name inscribed there?

Diana persuaded him along in that direction, aware of his reluctance, just as he was conscious that she recognised its source. Pausing to take a picture that encompassed the entire massively arched Gate provided further delay, yet he hadn't come this far to evade the ultimate issue.

The splendour of the memorial took his breath, overwhelming with its size, with its aura of compelling silence. Willing him to pause there, motionless.

They found his name – George Prescott. Diana read the details aloud, and quoted some battalion in the Rifle Brigade. Chris couldn't see the words: his eyes had blurred. He swallowed, hard. Twice. Feeling an idiot, he managed finally to speak.

'So, there we are – or there he is. At least ... well ... you know.' And perhaps it wasn't too wrong for a man who'd farmed the land to be returned to a field. Somewhere in Flanders.'

Diana knew. For yet another soldier from a long-past war, this memorial was the nearest he'd have to a stone marking his grave. She grasped Christopher's arm, hugging it to her side.

'Maybe it's better, in a way, being remembered alongside so many others. He's not alone.'

And nor am I, thought Chris, and thanked God for that. 'Glad you came with me.'

'Where's that camera?' she prompted.

There was barely enough light beneath the magnificent stone structure. He adjusted aperture and shutter speed with care, leaned against a part of the arch, steadying his focus.

Quite a crowd was assembling; he heard the march of feet. Just for the moment, a shiver traced his spine. *The sound of dead men marching?*

These men, though, wore a different uniform. Then Chris remembered – the local fire brigade. As he'd been told, they bore witness like this every evening.

They slowed to a halt, raised gleaming instruments. *The Last Post* went through and through him, scourging his emotions until eyes and throat were sore.

Diana's arm linked again through his; her free hand grasped his fingers.

'I never even knew him,' Chris said, and took a final look at the inscription.

'You do now,' said Diana softly.

They turned from the Menin Gate, wandered back through the town, marvelling again at the Cloth Hall, the rest of those elegant, reconstructed buildings which earlier he had photographed. The sinking sun shadowed the streets more sharply, emphasised gables and spires silhouetted against a sky that was slowly turning sapphire.

If he hadn't read such vivid accounts of the massive destruction which had left so little, he'd never have believed a town could be rebuilt so exquisitely. It was inspirational, Chris reflected, a scene to burn into his inward eye, willing memory to hold it there against times when everything seemed destroyed and when hope, like that solitary tower, was the only pointer to a reconstructed future.

Quietly, each savouring private thoughts, they travelled back to Ostend. Suddenly ravenous, he insisted they should dine, late though it was, in a good restaurant.

They slept entwined in his room overlooking the inner harbour, and wakened with the dawn, at last, to seek each other, urgently. Holding her closer than close, he pressed near until he finally was expressing the full intensity of his love. Chris felt a surge of joy echo throughout each vein of his body. He had needed Diana so much and for so long, he could not believe that even bliss this strong would ever sate his constant longing.

As though to prove that true, Diana drew him to her again almost before his rapid breathing grew slower.

This time she laughed softly into the hollow of his neck, teased the skin there with her tongue. 'You've soon taught me an appetite for this, but if we're to catch that ferry we'll be obliged to forsake any other hunger.'

They ate breakfast aboard, smiling their secrets to each other over the table, relishing their closeness and its promise of a partnership that was a special kind of maturing.

Hair blowing in the stiffish breeze, they stood on deck to watch the White Cliffs enlarging before them while the ferry headed towards Dover. Again, they had little to say, but much to occupy their thoughts. Hearts too, Chris supposed, which was certainly true for himself.

Driving off and going through the normal delays for Customs at the docks, they began chatting, animatedly, anticipating the new life which promised so many changes.

She would stay in his flat tonight, would pick up clothing and other necessities from her own home tomorrow. Or should she cook him a meal there in the evening?

'It's not really much further from the vineyard, is it, than your own place?'

It seemed not to matter where they might have a base – for the present. It would count in time, perhaps very soon, when they needed to establish their home, one that they would create together.

Passing the rail lines that converged as they approached the tunnel and, deeper into Kent, the still unsightly scarring that was destined to become the rail link,

Christopher thought of his stepmother. Caroline had always so hated this ruination of the area she considered *her* territory.

He must tell her about Ypres, let it symbolise the optimism that was reconstruction. The making whole – a healing, in a way. A reminder of the spirit of survival. And, as emphasised today, a family thing, of continuing generations – different, yet from identical roots. And like his beloved vines, finding the strength to stretch beyond the stony ground, beyond impeding barriers, beyond weighty boulders. To locate their source of life.